Emily Harvale lives i̶
– although she wou
French Alps ... or Canada ... or anywhere that
has several months of snow. Emily loves
snow almost as much as she loves Christmas.
Having worked in the City (London) for
several years, Emily returned to her home
town of Hastings where she spends her days
writing ... and wondering if it will ever snow.
You can contact her via her website,
Facebook or Instagram.
There is also a Facebook group where fans
can chat with Emily about her books, her
writing day and life in general. Details can be
found on Emily's website.

Author contacts:
www.emilyharvale.com
www.twitter.com/emilyharvale
www.facebook.com/emilyharvalewriter
www.instagram.com/emilyharvale

***

Scan the code above to see all Emily's books on
Amazon

Also by this author

The Golf Widows' Club
Sailing Solo
Carole Singer's Christmas
Christmas Wishes
A Slippery Slope
The Perfect Christmas Plan
Be Mine
It Takes Two
Bells and Bows on Mistletoe Row

Lizzie Marshall series:
Highland Fling – book 1
Lizzie Marshall's Wedding – book 2

Goldebury Bay series:
Ninety Days of Summer – book 1
Ninety Steps to Summerhill – book 2
Ninety Days to Christmas – book 3

Hideaway Down series:
A Christmas Hideaway – book 1
Catch A Falling Star – book 2
Walking on Sunshine – book 3
Dancing in the Rain – book 4

Hall's Cross series
Deck the Halls – book 1
The Starlight Ball – book 2

Michaelmas Bay series
Christmas Secrets in Snowflake Cove – book 1
Blame it on the Moonlight – book 2

Lily Pond Lane series
The Cottage on Lily Pond Lane – four-part serial
Part One – New beginnings
Part Two – Summer secrets

Part Three – Autumn leaves
Part Four – Trick or treat
Christmas on Lily Pond Lane
Return to Lily Pond Lane
A Wedding on Lily Pond Lane
Secret Wishes and Summer Kisses on Lily Pond Lane

Wyntersleap series
Christmas at Wynter House – Book 1
New Beginnings at Wynter House – Book 2
A Wedding at Wynter House – Book 3
Love is in the Air – spin off

Merriment Bay series
Coming Home to Merriment Bay – Book 1
(four-part serial)
Part One – A Reunion
Part Two – Sparks Fly
Part Three – Christmas
Part Four – Starry Skies
Chasing Moonbeams in Merriment Bay – Book 2
Wedding Bells in Merriment Bay – Book 3

Seahorse Harbour series
Summer at my Sister's – book 1
Christmas at Aunt Elsie's – book 2
Just for Christmas – book 3
Tasty Treats at Seahorse Bites Café – book 4
Dreams and Schemes at The Seahorse Inn – book 5
Weddings and Reunions in Seahorse Harbour – book 6

Clementine Cove series
Christmas at Clementine Cove – book 1
Broken Hearts and Fresh Starts at Cove Café – book 2
Friendships Blossom in Clementine Cove – book 3

ISBN 978-1-909917-81-1

Published by Crescent Gate Publishing

Print edition published worldwide 2022
E-edition published worldwide 2022

Cover design by JR and Emily Harvale

Emily Harvale

Saving Christmas

CRESCENT GATE PUBLISHING

Acknowledgements

My grateful thanks go to the following:

Christina Harkness for her patience and care in editing this book.
My webmaster, David Cleworth who does so much more than website stuff.
My cover design team, JR.
Luke Brabants. Luke is a talented artist and can be found at: www.lukebrabants.com
My wonderful friends for their friendship and love. You know I love you all.
All the fabulous members of my Readers' Club. You help and support me in so many ways and I am truly grateful for your ongoing friendship. I wouldn't be where I am today without you.
My Twitter and Facebook friends, and fans of my Facebook author page. It's great to chat with you. You help to keep me (relatively) sane!

To view a map of Norman Landing visit

the maps page on my website

www.emilyharvale.com

This book is dedicated to the wonderful members of my Facebook group who helped me choose the name of Aaron's rescued Westie, Ember. Thank You!
Special thanks go to Chelsea Best, Suzanne Garwood, Amanda Geeves and Jacqui Archer Ward, for suggesting 'Ember' in the first place.
XXX

One

Monday is not, and never has been, my favourite day of the week. Even allowing for the fact that it's my one day off. Or should I say it was! Now that I'm officially unemployed I'll have every day off until I can find a new job.

That's something I hoped I'd never need to do again after Cal and I opened our restaurant. Or more precisely, *his* restaurant. Callum Blake was the chef cum owner. His name was on the lease, and the restaurant, Blake's was named after him.

He had been saving since he was about twelve, determined to have his own restaurant and when he found a somewhat shabby one to rent in Lewisham, a now trendy, inner London borough, in a street that was off the main thoroughfare but not too far away to be too much of a problem, he made an offer right away without discussing it with me. I didn't mind. It was his money, after all.

It came with a one-bedroom flat above the premises and both the restaurant and flat had potential; even I could see that. When Cal asked me to move in with him and take a job as 'front of house', I jumped at the chance.

Cal may have signed the documents without discussing it with me but having our own restaurant was a dream we shared and we had both been working and planning and doing all we could to achieve that goal long before we moved to London five years ago. We worked together as a team and we worked hard to make our dream come true.

And when you've been with someone for almost six years and you're planning on spending the rest of your life with that person, everything that's his is also sort of yours and everything that's yours is sort of his. Right?

But what's that old chestnut? Tell God your plans and he laughs. Well, his sides must be splitting with laughter today. All my plans, along with all my hopes and dreams have just gone up in flames.

I'm glad someone's laughing but it certainly isn't me.

This Monday has been worse than most and it brought with it the hounds of hell.

Okay, maybe that's an exaggeration but it definitely had teeth.

It started taking chunks out of me right from the off, when I stumbled out of bed in desperate need of the loo and stubbed my big toe on a box just outside our bedroom door in the hall – a large box that shouldn't have been there in the first place.

I suppose I should've realised then that all was not well in my world, but at the time I was too tired and also in a bit of pain to take much notice of why a box was there.

Washing my hands in stone cold water made it clear it was going to be one of those days. The boiler was playing up again. Great. That's all we needed. As if we hadn't already had enough to contend with. When would our problems end and the sun shine on us again? But I told myself I mustn't complain. At least we had each other. And however bad things got and no matter what life threw at us, we'd get through it all, together.

Hmmm! Hindsight, they say, is a wonderful thing. Yeah, right.

I padded back to the bedroom, taking care to avoid the box but still not wondering why it was there and grabbed my fluffy fleece dressing gown from the hook on the back of the door. I wrapped it tightly around me and made my way downstairs.

The unmistakeable aroma of freshly brewed coffee pervaded my nostrils. Ah, heaven! My shield against the onslaught of the day. I need coffee like a string of fairy lights needs electricity, or a battery. Or like a vampire needs blood. You get the picture. It literally keeps me alive. That's no exaggeration. Without coffee, I could not get through the day. I didn't know then quite how much coffee I might need to get through this particular Monday.

Our bedroom and bathroom are in the attic of the tall and narrow building we rent. A living room and kitchen occupy the floor below and beneath that are two storage rooms, one of which doubles as our office. The restaurant is on the ground floor, needless to say. It, and the store rooms cum office came as one property, with a separate access to our flat, which came as another.

Cal's name was also on the tenancy agreement for our flat. Another document he signed without consulting me, but again, it was his money, so that was fair enough. He may have got us here but once we moved in, we split the bills equally. Or at least I thought we did.

Prior to moving here, we rented a two-bedroom flat, also in Lewisham with my best friend, Tori. It was the only place we could afford. The three of us had moved to London nearly six years ago, all starry-eyed and hopeful.

You may not know this, but to all intents and purposes, Lewisham *is* London. It is one of thirteen districts – twelve London boroughs, and the City of London which is a separate entity and even has its own police force – that make up inner London. Another twenty London boroughs make up outer London and all thirty-three lumped together form Greater London. Don't ask me why, because I have no idea, but I read it years ago when Tori and I first decided London was the place to be.

We had a certainty that 'this was it' when we first moved to London. This was our chance to make all our hopes and dreams come true.

Tori's dream was to make it big in the music industry. Not as a singer but as an executive for a large music label, preferably working in A&R. That's Artists and Repertoire, in case you're wondering and the job involves being responsible for finding promising new artists and bands to sign for a record label or music publisher. Tori didn't have much, if any, experience, but her enthusiasm was boundless and she would happily spend every night trawling pubs, bars and small or indie music venues in search of the next big thing. Not that that is what Tori's first job as a secretary in A&R entailed, as my best friend soon discovered.

Cal's dream was to own his own restaurant in central London, preferably in the West End or in Covent Garden, and to become a famous chef like those who have their own TV shows. The restaurant in Lewisham was supposed to be the first of many. So far, his dream, like mine, didn't seem to be going to plan. I don't know if he had any other dreams; he never mentioned any. Come to think of it, I suppose even that should've been a sign. But it wasn't.

My dream was to move to London. Check. What can I say? I'm a woman of simple pleasures.

But I had more than one dream. So maybe not that simple?

Shortly after I met Cal, I was sure he was 'The One'. I can't actually recall when I first knew I was in love with him and wanted to spend the rest of my life by his side, but I do remember the thrill I felt when he first said those three little words to me.

Everyone wants to hear those three little words, don't they?

'I love you.'

It's amazing how powerful those words can be. How life changing. How empowering. How absolutely incredible they can make you feel.

What no one wants to hear is three other words tagged on to them.

'I just don't love you anymore.'

There's nothing wonderful about hearing those words, believe me. And I should know, because that's exactly what I heard shortly after sitting at the kitchen table on that awful Monday morning. And to be quite honest, I still can't believe he said them.

Callum told me he had fallen in love with me just two weeks after we first met. We were having dinner at our favourite restaurant, Alberto's and I knew it was going to be a special night because of the way Cal kept looking at me. You've heard the phrase, 'His eyes were smouldering with passion,' right? Tori and I had often laughed when we'd read that in romance novels, joking about wafts of smoke streaming out from the man's eyes, fanned by his obligatory and impossibly long, dark lashes. We'd pictured flames bursting from his equally dark and dangerous eyes. We couldn't see it as at all romantic. It was more like something from a horror film. But that was before either of us had been in love, and no man had ever looked at us in any way that could be described as 'smouldering'. Until that night in the restaurant with Callum.

He took my hand in his and looked me directly in the eye and when I met his look, I finally understood what smouldering meant. He brushed my fingers with his thumb and shivers of delight shot through me faster than the speed of light. Until that night we hadn't slept together. Not because we hadn't wanted to – we had, but because we both lived with our parents. Parent in my case. Dad had left years before. We simply hadn't found the right time or had the right opportunity.

'I know we've only been dating for a few weeks,' he said.

'Two,' I confirmed, as if I needed to clarify that.

His brows furrowed momentarily but then he smiled that sexy smile of his.

'Two. Yes. Which isn't a long time, I know.'

'Unless you're a dog.' Did I mention I can be a bit of an idiot? I tend to say stupid things or make inane remarks at the most inappropriate times. 'Or a cat.' He didn't look happy and his eyes stopped smouldering briefly. 'Sorry. I don't know why I said that. What were you going to say?'

He gave me a devilish grin. Yes, I know I'm using clichés, but this was a sort of cliché moment. Bear with me.

'I think that's one of the reasons I love you, Katie Barr,' he said, his voice as smooth as silk. 'You're not like any of the other women I've ever known.'

I admit I wondered for a nanosecond, exactly how many other women he had known, and I was tempted to ask. We were both the same age but it was obvious we had spent our lives up till then very differently. I might have been twenty-nine at the time but Callum was only my third boyfriend. To say I had serious trust issues with men after Dad left us, was an understatement.

I'd been asked out a few times but in those days I would rather spend hours baking cakes in the kitchen than risk putting a bun in the oven with some man, who would ultimately run off and leave me. Mum and Nan (who is my nan, but her name is Nancy and everyone calls her Nan) taught me to bake before my sister, Emma was born and I've loved baking ever since. I find it therapeutic, especially when I'm stressed or upset.

It took many years – and a lot of baking – for me to come to terms with what Dad did to us and it nearly killed Mum. I still believe it did, in part, contribute to her death. Emma was relatively unfazed by Dad's betrayal, but then she is five years younger than me, so she was five when he left us, and nothing fazes

Emma. Absolutely nothing. If a meteor ever looks as if it might be on target to hit Earth, Emma should be the one they call. Not only is she cool, calm and collected, she's also a genius. Unlike me. She'll find a way to send that meteor packing.

When I did eventually forgive my dad – and I use that term loosely – and accepted that not all men were bad and they wouldn't all break your heart, I went out with my first boyfriend. At the ripe old age of twenty-four. Yep. Twenty-four and still a virgin. But that first relationship is hardly worth mentioning. And it wasn't much of a relationship either. He was more of a friend than a boyfriend. We hadn't even had sex and we dated for almost six months. Unbelievable, but true.

The second, a year later, lasted for a little over two years. We did have sex but actually not that often. And it wasn't something either of us yearned for. Or seemed to need. Smouldering looks never, ever passed between us. The first time was, simply put, a total disaster. I won't go into details; the thought of it still makes me cringe. I'm not sure what I expected but that definitely wasn't it. It did improve a little after that, but as I said, we didn't do it often. Again, I think we were more like friends than lovers. We got on well and enjoyed each other's company but the spark was more of a fizzle and the sex was never great.

So, sexually speaking, Callum was far more experienced than me, and I clearly wasn't Cal's third girlfriend. Probably his twenty-third, from what I'd heard about him.

That was one of the reasons Tori, my best friend since we were old enough to crawl, Emma and Nan were all so surprised when I said yes to a date with him in the first place. I was proud of myself. My trust issues with men were long behind me. And no sane woman would say no to Callum Blake. He was on every woman's wish list. Or a man who looked just like him was, at least.

I had been the one to end both of my previous relationships. Mainly because I couldn't see either of them going anywhere. I mentioned I had more than one dream, didn't I? Well one of my dreams was to marry one day, preferably by the time I was thirty-five. An odd dream to have for someone who had had such serious trust issues. But I wanted children. I wanted a family of my own. I still had Emma and Nan after Mum died, and they loved me as much as I loved them, but it wasn't the same as having a husband and kids of my own. And if my husband did ever leave me, I would have my children, just as Mum had Emma and me, and we'd be as happy as we could possibly be. I'd make sure of that.

Anyway, thankfully, I didn't go with the question of how many other women had been in Callum's life.

'One of the reasons you love me?' I said, surprised that there was one, let alone more than that. 'You're telling me you love me? Actually, *love* me?'

I'm not sure why I was so surprised about it but I was. The word 'love' hadn't come up in my two previous relationships of six months, and two years, respectively, and this one had only been two weeks so far. And this was Callum Blake.

I'm not ugly but I'm not beautiful either. I'm not fat but I could never be described as thin. I'm not short but neither am I tall. My hair is neither chocolate brown nor chestnut. Just brown. I'm really rather ordinary.

That's a word that could never be used to describe Callum Blake. Cal is drop-dead gorgeous, tall and athletically built, with hair the colour of an angel's and blue eyes as bright as a summer sky. Cal is really rather perfect. At least in the looks department. I also thought he was perfect in the boyfriend department too. Seems I might have been wrong. But that night, he was perfect. Perfect in every way.

'Yes,' he said, kissing my fingers and giving me that smouldering look. 'I love you. I really love you.'

'Oh Callum! I can't believe this. I think this is the best night of my life.' I didn't realise it then but I didn't say I loved him too.

'I think we can make it even better.' Now he was on fire. Metaphorically speaking, of course. 'My parents are away this weekend. I've got the house to myself. I was thinking that, after dinner, we could go back to my place and I'll show you just how much I love you. How much I want you. How much I need you, Katie Barr.'

I'm not sure why he kept adding my surname but it somehow made it sound more dramatic. More sincere. More intense. Perhaps I fell in love with him then. I was definitely in lust with him. I don't think either of us had ever eaten so fast in our lives. Or maybe Cal had. I had never wanted anyone or anything as much as I wanted him that night. And that entire weekend was the most perfect of my life.

It didn't take me very long to decide Callum was 'The One' – my future husband. The father to be of my kids. And after that first weekend we spent together at his parents' house, I realised why people raved about sex.

To say Cal blew my mind is putting it lightly. I experienced every cliché in the book that weekend. We made love in every room, including his parents' bedroom, although not in their bed. That would've been gross. We had sex on the chaise longue, right in front of the window. I didn't care if anyone saw us. Not that anyone would. The thirties, five-bedroom house with its white and black façade was set back off the road and the front garden was park-like, although not as big as a park.

Rabbits had nothing on us that weekend. Or in the weeks and months and years to come. Sex has never been a problem for us. Several other things have though.

When we first started dating, everyone else was a little concerned, but they all liked Cal and after nearly six years together, it appeared all their doubts were unfounded.

Except, perhaps, they weren't.

We met at Alberto's Christmas Eve party, which was why the restaurant was special to us. I was a waitress there, as was Tori, and Cal had come to the party with his mates. The place was full to bursting, as Alberto's Christmas parties always were. Luckily, a buffet was being served so Tori and I and the other waiting staff didn't have plates of food to manoeuvre through the throng, but carrying trays loaded with drinks was a test of skill and endurance. I was usually quite good at it but that night I was bumped by someone as I passed behind Cal and his friends, carrying a tray loaded with glasses of Prosecco. There was nothing I could do to stop it when the tray and all the contents slipped out of my hands and left Cal soaked with drink and surrounded by broken glass.

Amazingly, he laughed after the initial shock of being saturated and even helped me clear up the mess. He asked me out as the clock struck midnight on Christmas Eve. I'd said yes before he finished the question.

We had so much in common, or so I thought. We both wanted to work in the food industry. Cal was determined to own his own restaurant one day; I thought I might manage one. I wasn't quite sure exactly what I wanted to be but it had to have something to do with food. I love the stuff. Not just eating it but cooking it, preparing it. Even growing it. I didn't want to be a chef, but I loved baking. We both wanted to move to London. Cal had planned to go alone before he was thirty. I had planned, long before Mum passed away, to go with Tori at some point in the future. We'd been talking about it for years. We just didn't have the money. As it happened, all three of us went together. It was something we all should've done in our early twenties, not as we were coming up to thirty, but some plans take time and sometimes life gets in the way. We rented the two-bedroom flat and lived there happily for the first year and a half.

Tori didn't seem to mind when we told her about the restaurant and our new one-bedroom flat. She had just come into some money, left to her by her aunt, so she decided to invest it in a place of her own. All she could afford was a tiny studio, but it was hers and that was all that mattered to Tori.

Before we broke the news to her, I had suggested to Cal that Tori could have one of the storerooms as her bedroom, even though, at the time, it couldn't be accessed via the flat. One of Cal's plans, and one agreed to by the landlord, was to open up a previously closed off staircase and two doors, that did give such access. The work wouldn't take us long and Tori wouldn't mind a brief detour as a temporary arrangement. But Cal said we'd need both storerooms and one would need to double as our office, and besides, it was time it was just the two of us.

I actually thought that was quite romantic. Cal and I were taking the next step towards our future together but I was genuinely relieved when Tori said it was perfect timing because of her inheritance. She told me she would've felt uncomfortable if she had been the one to move out first, which is exactly how I felt before we shared the news. The future looked bright for all of us.

But not for long.

The restaurant, it turned out, was a bit too far off the main hub, after all. It began well but interest fizzled within the second year as more and more eateries opened up. Prices began to soar, takings didn't. We managed to keep our heads above water and for a short time, things improved, but this last year had got worse.

I hoped we could work our way out of our financial difficulties and had come up with all sorts of ideas to bring in clientele. I arranged singles nights, book club cocktail evenings, wine tasting events, cookery lessons with Callum, murder mystery nights and other themed events, and all of them worked, for a time. But money was tight for everyone these days, and winter had come early. The dark nights and the wet and windy conditions seemed to make even hardy Londoners want to go home after work instead of partying the night away. Cal became a little distant, and I had run out of ideas.

I knew the business was now in pretty serious financial difficulties and I wasn't surprised about that, but I was surprised just how bad things were. It was upsetting that Cal was so matter-of-fact about it, but it wasn't a total shock. Having to find somewhere else to live, was.

I had thought for some time that there had been a subtle change in our relationship, that Cal was not quite his usual kind, caring and passionate self, but each time I asked if something was wrong, he simply shrugged and dismissed my concerns with a tight smile.

'Nothing more than usual,' was his standard reply. 'The restaurant's struggling, just like so many other small businesses, and we've had a tough few years. Something will happen though. Don't worry.'

This year the lease of the restaurant and the flat above was up for renewal and the landlord had said he would be increasing the rent on New Year's Eve. Considerably more than either of us expected, it transpired. Bookings were down; costs were spiralling upwards but Cal told me he had it all in hand and that I shouldn't worry. He said he had a plan. What I didn't know was that he had kept to himself just how dire things really were. And that his plan did not include me.

When I entered the kitchen he was leaning against the worktop, cradling a mug of coffee and completely lost in thought.

'Good morning,' I said, in my usual cheerful manner, although it took considerable effort to sound cheerful this morning, before telling our home-hub to turn on the radio.

Christmas carols had just started playing even though it was early December, and *All I want for Christmas* blared out, cutting through the silence and the fact that Cal had not returned my morning greeting.

I assumed he already knew about the fault with the boiler because he'd obviously been up for a while. He was dressed in jeans, a black T-shirt and a grey V-neck sweater. He even had his boots on and not his slippers.

His eyes shot to my face as I approached him. I was intending to give him the usual quick kiss I gave him every morning but the expression on his face stopped me in my tracks. It was something akin to shock mingled with guilt and possibly a hint of fear.

'You know about the boiler then?' I said, thinking that must be the reason for his gloomy mood as I went instead towards the coffee pot. I took a mug from the shelf above and poured myself a much needed elixir of life.

The landlord was responsible for repairs, so, other than the fact that it was annoying not to have hot water, we didn't have to worry about paying for a plumber.

Which was just as well as we didn't have the money it might cost to repair or replace it. This wasn't the first time it had broken down. That was the upside of renting. We didn't have to pay when things went wrong. The downside was that we didn't own the place in which we worked or the home in which we lived.

Cal had paid for the initial lease and the tenancy but we had both ploughed almost every penny we had into bringing the restaurant up to date, opening up the old staircase and doors, and general refurbishment and redecoration. Cal had high standards and insisted we mustn't cut corners.

I spent most of my money, a lot of which had been left to me by Mum, on redecorating the flat. It had last been decorated during the 1970s by the look of it, so it took a substantial sum to make it the home we wanted. We did it in the belief that we would be living here and running the restaurant for some time so we thought it was worth the expenditure.

I admit that shortly before we first moved to London I had spent some of the money Mum left me, buying an almost new car. I needed one to visit Emma and Nan and trains were never reliable.

Cal and I soon found jobs working in other restaurants, learning more tricks of the

I laughed and hugged her. 'No one will ever be good enough for me or for Emma in your eyes, Nan. I love him and I intend to spend the rest of my life with him, so you can put your worries aside. He's not like Dad.'

'Hmmm,' she said, her eyes narrowing at the mention of Dad. 'Maybe he is, maybe he isn't. Time will tell. If you're happy, truly happy, that's enough for me – for now. But I'll just say this, and you take heed. When it pours with rain, there are men who will make a dash for it and find shelter for themselves. There are men who will hold an umbrella in an effort to give you both shelter. And then there are men who will take you by the hand and dance with you in the rain. Which one would you want to spend your life with? Dancing through any storm would be my choice. I don't see Callum Blake as a dancer. Do you? I think he's the dasher type.'

For some reason her words unsettled me, not that they made complete sense.

'Callum might not be a dancer, but neither am I. He'll hold the umbrella, and that's what I want.'

'Suit yourself. But you *are* a dancer, Katie my love. You try to make the best of any situation. You don't run. You once used to hide, but now you face life head on, and if a storm comes your way you'll force a smile onto your face and you'll be out there battling the elements and making the best of it at the same time.'

'Yes,' Callum said now, swallowing a slug of his coffee and choking on it, bringing me back to the present. 'And if I hadn't already made the decision, the boiler would've been the final nail in the coffin.' He sighed and ran a hand through his golden locks but his blue eyes didn't make me think of summer, more of a frosty winter day.

'Decision?' I queried. My legs started shaking as if I knew there was an earthquake coming. 'What decision?' Perhaps it was good news. Perhaps I was being silly and worrying for no reason.

'There's no easy way to say this, Katie, so I'll just say it, but I think maybe you should sit down.'

I staggered to the table as if drunk, and sat down on the first chair I came to. This was not going to be good news.

'I thought things would improve,' he said. 'What with Christmas coming. But we don't have any party bookings for the festive season and what with that and everything else, I've come to realise it's time we called it a day and closed the restaurant. It's best for both of us.'

I was stunned by the thought of closing the restaurant; a restaurant we'd worked so hard to open just over three years ago. But at least we had a roof over our heads. And each other.

Except we didn't.

'I'm broke,' Cal added. 'As are you. I can't afford the rent hike and with no money coming in, neither can you. And it's worse than that. I hoped to keep this from you, but I've been borrowing money from Mum and Dad. They've agreed to pay off our debts, but they said enough is enough and they can't keep bailing us out. Which I can't argue with. I hoped I could get through this, but I can't. We've got no choice but to move out.'

Just like that. As if leaving our home of the last three and a bit years, a home we'd built together, meant nothing at all to him.

I wasn't surprised about us not being able to pay the increased rent, but I did think we might be able to work something out with our landlord. He wasn't an unreasonable man. As for us having to move out, well, I had known it was a possibility but I still wasn't prepared for how numb it made me feel.

The debts though were a total shock. I also had no idea Callum had borrowed money from his parents.

'Why didn't you tell me, Cal?' I asked when I could find my voice. 'How much have you borrowed and how much do we owe in other debts?'

'We don't owe Mum and Dad anything. They've written it off. And they've cleared all the other debts so right now, we don't owe anyone a penny. Providing we're out by New Year's Eve.'

'New Year's Eve! That can't be right. That's less than four weeks away. Surely we have to be given more notice than that? I thought it was at least two months.' Cal's sheepish expression said as much. 'How long have you known?'

He paled visibly and gave a small cough but avoided looking directly at me when he mumbled, 'A while.'

I wanted to ask how long 'a while' was but what was the point? It didn't change anything. Callum had obviously delayed telling me this awful news in the hope he could prevent me worrying about it. I do have a tendency to worry where money is concerned these days. That is thanks to my early teenage years being spent living hand-to-mouth with Mum, Emma and Nan after Dad decided to move on to pastures new. Once I realised that the restaurant might fail, all those doubts and worries and fears had come back.

'We'll find somewhere else,' I said, still not quite able to take this all in but trying my best to put a positive spin on it. That is something else I try to do whenever possible:

see the bright side of any situation, even if I
might be secretly worrying about it. I am a
contradiction and well aware of that fact.
'We'll find somewhere cheaper. We'll both
get new jobs, and although it'll be hard to
leave here, and the future we had planned
together, we'll have a fresh start. Somewhere
new.'

He shook his head and sighed. 'No. We
won't. At least, not together. I think it's time
we faced facts, Katie and accepted this is
over. We both knew this was coming.'

What? I certainly didn't.

'Over? Us, you mean? Are you … are you
breaking up with me as well as telling me I'm
jobless and homeless?'

'We had a good run, didn't we? We did
the best we could. But the thing is, Katie, I
just don't love you anymore.'

And there it was. Those awful words that
no one wants to hear, made even worse by
the matter-of-fact manner in which they
were delivered.

It was as if he were saying he didn't like
marmalade on his toast anymore. Which was
something he actually had said a few weeks
before. And that had also been a surprise. Cal
had had marmalade on his toast ever since I
had known him; well since I'd slathered it on
his toast that very first weekend we spent at

his parents' house, and he'd done so every day since. Until about four or five weeks ago.

'The problems with the restaurant made me re-evaluate everything,' he continued, sticking the knife further into my heart. 'We're more like friends than lovers now, and that's the problem. We both need a fresh start. Both the lease and the tenancy are up for renewal so this is the perfect opportunity. The perfect time to call it quits.'

Now I was completely numb with shock. I couldn't speak. I couldn't think. I couldn't even drink my coffee.

'You need time to think this through,' he went on, clearly on a roll. 'I've arranged to meet a mate for breakfast, and I'm meeting someone I worked with when I first came to London, for lunch. He might know of a job for me. I've already started packing and I'll do more when I get back. You'll want to start that too. I'm really sorry about this, Katie. But it's for the best, you'll see.'

I was about to open my mouth although I had no clue as to what I might be about to say, that's how dazed I was. I don't think I've ever seen Cal move so fast. He was out of the kitchen and closing the door to the flat before I'd made a sound.

This was the worst Monday of my life. And the day had only just started.

No. That's not true. The worst Monday of my life was the Monday Mum died. And the second worst Monday was the Monday Dad left Mum, me and Emma and Nan.

So this was the third worst Monday of my life.

You can see why I'm not a fan of Monday.

Two

I sat, statue-like, for several minutes after Cal left, trying to digest what had just happened and to make sense of it all. Was this some sort of nightmare I was having? Would I awake to find Cal lying beside me, snoring softly? Unable to take it in, I pinched myself just to check. The fact that it hurt didn't mean I was awake; I've felt pain in dreams before. But it did mean there was a greater chance of this nightmare being real.

The first person I phoned to share my horrendous news with was my best friend, Tori, but even as I regaled her with every detail of the breakup, I still couldn't believe it had actually happened.

'The guy's a scum bag and you're better off without him,' Tori said, in the no-nonsense way that was uniquely hers. 'That he could treat you like this after you've been together for six years is unbelievable.'

'Six years on Christmas Eve, to be exact.' I'm not sure why I needed to point that out. 'We met at the Christmas party at Alberto's restaurant, remember?'

Tori's tone changed momentarily and she even giggled. 'Oh blimey, yes! Who could forget, Alberto's? I still miss that place. I know I wasn't really cut out to be a waitress and some of the customers were utter twats, as I believe I may have told one or two, but the tips were great and the food was to die for and Alberto knew how to have fun. We had such a laugh, didn't we?'

'Yes, we did. But I don't feel much like reminiscing. I'm heartbroken.'

Tori coughed. 'Of course you are. But not for long. We'll show Callum Blake that he's just made the biggest mistake of his life. You'll meet someone new and when Cal comes crawling back, which he will, you can laugh in his face and tell him to go where the sun doesn't shine.'

'But I love him.' I couldn't believe how calm I sounded. I certainly didn't feel it. Although to be honest, I think I was still too numb to feel anything. But I was struggling to hold back the tears that had been building since Cal's bombshell. Or more precisely, bombshells. There had been three. One after another. I was jobless, homeless, and single.

And all just a few weeks before Christmas, my favourite time of year.

'I know you do. But you'll get over it.'

Tori is one of those people who believes that, no matter what happens in life, you simply put on a brave face, smile and move on. But she is also one of those lucky people who has never had anything particularly bad happen in her life. I'm not saying her life's been a bed of roses without thorns, but the worst thing that's happened to her so far was when her parents decided to move, which meant she wouldn't be living next door to me. At the time, that was the worst thing that had happened in both of our lives.

'I won't. My heart's smashed to bits. I'll never love again. I'll die alone, surrounded by cats. I'll be like Miss Haversham.'

'Don't talk such crap. Your heart will mend. Cal's clearly not the nice guy we all thought he was and once you come to terms with that, you'll realise he's a waste of space in your heart. You'll meet some gorgeous hunk, fall madly in love and have five kids. Not all at once, obviously. And what's wrong with cats? You love cats. But who the hell is Miss Haversham? Oh wait. Was she that old battle-axe who lived at number 24? God she was awful, wasn't she?' Tori snorted with laughter. 'That woman had super powers. She always managed to be peering out of her front window whenever you and I were doing something we shouldn't. Which was frequently. And she was constantly reporting people to the local council for noise violations or to the police for some minor indiscretion. I think she had a dedicated phone line to both and I'm sure she was one of the reasons my folks decided to move, even though they maintain it was for Dad's work.' Tori took a breath. 'But that old bag didn't die alone. She was shacked up with someone else's husband the last I heard. Someone should've reported her for stealing another woman's man.'

Tori and her family had lived next door to me and mine for as long as either of us could remember and as I said, I had been equally heartbroken when Tori told me they were moving because her dad had been offered a better job. Thankfully, it hadn't been that far. Brighton was about fifteen miles away, or thirty-five minutes by bus, and for the first few months after the move, Tori remained at the school we'd both attended since we were five, so we still saw each other every day. Even when Tori transferred to a more local school, we saw one another whenever we could and our friendship hadn't suffered one bit as a result of the distance.

'Tori, you can't 'steal' a man. People aren't possessions. You can't keep them chained to your side, however much you might want to. And that was Miss Havant. Miss Haversham is from *Great Expectations*. The classic by Charles Dickens. The remake of the film was on TV the other night.' I sighed dramatically. 'Little did I know then that the love of my life was about to dump me a bit like the love of her love dumped her.'

'Callum Blake is not the love of your life. Okay, maybe you thought he was, and maybe it did seem, for a while, that he might be. But he's not. And there's no chance you'll end up like either Miss Haversham or the old battle-axe, Miss Havant. Stop being so dramatic. Honestly, Katie. You'll be laughing about this before you know it.'

'Laughing! Are you mad? You are mad. We all know that. You don't seem to understand. He *was* the love of my life. He's my soul mate.'

'No, he wasn't. And he isn't. If that were the case you'd still be together. He wouldn't have dumped you when things got tough. He was – and is – a total and utter prat. Once you get over the shock, you'll realise you're better off. Believe me.'

'How can I possibly be better off? I'm devastated. Heartbroken. Crushed. Not to mention jobless. And homeless. What am I going to do, Tori? Where am I going to live?'

Tori didn't even hesitate. 'With me. You can live with me for now. You'll find a new job and you'll find a new flat. Or maybe I'll see if I can sell mine and we'll find somewhere slightly bigger where we can both live. A bit like we did when we first came to London. Only this time without Callum Blake. And as I keep saying, you'll find a new man. But we can do all that tomorrow. For now, pack your things and get out of there. I'll tell you what. I'll get off work. I'll say I've got a migraine or something, and I'll come and help you pack. Then we'll go back to my place, get drunk, drown our sorrows and watch Christmas movies. You love Christmas movies.'

Tori's offer was heartfelt, and I know she meant every word. The problem is Tori's studio flat puts the 'T' in tiny. Property in London isn't cheap and a studio flat was all Tori could afford when she bought it just over three years ago. It was her first step on the property ladder. And it isn't much bigger than a step on a ladder. The front door opens directly into the lounge-cum-kitchenette and you do have to climb a ladder to get to the bed which is situated on a raised platform. The estate agent optimistically referred to it as 'the mezzanine floor' when he showed us the property. I'd gone with her and had tried to talk her out of buying it because the entire flat was smaller than her then bedroom in the flat we'd shared, but she had fallen in love with the place at first sight. And we all know what that's like, don't we?

I love Tori to bits, but there was no way we could both live in that flat for four days let alone four weeks. Not if we wanted to remain best friends.

'Thanks, Tori. But the last thing I want to do right now is watch other people get their happy ever afters. Everyone knows it's not real. Real life sucks. Romance sucks. Men suck. And as much as I love you, we can't both live in your flat.'

'Of course we can. We'll spend the next three weeks having fun and then we'll spend Christmas and New Year with my parents. They'll love that.'

Tori's parents' house in Brighton was huge, so at least there'd be plenty of room, and it would only mean spending three weeks in Tori's teeny-tiny flat. But that posed another problem. Tori and her family are ... a little mad. In a good way. Christmas, to them, means playing games every single day; dressing up like elves – or worse: I had once been a Christmas donkey. Don't ask. It also means drinking and partying till all hours, and basically behaving more outrageously than was good for anyone. In normal circumstances, that would be great. I love to party as much as the next person. But these were far from normal circumstances. Right now, the thought of partying seems like a nightmare.

How can I think of having fun when my life has just been blown apart? All my dreams have been dashed and my heart shattered into a thousand tiny pieces that would never, ever be whole again, no matter how many times Tori might try to reassure me that it would.

'That sounds great,' I lied, 'but Emma will probably ask me to spend Christmas with her, once I tell her what's happened. And you know how much she likes to take control of everything.'

I could almost see Tori rolling her eyes.

'Doesn't she just. You'd think she was the elder sister. Okay, but that still leaves the next three weeks. You can't stay in your flat. Seeing him every day will be like torture. You'll have to come and stay with me. Where else are you going to go?'

Tori had a point. Where else could I go?

But why couldn't I stay in the flat? Cal had said we had to be out by New Year's Eve. He didn't say anything about leaving right away. Well, not in those exact words. All he'd said was that I should start to pack.

And three weeks was plenty of time for me to remind Cal why he fell in love with me. Not that I actually know why he fell in love with me. I don't think I'm that different now from the way I was when we first dated. And if he's loved me for almost six years, what has suddenly changed?

No. I think this is because of the financial situation we're in. That's clouded his judgement and he's not thinking straight. All I need to do is come up with a plan and make him see our future could still be as bright as we hoped it would be. Once I do that, Cal will realise he still loves me and my life will be back on track. *Our* lives will be back on track. There's plenty of time to make our dreams come true. There's no time limit on success.

'You're the best friend ever, Tori,' I said. 'But I think I need to be alone today. I need to get my head around this and ... ooooh! I've got another call trying to get through. I'd better take it. I'll call you later. Love you!'

I rang off as fast as I could. I didn't want to say so to Tori, but I silently hoped it was Cal calling to tell me he'd realised what a fool he was being and that he'd changed his mind and he did still love me.

I wouldn't need to stay with Tori after all. Yay!

Sadly, it wasn't Callum; it was my sister, Emma, calling me with news of her own. And I didn't know it then but luckily for me, Emma was about to make me a better offer.

Three

'Why don't you come to New York with me?' Emma said, once I explained, in great detail, what had happened.

She had called to say she had just been told she would need to go to the States on business. The company she worked for had offices in New York and Emma was in charge of a new joint project. She'd told me about this project last week, but not that she might have to go to the States to help move it forward. But she had been genuinely excited about it so the fact that she would now be going away, and would be leaving the day after tomorrow didn't seem to bother her at all. Nor did it worry her that she would be gone for at least four weeks, including Christmas and New Year. But that was Emma. Nothing ever fazes her.

That was as much as I heard about the project because as she was talking, her tone was changing.

'Is everything okay, Katie?' she asked, right in the middle of explaining what was involved.

'Yeah. Tell me more.'

I didn't want to dampen her enthusiasm. I could tell her my problems later. She works really hard and deserves every opportunity her company gives her. This project involved a promotion for her and an increase in salary, although the package she had before involved figures Cal and I could only dream of.

'It's clearly not,' she said, her tone already sympathetic. 'What's wrong, Katie? What's happened?'

'I don't want to spoil your exciting news,' I said, really struggling now to keep it together.

'Stuff that. Tell me right now, Katie, or I swear I'll get in my car and come up there.'

She would. Believe me.

I let out a sorrowful sigh and a flood of tears came with it.

'C-Cal's dumped me! He ... he says he doesn't love me anymore.'

There was a momentary silence. Well, not silence exactly. I was blubbing like a world champion, but neither of us spoke. It was almost as if Emma wasn't totally surprised.

'I'm so, so sorry, Katie,' she eventually said. 'I know it probably feels like the end of the world right now but I promise you, it isn't.'

'Oh y-yes it is! I'm jobless, too. And ... and homeless! I don't know what I'm going to do, Em.'

'You're going to tell me exactly what he said and when he said it. It's always best to get these things off your chest. And then you're going to pull yourself together and we're going to sort something out.'

Easy for Emma to say. Not so easy for me to do. Especially now the floodgates had opened and I couldn't speak without hiccupping between sobs. Eventually, I got to the part where Callum had walked out and then I told Emma about Tori's offer. That's when Emma made me a better one, or so she thought, of joining her on her trip to New York.

'The hotel room is three times the size of Tori's flat. And as lovely as Tori and her family may be, we all agree they can also be as noisy and annoying as a swarm of bees with a hangover.' Emma laughed good-naturedly. 'I won't be working all the time. Just during the day. And maybe a couple of evenings. But I'll have Sundays off. You can see the sights of New York, watch trash TV, be pampered in the spa, drink Manhattans every day, ice skate at the Rockefeller Center, spend a fortune on Christmas delights in Macy's. It'll be great. And I'll have a couple of days off for Christmas and New Year.'

At any other time in my life, it would've been great. Right now it wasn't much better than Tori's offer.

'Thanks, Em. But there's no way I can go to New York. It'd bring back too many memories. Cal and I went there on our one and only weekend break together, remember?'

Memories of that wonderful, long weekend came tumbling back. It had been Thanksgiving and we had watched the Macy's Thanksgiving Parade, taken an invigorating carriage ride through Central Park, had the most deliciously decadent desserts in the famous Serendipity3 restaurant: the setting for one of my favourite Christmas movies, Serendipity, and 'shopped till we dropped' in the world-renowned stores of Macy's and Bloomingdale's. Well, shopped until we stopped to drink cocktails in several of the city's landmark bars and clubs. We'd gone to check out the restaurants. A flying visit and a treat paid for by Cal's parents for his thirtieth birthday. We'd been dating for almost one year, Christmas Eve being less than a month away, and we fell even deeper in love that weekend. It was absolutely magical.

One day, if Cal and I don't get back together that is, I'll be able to treasure those memories. But not just yet. Merely thinking about them hurt like hell. I pushed them to the back of my mind, with considerable effort.

'Besides,' I continued, my voice crackling with the weight of those memories, 'I wouldn't be good company. And I'd be in your way. I'll probably be crying my heart out for the foreseeable future and you won't be able to concentrate on work with me blubbering in the corner.'

'At least you can joke about it.'

'I'm not joking, Emma. I'm serious. I didn't shed a tear when he told me, but now, as you've probably guessed, all I want to do is cry and cry and cry. I think I need to be alone for a while. I need to wallow. I didn't think I was the wallowing type, but the thought of it appeals to me right now. Maybe a good wallow will make me feel a little better. Not that I'll ever feel happy again. And I need to find a job. And a place to live. Because you're right about Tori's flat. It's far too small for two people, I realise that. And you're right about her family. And although they'd welcome me with open arms, I can't face being surrounded by happy, jolly people twenty-four-seven.'

'You're not the wallowing type. You and I both know that. But sometimes a good cry and a day or two of solitude can help. I agree. That's what I did when I missed out on what I thought was my dream job, remember? I spent two days in my PJs, eating ice cream and watching old movies and I realised that stupid job wasn't my dream job after all. And look at me now. Now I do have my dream job.'

'Right now, any job would be my dream job. I need to earn a living. I don't know what I'm going to do, Em. But I do know that I'm not going to stay with Tori, and I'm not going to New York with you.'

'That's a start. You're already making decisions. That's a good sign. And come to think of it, there is another option.' Emma's tone suggested the problem had been solved. 'You can house-sit for me.'

'House-sit?' It certainly was an option. And one far preferable from squeezing in with Tori. 'While you're in New York, you mean?'

'Yes. Nan's been moaning about me leaving her all alone over the holidays. Even though she's never alone at Conqueror's Court. But you know what she's like. She'd love it if you came home for Christmas. And if Tori's going to be in Brighton with her folks over the holidays, she won't be far away. Not that London's that far away either. Anyway, you'll have some company if you want it, and you can be alone when you don't. It's the perfect solution. For everyone.'

It wasn't exactly the perfect solution; that would be Cal saying he'd made a mistake and we'd stay together and build a new dream. But it was better than the alternative, and beggars couldn't be choosers, as Nan always says. Plus it would be lovely to spend more than the few short hours I usually did with Nan, during one of my flying visits to my home town.

Nan, whose name as I said, is Nancy so everyone calls her Nan, which can seem a bit confusing at times, moved into the residential care home, Conqueror's Court when Mum passed away five years ago.

Prior to that, Nan lived at our family home with us. She moved in soon after Dad left, many years before, having sold her own small cottage to help Mum pay the mortgage on our house. Dad only took two suitcases and his clothes and personal belongings when he left, saying Mum could keep the house. What he failed to mention was that he wouldn't be paying anything towards either the mortgage or the upkeep, and Mum stood more chance of seeing a flying pig than she ever did of seeing any maintenance payments from him for me and Emma.

Mum had to find a job; she'd been a full time, stay at home mum beforehand and she had to pay not just the mortgage but also for all the repairs to the house. And there were a lot. It might have been a bargain when Mum and Dad first bought it, but there was a reason for that as they soon discovered.

Even with Nan's help, sometimes the four of us weren't sure if we could afford to keep the lights on. Layers of extra jumpers and socks, and snuggling together under fleece blankets were our main form of heating during winter. Fish and chips were a special treat for us and birthday parties were put on hold for several years. Mum and Nan always made birthday cakes for me and Emma, and we would always get a present. Either something homemade or something 'preloved' as Nan and Mum called it; namely something purchased from one of the many charity shops on the high street.

But even so, Emma and I had the happiest childhoods we could – without our dad, and we both have many very special memories of those days.

At times like this, I miss Mum even more than usual. I miss her warmth, the smell of her homemade lavender soap, the trill of her laughter, the soft caress of her reassuring words, the tight hugs she would give us, and the boundless love she had. And her smile. I miss her smile more than I can possibly say. So do Emma and Nan.

It had been Nan's choice to move to Conqueror's Court. She told me and Emma that she didn't want to cramp our style but when we tried to get her to change her mind, she said that in truth, she didn't want us to cramp hers. She was going to have some fun during her final years on Earth, she told us, and she wanted to be with people her own age.

I'm not entirely certain which one of those is true, but she's definitely having fun at Conqueror's Court. It's more than just a care home. It has studio apartments for the elderly, which are twice the size of Tori's, and that gives the residents their own front doors and doorbells, and a great amount of independence.

Nan joked that the apartment was the first of three 'boxes' she'd be in, on her way to rejoin her late husband and her beloved daughter, my mum. The second was a room in the care home section of the building that she'd occupy when she grew either too infirm or too incapable to take care of herself, and the third, was her coffin. Nan has a weird sense of humour. But no amount of reasoning would make her change her mind.

At the same time as Nan moved to Conqueror's Court, Emma bought herself a small flat in the centre of town with her share of the money we received from the sale of the family home. We didn't want to remain in that house, not without Mum, and even if we had, we weren't sure we could afford to. Something was always going wrong, or breaking down, or falling apart.

We should've moved somewhere else long before, but Mum didn't want to sell it. She said it was because of all the upheaval it would entail, and the fact that the bank probably wouldn't give her another mortgage, but I think part of the reason she didn't want to move was that she hoped, in spite of what he did, that Dad might return. If we moved, he might not know where to find us.

It had been a fight for Mum and Nan to take over the mortgage when Dad left. I don't know exactly what it entailed but I do remember the nights Mum was in tears about it, when she thought Emma and I were tucked up in bed, and how Nan had comforted her.

I tried to comfort her once but she told me I shouldn't be worrying about such things and it was clear it hurt her for me to see her like that. It wasn't because she was too proud or anything; it was because she didn't want me to be upset or worried. Mum did her very best to put on a brave face for us. She was an incredibly selfless person.

Mum left everything she had to Nan, Emma and me, although she had no expectation of passing away before her own mother. But Mum wanted to be sure that Nan was repaid the money she had sunk into the family home. If Nan had died before her, as we had all anticipated, not unreasonably, the bequest to Nan would've been split between me and Emma.

Mum's death had been completely unexpected. She was only fifty-eight and had rarely been unwell, other than with the occasional cold. There had never been the slightest indication that anything was seriously wrong with her health.

Sudden Adult Death Syndrome, the doctors called it. That was basically a cover all; a term used whenever an adult dies suddenly following a cardiac arrest and no obvious cause can be found.

I wanted answers even though I knew I would never get them. Mum's death ripped my world apart and there was nothing I could do about it.

It took a few months for probate to be granted but the house sold fairly quickly. The plot it sat on was big enough for three houses apparently, assuming permission was granted, and the purchaser was prepared to take that chance. It didn't sell for a fortune due to the state it was in; we'd never really had enough to spend on it to bring out any potential it might have. Emma and I both offered to help out financially, once we started work, but other than a nominal sum towards our living costs, Mum wouldn't take anything from us. In fact, she actually got cross with us about it.

'You save your money, my darlings,' she said. 'I want you to use it to buy homes of your own, one day. Or to help you achieve your dreams. You're certainly not going to throw it away by spending it on this old place. I know you want to help, and I love you both for that, but I never want to hear you say this again.'

I wish Mum would've let us carry more of the burden, but she was as stubborn as she was determined.

Emma said I could move into her new flat with her, but instead I moved to London with Callum and Tori. It was something the three of us had planned to do long before, and I had actually tried to persuade Emma to go with us. But Emma loved our home town, and she already had a great career. London wasn't very far away and we saw one another as often as we could.

'Aaron said he'd keep an eye on the place for me,' Emma now continued. 'But he works shifts so he's not always around. I'd feel so much happier knowing you were living here.'

'It would be good to have somewhere to stay where I can sit and think about my future,' I agreed. 'As bleak as my life's going to be, I suppose I've got to sort something out. Wait. Who's Aaron? Have you got yourself a new man? And if so, why haven't you mentioned him before?' I tutted, putting my own heartache to one side for a moment. 'It's not like you to keep such things a secret.'

Emma laughed. 'He's not my new man. He's my neighbour. The hunky firefighter. I told you about him. Tall, dark-haired, handsome. He's a bit too old for me. I draw the line at thirty-five and he's thirty-nine.' The timbre of Emma's voice altered noticeably. 'The perfect age for you.'

'What? No way. Forget it, Em! I'm heartbroken, remember?'

'Yeah, yeah. But what better way is there to get over Cal and show him you don't care than to start dating someone new? Aaron's gorgeous, Katie. As I said, he's tall, broad shouldered, fit, obviously. And he's single. He does have a bit of a mean and moody vibe about him but maybe that's because he's lonely. Not that he seems lonely. People are always coming and going to his house. And he's not mean. Far from it, actually. I don't know why I said that. Maybe distant, is a better description. Anyway, you can make up your own mind when you meet him. Both times you've visited, he was working, so I don't think you got to see him, did you?'

'I wouldn't have asked you who he was if I had. But please don't get any ideas about trying to fix us up, Em because I'm seriously not in the mood to meet someone new. I'm still in love with Callum. Even if he's no longer in love with me.' Which I still hoped wasn't true.

I had only spent a couple of weekends at Emma's new house. The first was when she moved in six months before, in July, during what turned out to be the hottest weekend of the summer. Emma had got a good price for her flat and the new house was a bargain. The second was at the end of October, for Emma's thirtieth birthday. A hunky man would've come in handy on both occasions, but not for the reasons Emma was now clearly suggesting.

Emma had employed a removal firm to pack and deliver everything for her when she moved out of her flat into her house, but removal firms don't help with the unpacking. They did put the double beds back together in each of the two bedrooms, and the small dining table and sofa in the large living room but other than that, Emma and I, along with some of Emma's friends did the rest.

Not one of Emma's friends could ever be described as 'hunky'. One was chunky, possibly, but the others were leaning towards skinny. Computer software companies didn't seem to attract hunky, outdoorsy types very often. At least, not the company Emma worked for.

A hunky man would've come in handy on Emma's birthday weekend too. Why Emma had thought it would be fun to have a marquee in her garden at the end of October, draped in fairy lights and bunting was still a mystery to me. And that weekend had turned out to be the windiest and wettest weekend of the year so far. All the guests, including me, had spent most of the evening trying to ensure the marquee didn't fly off into the stratosphere. We failed, and ended up like drowned rats in the process. We never did find the marquee. Cal said, when I told him about it later, that someone probably stuck it in their shed and would use it the following summer.

Cal hadn't been able to come to Emma's party. He had promised to help his dad with something, although I can't remember what, come to think of it, but he said he couldn't break his promise, especially not as his parents had done so much for us.

I'd actually questioned that statement at the time; they'd helped us out a couple of times and they'd paid for the trip to New York, but other than that, I didn't feel we owed them any particular debt. Of course, now I know about the money they've given Cal that puts an entirely different light on it. But I was hurt that he hadn't come to Emma's party. Not that Emma minded in the least.

Emma never did anything by halves. But she couldn't really be blamed for the weather. Not even Emma could control that. She did try to control anything else she could though. Including her elder sister's life, namely mine, given the slightest chance.

'This is a new beginning, Katie,' Emma said. 'I'll let Aaron know you'll be staying here for the next four weeks. I'm sure you two will get on like a house on fire.' She gave a snort of laughter. 'That's apt as he's a firefighter. It's all going to work out brilliantly. I can feel it. You wait and see.'

I didn't want to wait and see. I didn't want my younger sister to fix me up with the neighbour, however handsome and hunky he might be. I want things to be the way they were before the love of my life had dropped his bombshell and blown my world apart.

Four

My fingers clenched the steering wheel, my knuckles as white as the snowflakes swirling around my car. At this rate I'd be lucky to reach Emma's house by eight p.m., several hours later than promised. Emma had already forgiven my late departure, given the circumstances, via an exchange of hurried texts, but Emma did not like people being late, not even her only sister, and this additional delay did not bode well.

Perhaps it was a sign? Maybe I should've accepted Tori's offer instead of Emma's. Spending the next four weeks, including Christmas and New Year with my best friend as opposed to spending it house-sitting – alone – for Emma who was off to the U.S.A for her work, might have been a better idea, all things considered.

'God! That man is a cold-hearted bastard,' Emma had said when I had phoned to tell her why I was running so late. 'I've never understood what you saw in him. He always seemed wrong for you somehow. I didn't say so yesterday because you were so upset, but at least you're out of it now. You may not think so, right at this moment, Katie, but this is the best thing that could've happened.'

'Yeah right. I thought you liked him?'

'I did. Sort of. Nan didn't like him. And she always said this would happen.'

That was true.

'Nan never thinks anyone is good enough for either of us. But you and Nan didn't know him the way I did.'

'I hate to point this out, but it seems you didn't know him that well either. You said this was a bolt out of the blue. That you had no idea he felt this way. No clue that he didn't love you anymore. No notion that you were about to lose your home. Only that the restaurant and therefore your job, might be at risk.'

'Yes. Thanks for rubbing a barrel of salt into my open wound!'

'Sorry. But it's the truth. And Tori didn't know what you saw in him either so it wasn't just me and Nan.'

That was also true.

Truth can be bloody irritating.

What could possibly be causing this hold-up? There had been no mention of traffic jams or road works on the local news and none appeared on the screen of my infotainment system on my car dashboard. But this was a jam to beat all jams. Cars snaked along the motorway, their rear lights and brake lights flickering like the longest string of fairy lights known to man. Or woman.

I had no one to blame but myself. I should've left at four. I had told Emma I would. But Cal, who had spent the night at a friend's place to give me some space and some time to "come to terms with the situation", had come home earlier than expected and, once again, I had done what I had promised myself I wouldn't: I'd asked for an explanation.

No. I'd pleaded for one. Begged, even.

'These things happen, Katie,' Cal had said. 'People fall out of love just as often as they fall into it.'

The shoulder shrug annoyed me as much as the eye-roll. How could he be so cavalier about it? So nonchalant? So unfeeling? Tears welled in my eyes but I blinked them back. I hadn't cried in front of him when he first broke the news. I wasn't going to cry in front of him now.

'So that's it?' My screech made me wince just as it had him. I coughed to clear my throat. 'After almost six years, you've simply fallen out of love with me?'

He avoided my teary stare and blinked several times as if he might be fighting back tears of his own, but his words made that seem unlikely. 'Yes. And you can keep asking me the same question until you're blue in the face but my answer won't change. I don't love you anymore, Katie. Please don't make this more difficult than it has to be. Don't you think we both have enough to deal with right now? We've lost our business and our home. I hoped we could still be friends.'

'Friends?' That screech actually hurt and I swallowed to ease the scratchy feeling at the back of my throat. If he'd said that yesterday I'd have jumped at the chance. Anything was better than nothing, but now I was cross. Cross that he seemed to care so little. Cross that he had hidden just how bad things were from me. Cross that he had given me so little time to prepare. Cross that I still loved a man who clearly did not love me. 'You're dumping me, just weeks before Christmas, leaving me with no home, no job, no boyfriend ... and no explanation, and you think we can still be friends?'

Another shrug, this time accompanied by an audible sigh, told me I was fighting a losing battle.

'I had hoped so. Clearly we can't. And I have given you an explanation. Several times last night and God knows how many more times today. Calling me every hour when I told you I was going to be busy and had various meetings all day didn't help, you know. Stalking me isn't going to make me fall back in love with you.' He sighed again and shook his head. 'Sorry. That was mean. And I don't want to be mean. I just want ... I just want you to see things from my perspective, Katie. It's over. If you had simply accepted it, and been reasonable, then perhaps you could've stayed here until we both have to move out. But bombarding me with several text messages and numerous calls last night and then more calls and texts today, made it obvious that wouldn't be a good idea.'

I cringed at that rebuke. Cal was right. Last night had not been my finest hour. Nor had today.

When he told me he was going to stay with a friend and had left, I had tried to come to terms with it, as he had suggested. But how do you come to terms with something you don't understand? This was just like it had been when I'd lost Mum. These things happen, the doctors had said then, just as Cal had told her now.

When I told Tori that I wanted to be alone, I knew, deep down, she wouldn't let me. I was right. She arrived just before lunchtime with two large, meat-feast pizzas, a tub of Christmas Pudding flavoured ice cream, two bottles of Prosecco because she was determined that I would see this as a reason to celebrate, not to regret – and a bottle of Bailey's. I hadn't drunk very much, I never do, but what I had drunk had gone straight to my head. Encouraged by Tori, I'd called Cal to give him a piece of my mind. And then I'd called him again to give him some more. And then again because I'd forgotten one or two choice words, and then once more because ... well, I can't exactly remember, but I hadn't stopped at that.

This morning, with a hangover in spite of only drinking two glasses of Prosecco and none of the Bailey's, and a queasy tummy from definitely eating too much pizza, and ice cream, I'd called Callum to apologise, been angry that he hadn't taken my call, and called him again. Several times. Followed by some slightly insane and desperate-sounding texts. My final text had said that I thought I'd temporarily 'lost my mind' due to the shock of it all.

Cal had eventually replied saying that it shouldn't have been a shock and that it had been coming for ages. That had, unfortunately, made things worse, so that final text wasn't my final text, after all. The final one was a stream of foul language and name-calling.

Feeling awful about that, I'd phoned to apologise. By the time I was due to leave for Emma's, I'd done nothing except text and phone and fume, which was why I was still packing when Callum had returned at five p.m.

And then I'd gone a little crazy once again, as if the bombardment of texts and calls during the night and several more frantic texts and phone calls today, weren't quite enough. I think it was because it suddenly all felt so final. It was the end of an era – the end of my dream.

'I can be reasonable!' Even as I said that I knew that wasn't exactly true, given the circumstances.

Cal's eyes were blue balls of ice. 'No, Katie. You can't. Do us both a favour and just go. Please. Before I say something we might both regret. I'm going to get changed. I hope that you'll be gone by the time I come back down. I thought you'd be gone already. You'll be driving to your sister's at night now and you hate driving at night.' One of the many messages I had left on his phone was that I'd be going to stay at Emma's … and that I hoped the distance would give him time to think and make him see this was a mistake. 'And before you say it again, no, I won't change my mind. I don't need time to think. I've done nothing but think for several weeks now and believe me, Katie, this is for the best. You'll realise that in a day or two. If you'll just stop texting me and phoning me every five minutes and give *yourself* time to think.'

All I could think about was everything I'd lost. My boyfriend. My home. My job. I'd always thought we'd get through the tough times together and if needs be, start a new future, side by side. Instead, Cal had decided to go it alone.

'So how far away are you?' Emma said now.

'Not that far, annoyingly. I'm tempted to pull over, abandon the car and walk. But they fine you for leaving your vehicle on a motorway unless it's broken down, don't they? I'm within spitting distance of the slip road, and I can almost touch the bridge from here, but the queue isn't even moving. You'll have to come and dig my frozen body out of two metres of snow in the morning.'

'Don't exaggerate. And anyway, I can't. I'll be on my way to Heathrow tomorrow morning. Hello, New York!'

'Leaving your broken-hearted sister, alone.'

'I said you could come with me. It's not too late. We could probably still get you a ticket. Assuming my flight isn't cancelled, that is. If the snow is as bad as this all night, there might not be any flights tomorrow. But if there are, you could come. Why don't you? I'll have most of my evenings free. I'll have to do a bit of work out of hours, but I can do that with you there.'

'Thanks. But I told you. New York will only bring back memories of happier times for me. And if I'm going to spend all day every day crying for the foreseeable future, I'd rather not do it in a hotel room, thanks all the same. Besides, Nan won't be happy if one of us doesn't stay and spend Christmas with her. You said so yourself. You've got to go to New York for your work, so it's got to be me.'

'Lucky Nan.'

'Don't be sarcastic. Wait! Woohoo! We're moving. We're actually moving.' I put the car in gear and edged forward. 'Snails go faster, but at least I've moved a couple of feet. The junction is tantalisingly close now. Hold on. We're moving again. And this time it looks ... yes! Oh. My. God. I'm just about to turn off onto the road to paradise.'

'I think you mean the road to Norman Landing, don't you?'

'After the last twenty-four hours I've had, Em, believe me, even Norman Landing seems like paradise. At least the large glass of red wine I know you'll have waiting for me does.'

'Yay. I'll get us a take-away. If I order it now, it'll be here by the time you arrive.'

'I'm not that hungry.' My stomach told me otherwise.

'Was that a stomach rumble or thunder?' Emma laughed. 'I heard that from here.'

I'm pretty sure she didn't; she just knows how much I like food. But then again, with hands free mobile, you can never be quite sure what the other person can hear. I remember being on the phone with Nan when I was driving home for Emma's birthday in October. Nan was giving me the 'benefit of her wisdom', as she likes to call it, and I mumbled something sarcastic. I can't remember what it was now and I swear I could hardly hear what I said myself. Nan's in her eighties and yet she heard every word.

'If you don't want my advice,' she said, 'you only have to say so.'

Yeah right. Like that would ever stop her.

Since then I've been more careful with making sarcastic asides when on the phone.

'I'm not sure I can face food,' I said to Emma. 'But okay. Get me the usual, please. Oh bloody hell. I don't believe it.' I sniggered. 'They're still defacing the welcome sign at the top of the turn-off, I see. Someone's scrawled an apostrophe and then an 's' after Norman. But someone else has tried to scrub out the first apostrophe and add one after the new 's'. It's almost comforting to know that some things never change here.'

Emma laughed. 'Ah. The good old debate about what the name of this town should be and what comes first. The apostrophe or the 's'. But that might change before too long. The powers that be have agreed to fund a couple of cameras to be placed somewhere nearby each of the welcome signs at either end of town so that they can see who keeps defacing them. They've had to replace those signs too many times over the years and they still can't agree whether it should be *Norman's* Landing, *Normans'* Landing or the completely incorrect, Norman Landing that we've all now grown accustomed to.' Emma emphasized the relevant words. 'I think it should be *Normans'* Landing. If this really is the place William the Conqueror and his band of merry Normans landed before they sacked and pillaged all the towns nearby and gave old Kind Harold one in the eye, then it should be Normans'. Nan, of course, still says we should change the name entirely, but no one listens to her these days. Or so she keeps saying.'

'I'm with you on the name. And where the apostrophe should be. Although I can also think of somewhere else they could stick it. I'll hang up now as the traffic seems to have miraculously cleared.'

'Any indication of what caused it?'

'Nope. Order my curry and pour the wine. I'll be there in the jingle of Santa's bells.' I felt more cheerful now that I was on my way once again, especially as the snow was really coming down. I love snow, but I didn't want to be driving in it for much longer. Visibility was poor and getting worse by the second.

'At least you're sounding jollier,' Emma said.

'It's the thought of sitting in front of your roaring, log fire with a curry and a glass of wine.' I managed a smile, although Emma couldn't see it. But it slid from my face like melted snow as I drove over the bridge which crossed the motorway and led into town. 'Oh no!' I caught a glimpse of flashing lights and a big red truck and slowed to get a better look. 'I think I just saw a fire engine and a police car ... and an ambulance. There're some of those pop-up floodlights on the motorway, a few metres past the slip road. There's been an accident, Em!' Not wanting to be one of those people who stare at others' misfortune I looked away and sped up a little, still taking care in the snowy and icy conditions. 'I really hope they're all okay.'

Five

Aaron removed his yellow safety helmet and swiped the back of his right hand across his forehead. Despite the swirling snow and the temperature hovering a little above freezing, he was sweltering and he gratefully accepted the bottle of water, Bert, one of the other crew members of Blue Watch, tossed in his direction. Aaron had been working non-stop for almost an hour and the cutters, spreaders, or 'the jaws of life' as they were called, were not exactly light. But the surge of relief, once he and his fellow firefighters had cut the man free from the crumpled wreckage of what was previously a gleaming new sports car, was worth every second.

'Christmas is a time for miracles,' Bert said, opening his own bottle of water, 'and that guy definitely had a miraculous escape.' He nodded in the direction of what was left of the car.

Aaron tensed. Christmas and the word 'miracles' did not go hand in hand in his experience. But Bert was right about the guy's escape. It had been nothing short of a miracle for the drunk driver in question.

It had started snowing late afternoon and had been doing so on and off ever since. As the evening progressed, the temperature dropped and conditions were becoming more treacherous by the minute. Drivers should be taking more care than usual, not less.

When Blue Watch arrived, less than five minutes after the tele-printer clicked into action with details of the call out, they were the first of the emergency services on the scene, followed less than ten seconds later by a couple of police patrol cars and shortly after that, an ambulance. Bert was the designated driver this shift and he had positioned the fire truck, complete with its snow chains, across the motorway to stop the oncoming traffic; the police immediately began cordoning off the road and the paramedics prepared to assist any casualties.

Aaron was the first out of the truck and initially thought the driver of the badly wrecked car possibly hadn't survived, but that didn't affect how he did his job. It looked as if the car had crashed into a lorry that might've been stationary and parked on the hard shoulder. Other vehicles seemed to be involved in a separate but clearly related incident. The drivers of those five cars had either braked too hard to avoid the first car, or been unable to control their vehicles and swerved on the icy road. None of those drivers or their passengers were probably seriously hurt as the damage to those vehicles appeared to be fairly minor. But you could never be sure.

The priority was the badly wrecked car and this wouldn't be a cool, calm extraction of the casualty. Smoke was rising from the car bonnet which was half way under the rear, right side of the lorry, and although the lorry bore no red diamond symbols or other safety hazard warnings, again, you could never be certain what load it might be transporting.

Aaron grabbed the hooligan, as it was known, the correct name being a halligan tool, and smashed out the already badly damaged car windscreen so that he could get a better view of who and what was inside. While other crew members dealt with the prospect of a fire, Aaron and another crew member, Steve set about removing the driver's door using the heavy cutters. The weather hampered their efforts but it took them less than twenty minutes. Freeing the driver from the inflated airbag and the mangled remains of the steering column took a little longer, but they had him out and on a stretcher within thirty minutes of arrival at the scene.

Inwardly, Aaron now fumed at the man's selfishness and stupidity but neither Aaron nor his crew mates let their personal feelings affect the way they worked. They were there to save lives and that was exactly what they had done. Not that they would get any thanks for it, and not that any of them expected thanks.

Aaron was glad that, on this occasion, no one had died. Even the drunk driver appeared to have only minor injuries. He had to agree, that was miraculous. Although that prognosis might change on further examination. But that wasn't Aaron's concern.

He and his crew from Blue Watch had rescued the man, who was probably around Aaron's age – late thirties, and helped the other five drivers involved along with their passengers. A total of fifteen stunned but otherwise relatively unharmed people, two barking dogs, one cat (amazingly still fast asleep in its basket) and one caged and noisy parrot were assisted to safety. The police would take statements and help with arrangements for onward journeys.

It transpired that the collisions had been caused by the drunk driver losing control of his flashy new car, exactly as Aaron had thought. The man skidded, as could still be seen from the tracks on the snow and ice-covered motorway, although the falling snow might quickly hide that evidence, but not before the police took photos, Aaron was sure of that. The man had seemingly been unable to control the skid and his car went into a spin, finally crashing headlong into the rear, right side of the lorry. The drivers of the other vehicles had either been too close to the sports car, or unprepared for what was happening and had been unable to avoid crashing into one another.

'It just seemed to be spinning,' Aaron heard one of them say to a paramedic. 'Like an ice skater doing one of those fast twisty spins, you know? Round and round and round. Almost on the spot. I didn't know what to do. Or how to avoid crashing into it. I braked too hard, I think, but I managed to avoid it. Then someone slammed into me. Do I have whiplash? Will I be okay?'

'Is that guy dead?' another asked.

'Will I lose my no-claims bonus,' queried a third.

Aaron left the paramedics and the police to answer those questions.

That was another problem in weather like this; so many people had no idea how to drive on ice and snow. And not one vehicle, other than the police and rescue service vehicles had snow chains. Then again, heavy snow was a rarity in this part of the UK so snow chains wouldn't often be required. But it only took one night of bad weather to cause traffic and transport chaos. This section of the motorway would be closed for several hours. The highways authorities would have to do a thorough clear up before traffic could flow freely again. Mind you, if the snow continued coming down as hard as it was now, even slower speed limits would be imposed. Not that everyone took notice of speed restrictions; the drunk driver clearly hadn't.

'I'm surprised no one was badly hurt,' Steve said, tucking his hand through the strap of his helmet so that it swung from his forearm and letting out a long sigh. 'When will these stupid sods ever learn?'

Aaron took a slug of water from the bottle Bert had given him and shook his head. 'Sometime never. You've been doing this job long enough to know that some people are idiots and selfish bastards and always will be.'

'Yeah,' Bert agreed. 'That jerk will probably blame the snowy conditions for his loss of control, not the fact that he was six sheets to the wind and clearly speeding. He's lucky the car didn't go up in flames.'

Steve scowled. 'With that much alcohol in his system it was a miracle *he* didn't spontaneously combust.' He slapped Aaron on the back. 'Great job, mate. For a minute there I thought we might have to saw the jerk out. What a plonker! I'm almost light-headed from the alcohol fumes. The coppers will be reading him the Riot Act. Hope they throw the book at him.'

'We will.' Tony, one of the police officers at the scene and a man Blue Watch knew well as he had a brother who was a firefighter in Green Watch, approached, shaking his head. 'It really pees me off when morons like that risk not just their lives but the lives of others. Don't they watch TV? Haven't they seen the warnings? We spend enough on the sodding things.' He shook his head again. 'Sorry. I'll get off my soapbox. Just feeling it a bit tonight. It's Josh's birthday tomorrow and I got nagged at for forgetting to pick up his present when I got up today, so the missus will have to do it first thing tomorrow before she goes to work. I said I'd go but you know Jane. She says I'll forget again.' He shrugged and leant against the open side of the fire engine, surrounded by the rows of equipment the firefighters needed for their job. 'She was in a right mood. I was glad I was on duty tonight until we got this call out. Hate RTAs, especially in these conditions.'

'Me too,' Bert said. 'That guy's one lucky bastard. It could've been a completely different story.'

Road traffic accidents weren't on Aaron's list of favourite call outs either. Not that he had such a list. Even a seemingly minor incident, like a cat stuck in a tree, could turn into a disaster if things went pear-shaped. Thankfully, that rarely happened. But until you reached the scene you could never be entirely sure what the call involved from reading the print-out sheet.

Steve grinned at Tony. 'Jane's right. You would forget.'

Tony cocked one eyebrow, shrugged and grinned. 'Yeah. Probably.'

Aaron shook his head. How could anyone forget their own son's birthday? Especially such a great kid like Josh.

'Wish Josh a happy birthday from us,' Aaron said, screwing the cap back on the water bottle as he watched the ambulance crew load the first casualty, the drunk driver.

A second ambulance had arrived and paramedics were dealing with the others involved in the incident, most of whom were able to walk unaided, thankfully. Aaron went to see if any of them needed his assistance, just as the first ambulance drove off, sirens blaring and lights flashing, heading for the hospital two miles away.

Ambulance services were so short-staffed that these days, fire crews often gave assistance. They were now frequently called to aid paramedics with tasks such as getting housebound people out of their homes and into the ambulances. Or lifting patients; gaining access to injured parties who had fallen or were trapped in inaccessible places; or anything else that was required of them. They sometimes assisted the police too. A firefighter's day was not often spent actually fighting fires. Thankfully.

When Aaron had first joined up at eighteen, after completing his A levels, he thought he'd be dashing into flames to rescue people on a regular basis and the idea of that excited him. He soon discovered that wasn't the case. And these days he was grateful it wasn't. He had seen his share of fires – one too many, in fact. Or one in particular. One he was sure he would never forget.

For a time, after that one, he wondered if he could continue as a firefighter, and almost quit. But quitting wasn't in him. It wasn't who he was. He had taken time off, having been told he had to, and he'd received counselling, but when he returned to Blue Watch, he was oddly relieved to be back.

The first fire his watch responded to on his return had been in a small block of flats and flames were billowing from the building when they arrived. He felt things he never had before. A momentary panic. Doubt as to whether he could do a good job. Fear of what he might find. But within seconds his instincts and his professionalism kicked in and all he was thinking about was saving everyone he could. That night he and the crew, along with another crew called to attend, had rescued everyone from the fire. But sadly, one person had died. Not from smoke or flames, but from a heart attack.

Aaron and Steve had found the elderly man and Steve, assisted by Bert, took care of the deceased; Aaron checked the rest of the flat. There was no one else in occupation. But just as Aaron was about to leave, a movement caught his eye. He knelt down to get a closer look and his heart melted. Hiding under the armchair in which the owner had died, was a little white dog. A dog who backed away at first when Aaron reached for him.

'Come on, little one,' Aaron had said, although the dog probably couldn't hear him above the noise of the flames and engines and sirens and shouting. 'This is no place for you right now. Come to me and we'll get you somewhere safe. I bet you'd like a drink of water.'

Flames were licking the walls within a metre or so of them and Aaron had to act fast. The dog gingerly stretched forward to sniff Aaron's glove and Aaron reached out and grabbed the dog by the scruff of his neck, pulled the bundle of blackened fur towards him as he got to his feet, and hurried from the flat as the entire ceiling of that room caught fire.

'All clear', came the shout to confirm that the rest of the building had been searched and that everyone was out, as Aaron made his way to Blue Watch's truck with his tiny bundle.

'Is that a rat?' Bert asked, grinning.

'A Westie, I think,' Aaron replied, smiling for the first time in a long while. 'A puppy. Chuck me some water.'

He cradled the dog in his right arm, removed his helmet, and rinsed his left glove with some of the water Bert handed him and then poured a little of it into his cupped hand and offered it to the puppy. The little thing lapped it up and then licked Aaron's glove and looked up at Aaron as if to say, 'thank you.'

'I wonder if this little guy has anyone who'll look after him,' Aaron said.

Steve, who was now stacking equipment close by, laughed and stepped towards Aaron, slapping him on the back.

'I think we can safely say, he does now.'

Aaron drew his brows together and then relaxed them. He lived alone and worked shifts of two days followed by two nights and then had four days off. Owning a dog would be a problem when he was on shift, but his mum and dad lived nearby, not to mention, his sister. If no one else claimed this little soul because the deceased owner might not have relatives, Aaron would adopt him and work something out. He had already thought of a name. He would call the little guy Ember.

Now, Aaron often wondered who saved whom that day. Did he save Ember, or did Ember save him? Aaron's dark moods had definitely been growing worse until that night when a little bundle of smoke-blackened fur trusted Aaron with his life.

No one claimed the puppy, and Aaron officially adopted Ember. As he had assumed, when he was on shift, his parents, or his sister, Meg were more than happy to look after the little guy. Ember was being spoilt rotten. But he deserved it after such a shaky start.

Now, four years later, Ember ruled not only Aaron's house, but also Meg's and their parents' houses too. And for a West Highland White Terrier that was under twenty-eight centimetres tall, that was some achievement.

Six

Saying goodbye to Emma the next morning made me wish I'd got to her place earlier; that I hadn't stayed and tried to talk to Cal. For all the good that did me.

I hadn't seen Emma since her thirtieth birthday weekend and now I wouldn't be seeing her until next year. I know the New Year was only four weeks away but when she got into the limo her company had sent to transport her to the airport, and we waved goodbye, I wanted to run to the car and beg her not to go.

I wasn't sure exactly what was wrong with me at that moment but I seemed to be having a problem with people leaving me.

I felt the same when Dad left, and again when Mum died, but on those occasions, I had other people around me, comforting me and reassuring me that it would all be okay. Even when Cal left, I had Tori.

With Emma on her way to the airport, and Tori still at work in London, I had no one, once I closed Emma's front door. That was a very strange feeling. I can't remember the last time I was ever on my own. Completely alone.

I was being dramatic. I wasn't completely alone. Nan's studio flat in Conqueror's Court was less than ten minutes' walk away, if I cut across the park. Fifteen to twenty if I took the roads, but only a couple of minutes by car. But Emma's house seemed oddly empty, in spite of the fact that I loved the place. I've felt at home at Emma's both times I've stayed and this time shouldn't have been any different.

Except it already was. This time I didn't have a boyfriend. Or a job. Or my own home to return to when I left.

Part of me was hoping Emma wouldn't be able to go, that her flight would be cancelled or delayed. It had snowed on and off all night and we awoke to a sparkling white blanket of it, at least five or six centimetres deep. But only a flurry of snow had made it as far west as Heathrow, it seemed, where it had promptly turned to rain, and Emma's driver had called to say, having checked all the traffic reports and travel conditions, the roads from Norman Landing to the airport were all surprisingly clear. No doubt due to prior gritting by the relevant authorities, together with some people deciding to stay at home.

There was a brief mention of the accident of the night before but all the news reporter said was that the motorway was now clear after an accident involving several vehicles; that fire and rescue, together with the police and ambulance had quickly been at the scene, and it had resulted in three people being taken to hospital with minor injuries but there had been no fatalities.

'I wonder if Aaron was there,' Emma said when we heard it. 'He was working last night, I believe.'

'I'm glad no one was seriously hurt. I know accidents are dreadful at any time of year but they somehow seem worse around Christmastime. I hope your driver takes care.'

Emma rolled her eyes. 'Don't you start worrying about me. He once worked for the police, so if anyone knows how to drive in these conditions, it's him. They receive special training, you know.'

I don't know if he was once in the police or if Emma was just saying that so that I wouldn't feel anxious, but as she also reminded me, 'Nan always says, "Worrying won't make things better. All it'll do is give you indigestion." And no one wants that.'

Instead of leaving later as I'd hoped, Emma left a little earlier, just in case the roads weren't as clear as believed. I stood and watched the car until it was out of sight and after closing the front door, I burst into floods of tears.

Maybe staying at Tori's teeny-tiny flat might've been a better idea after all.

Emma's house is a new-build, two-bedroom, one of which has an en suite comprising of a toilet and shower. That seems a bit pointless for a two-bed house, but I suppose it's handy if you need the loo on a freezing cold night. You don't have so far to dash from your warm and cosy bed. The main bathroom is small but there's enough room for a proper-sized bath, a full-sized sink and a toilet. Downstairs is the lounge diner, a good-sized kitchen, a cloakroom and an understairs cupboard, all off a square entrance hall spacious enough to fit two people at a time and still be able to open the doors.

It's a light and bright and airy yet cosy home and somewhere I wouldn't mind living myself. Emma's choice of soft, delicate colours gives it a calming feel. All the floors are light wood, and some rooms have rugs either matching or complementing the colour palette. The hall is light grey, the kitchen pale green and the lounge diner a soft blue with midnight blue rugs in both the sitting and dining areas.

Upstairs, the master bedroom is pale lavender but does have a shocking pink rug near the bed. The guest bedroom is a soft baby pink with a white rug, while the bathroom is light grey with a matching bathmat.

Emma had said I could use her room, or remain in the guest bedroom if I'd prefer. Her bedroom is at the back of the house overlooking her lovely garden, from which we lost the marquee. It's a surprisingly large garden for the size of the house, as is the garden next door. That's the house where the firefighter lives. The one Emma says is a hunk called Aaron.

Emma's house and his are detached but the space between each is only large enough to accommodate the wheelie bins on either side, so the houses are about two metres apart at most with a wooden fence of just under two metres between them.

Each house has a small driveway large enough for two cars, and each has a garage on opposite sides. They are at the end of a cul-de-sac with rows of four similar houses either side, leading out onto another road with identical-looking houses. It's a small estate of four roads, each of which is named after a fruit or nut tree.

Emma's house is in Cherry Tree Close, which leads onto Pear Tree Lane. Further along is Chestnut Crescent and then there's Hawthorn Road. That's the longest road with the most houses. They all surround or lead onto an area of common land called Mulberry Park where there are swings, a slide, a duck pond and a large expanse of grass. Emma's garden backs onto the park and in the early mornings you can hear the ducks quacking on the pond.

There were no ducks this morning. It was probably far too cold for them. I suddenly realised I was shivering and went and stood beside the radiator in the kitchen while I made myself another cup of coffee.

I'd had breakfast with Emma around six a.m. and it was only just gone nine now but I could feel a rumble in the pit of my stomach. Emma had told me to help myself to anything, so I rummaged through her cupboards looking for either biscuits or cakes. The cupboards were far from bare but there was a definite lack of anything sweet. Not even a bar of chocolate. That was something I would have to change.

Norman Landing isn't huge by any means but it does have more than its fair share of supermarkets; six to be precise. All the usual suspects and a local store that has

been around since 1066, or so the sign on
Conqueror's Convenience Store states.

That was the year of the Norman
invasion, so we all suspect there's no way
that is true, but no one has as yet been able
to prove it isn't. Records do show that there
has been a 'shoppe' on the site since way back
when such records began, so who am I to
argue?

From the outside it definitely looks as if
it's been there since before the Elizabethan
age; the first one, not the second. And inside,
in parts, you have to duck your head if you're
more than a certain height. The Health and
Safety people have sent them all sorts of
notices about it but the owners, Mr and Mrs
Williams have always managed to get around
such things. The local authority even went to
court about it. Don't ask me what happened
or why because to be honest, I wasn't that
interested at the time and I'm still not, but I
know the Williamses won. It was around the
time of Mum's death and I had far more
personal things on my mind.

I hadn't yet had a shower as I wanted to
spend as much time as possible with Emma
before she left so I went upstairs and got
showered, and dressed in jeans and a
jumper. I put on a pair of reindeer-patterned
socks and slid my feet back into my slippers.

I could hear shrieks of laughter and shouting at the front of the house so I went to the hall window to look out. A group of five or six kids were playing outside in the snow. It was still only around nine thirty or so but it was a Wednesday and they should've been in school.

Perhaps the schools had declared a 'snow day'. The kids were having a whale of a time throwing snowballs, building snow people, slipping and sliding on the snowy and icy pavements.

One set of parents appeared with what looked like two homemade sleds, and the kids jostled with one another to be the first to have a go on them. Obviously, the parents let their own children go first. I didn't know any of these people although I had met one or two of Emma's neighbours during the flyaway marquee incident, but two of the kids looked like little clones of these particular adults. All four had bright ginger curls and glasses and all four were dressed as if they'd stepped out of a catalogue. I could see from the window they had identical smiles and the kids were called Justin and Jade.

I decided to go outside and say hello. Emma had told me that she would tell her next-door neighbour, Aaron that I was staying while she was away, but I wasn't sure if any of the other neighbours knew. It wouldn't hurt to introduce myself.

I hurried downstairs, grabbed my coat from the cloakroom, pulled on my boots and gloves, wrapped a scarf of Emma's around my neck and tugged a bobble hat of hers that Nan had knitted, onto my mass of brown wavy hair and dashed out into the snow.

Sadly, I hadn't checked for ice on the path. Emma had held onto the railing at the side when she had left but I didn't think about doing that. My feet slipped like ice skates and my arms swung in the air like the sails of a windmill but I couldn't retain my balance. My feet flew up in the air followed by the rest of me and I landed on my backside with a thud and toppled onto my back.

'Are you okay?' a woman said, as a fluffy white dog wearing a bright red and black checked coat, came bounding over, jumped up onto my chest and unceremoniously licked my face. 'Ember. Naughty boy. Leave the poor woman alone.' The dog ignored her, no doubt because the woman was laughing.

I managed to grab the dog's collar and tried to push him off as gently as I could. I like dogs but I didn't want this display of friendship right now.

'Sorry!' The woman now towered above me, still smiling. She lifted the dog into her arms and put him down on the ground beside me. 'Stay, Ember. Good boy.' She tossed the dog a treat she had taken from her coat pocket and turned her attention back to me. 'Can you get up? Do you need help? Are you hurt?'

'The answer to all three is, I'm not sure.'

I took a deep breath and let it out. I was alive and I wasn't in pain. That was a good sign.

I tried to sit up and she reached out her gloved hand to help me. I took it and pushed myself upright with my other hand. So far so good.

'You're probably just winded,' she said, smiling but with a hint of concern in her deep brown eyes. 'I think the snow cushioned your fall.'

'It caused my fall,' I said, smiling back at her. 'I think I'm okay. No bones broken. Just my pride that's bruised.'

I realised everyone was staring at me. The kids all gaped and giggled; the ginger-haired adults moved towards me as if they were about to offer help. I scrambled to my feet and brushed myself down, giving the couple a friendly wave.

'I'm okay.'

They gave me a small wave back and went about their business which was making the kids form an orderly line for each one to take their turn on the sleds.

'I think they're all more interested in having fun,' the woman with the dog said. 'Are you sure you're okay?'

'Yes, thanks.' I smiled down at the dog who had finished his treat and was now on his hind legs snuffling against the woman's pocket in search of another, his bright red and black checked coat, almost the same colours as the woman's. 'And thank you for those lovely kisses.' I petted him by stroking his ears and he glanced briefly in my direction but what he wanted now was that treat, not to make friends with me.

The woman tossed another into the snow and he ran off to retrieve it.

'I'm Meg. I haven't seen you around here before. Are you visiting someone?' She laughed aloud and shook her head, holding up the palms of both hands in front of me. 'Sorry. None of my business. I work for the local paper so I tend to ask questions without thinking.'

I laughed too. 'That's okay. I'm Katie. I'm staying at my sister's for a few weeks. She's not here though. She's gone to New York for work.' I turned and pointed at Emma's house.

'Oh. You're Emma's sister! It's lovely to meet you, Katie. Emma told us you'd be here.'

'Us?' I queried.

She pointed to the house next door. 'Aaron and I. He's my older brother. Have you met him?'

'Oh! No. Not yet. I only arrived last night. I think he was working when I've been here before.'

'Probably. He works shifts. Two days on followed by two nights and then he gets four days off. He was working last night and the night before so he should be home any minute.' She leant forward. 'Word of warning. He can be a bit like a bear with a sore head sometimes but he's really a teddy bear when you get to know him.' Ember came bounding back and Meg bent down and ruffled his fur. 'This little devil is Ember. He's Aaron's dog but either me, or Mum and Dad look after him when Aaron's on shift.'

'Pleased to meet you, Ember.'

He barked as if saying the same to me and Meg and I laughed but her phone distracted her.

'Sorry,' she said, pulling it from the same pocket as the treats and glancing at the screen. 'It's work.'

'Don't mind me,' I stepped back, carefully this time, to give Meg her space but she didn't seem bothered about me overhearing her call.

'Right now?' She grimaced. 'I was supposed to be having the morning off because I was up late working on the RTA last night.' She let out a sigh. 'Yeah, yeah. I know. No rest for the wicked or for local reporters who want to be word famous photojournalists, right? Fine. I'll be there in ten minutes. I'm just dropping off Aaron's dog.' She rang off, sighed again and stuffed her phone back in her pocket. 'Damn. Where the hell is Aaron?' She glanced around as if expecting her brother to appear. 'Trust him to be late the one day I need to dash off and I've forgotten my bloody key. Sorry, Katie.' She pulled a semi apologetic face. 'I can be like a bear with a sore head too. I usually drop Ember inside if Aaron's not here yet, but I got a new key ring yesterday and as ridiculous as it sounds, I forgot to add Aaron's key to the damn thing, so I can't get in. Oh well, Ember. I suppose I'd better get you to Mum and Dad's and Aaron can pick you up from there.' She gave me a direct look. 'That'll please him no end when all he'll want to do is come home and sleep. It was great to meet you. Hope I'll see you again soon. We should grab a coffee or something.'

'Can I help at all?' I asked as she was turning to hurry away. 'If your brother will be home soon, I could look after Ember until he gets here, assuming he'll come with me, that is. I can keep an eye out for your brother, or put a note through his door telling him I've got his dog.'

Meg's eyes opened wide. 'You'd do that? Seriously? Wow.' She handed me the lead before I had a chance to change my mind. 'Ember will go to anyone. Sorry. I didn't mean that quite the way it sounded, but you know what I mean. Ember's very friendly. As you discovered just now. This is fantastic. Thanks so much. I'll return the favour, I promise. And so will Aaron. Don't worry about feeding him or anything. Just give him a bowl of water and a cuddle and he'll be fine.'

'I assume you're still talking about Ember and not your brother,' I joked. I had no idea why though.

Her brows furrowed momentarily and then she laughed. 'Good one! Yes. Try to cuddle my brother and he'll rip your hand off. Only joking. He's not that bad. Usually. Anyway, thanks again. Oh. I should give you my number in case there's a problem. Which there won't be.'

She dashed back towards me and we exchanged numbers and then she was gone, leaving me with my neighbour's dog and a feeling that I might've just bitten off more than I could chew.

Seven

'Hey you!' a male voice boomed out in the distance as I was about to take Ember for a short walk.

The little dog had been scratching at the door for the last five minutes and I didn't want Emma's paintwork to be ruined or for there to be a puddle of dog pee on her wooden floor.

We'd only been indoors for about ten minutes prior to that, so I wasn't sure if Ember wanted to pee, or if he was simply trying to get to his own home. Either way, a walk seemed the best option. Or it had done. I had put the bright red and black checked coat back on him, having removed it in the warmth of Emma's house, and we'd just turned out of the driveway and made it a few metres down the road before I heard the shout.

I turned around to see a man barrelling towards us. The snow and icy pavement didn't seem to be hampering his advance and I wondered at whom he was yelling. Apart from me and Ember, the ginger adults and the group of kids, only one other adult was on the street, busy scraping ice from her windscreen. Meg had told me she would text Aaron and tell him I had Ember, so this couldn't be Aaron concerned about his dog. This man looked angry even from the distance between us and Aaron wouldn't be angry. He'd be grateful.

I turned away, deciding whatever the man's intention it had nothing to do with me. I did suddenly wonder if the man was drunk or something. Even at this time in the morning. You hear about people being accosted for no reason at all and I considered dashing back indoors until the man had gone but before I had time to react, he was towering in front of me and was grabbing Ember's lead.

A dog thief! Oh no. I couldn't let this thug steal Ember.

'Get off!' I screamed, pushing the man away with all my might; an action that had no effect on him whatsoever. He was as solid as an oak tree. A snowflake might as well have tried to push away a snowman. 'Someone call the police!'

Only then did I notice that everyone was looking at me and this man as if we were putting on a show for them.

'I'll call the police,' the man said, his voice as cold as an iceberg, 'don't you worry about that. How the hell did you get in?' He yanked the lead from my hand, twisting my wrist painfully in the process.

'Owww!' I yelped. 'That hurt!'

I instinctively lunged at him, as Nan had taught me when she decided Emma, Mum and I needed to learn some self-defence moves that she herself had learnt at her OAP friendship group.

'We old age pensioners need to know how to look after ourselves these days,' she had said. 'And so do you, your mum and Emma.'

I shoved the flat of my other hand beneath my assailant's chin and pushed up hard. I couldn't reach his nose. The man was too tall. But his head snapped back and he too let out a sort of 'ugh' sound. He grabbed my arm in a hold so tight I could feel his fingers digging into my skin.

Ember was barking but oddly enough, not at the man – at me. And then it dawned on me what had happened. Meg had not texted Aaron. *This* was Aaron and he thought I was stealing his dog.

'Aaron!' I gasped, my eyes wide in horror. 'You *are* Aaron, aren't you? I'm not trying to steal your dog. Meg gave him to me!'

He glowered at me, a mixture of shock and doubt on his face. His dark eyes looked dangerous and the scowl on his lips gave him a murderous expression. His dark brows drew together and his eyes searched mine as if he was processing my words.

'Meg?' he said, his voice not quite as icy and his grip loosening slightly on my arm. 'Meg gave him to you? When? Who are you? Are you a friend of Meg's? I'm calling her right now. Don't move.'

I couldn't if I wanted to.

'You were late,' I said crossly. 'Her work called and she had to go. I'm Katie. Emma's sister. We're neighbours. I was trying to do you a favour. But I'm seriously regretting it now. I think you've just broken my wrist!'

'K-Katie!' His Adam's apple shot up and down as he swallowed hard. 'You're Katie?'

His phoned beeped and he dragged his astonished gaze from me and stared at the screen. A moment later he met my eyes and I couldn't believe the change I witnessed.

'Yes,' I said, sticking out my chin. 'I am. And you owe me an apology.'

I assumed he had just received Meg's text and he now realised his mistake. He let go of me so fast that I almost fell. I'd been tensing against his hold. He steadied me and a smile swept across his mouth, so full of apology but also so sexy that it was hard for me to stay cross.

'Oh shit! I'm so sorry. I ... I had no idea. Meg's only just texted me to explain.' He raised his phone a little as if to show me. 'Did I hurt you? Are you okay? I really am sorry. I thought ... that doesn't matter. I'm truly sorry.'

'Maybe next time you'll ask before you assault someone.' I rubbed my wrist.

'Are you hurt?' He reached out but I stepped away.

'Yes!' I snapped. 'But I'll probably survive.'

'Let me take a look at it. I know first aid.'

'No thanks. You've done enough for one day.'

'I said I'm sorry.' He sounded a little cross now. 'How was I supposed to know who you were?'

'You automatically assumed that I'd somehow gained access to your house and stolen your dog. Or that I'd overcome your sister and tossed her in a bush or something? You couldn't just come and ask me?'

He frowned at me and glanced at Ember, bending down to pick him up. I was surprised to see him smile at the dog and to give the dog a tiny kiss on his head.

'I didn't think. I didn't have time. I saw you with Ember and I ...' He shrugged. 'Okay. Now I realise I may have overreacted. But in my defence, I had no idea who you were.'

'That's not a defence. That's an excuse.'

'What more do you want me to say? I've said I'm sorry. I was concerned about my dog. I've asked if you're okay. And you gave me as good as you got. That shove you gave me made me bite my tongue, you know.'

'Good. You deserved it.'

I'm not sure why I was so cross. I would've behaved exactly as he had if I'd thought someone was stealing my dog.

'Fine. Well ... thank you for taking care of Ember.' His tone was flat.

'You're welcome.' I matched it.

We stared at one another for a second or two and then he looked away.

'I've been working all night and I'm shattered. If you're sure you're okay I'll get Ember indoors. Thanks again.' He turned away but quickly glanced back. 'Oh, and it was ... nice to meet you, Katie.'

'Huh! I wish I could say the same.'

I turned away too but then I realised I had to walk in the same direction as him. I hesitated for a moment as he continued to stare at me and then, when he looked away again, we walked along the road, me a few steps behind him, both in silence for the short distance until I could dart into Emma's driveway.

Eight

I closed the front door behind me and leant back against it, releasing a relieved sigh. My wrist was sore but it wasn't broken or sprained, just slightly bruised.

The man was certainly strong. And tall. And now that I wasn't terrified for my life, I realised Emma was right.

Her neighbour, Aaron, was rather gorgeous.

His face appeared in my mind's eye; those intense dark eyes, the firm jaw with a shadow of stubble, that warm and sexy smile, although the warmth had only appeared for Ember not for me. His hair was the deep, dark brown of roasted chestnuts, several thick strands of which had fallen across his forehead as he had run towards me; his skin had that healthy glow that outdoorsy types always seem to have. He oozed strength and solidity. Even his voice was deep and strong, albeit slightly gruff when he was cross.

I could picture him on the front of one of those calendars of sexy, half naked firefighters and my mind began to wander.

I quickly pulled myself together and pushed away from the door. What was I thinking?

Aaron might be gorgeous but he definitely wasn't Cal.

I removed my coat, gloves and scarf and put them away in the cloakroom. I kicked off my boots and left them in the hall.

I'd certainly given a few of Emma's neighbours something to talk about. The exchange with Aaron had been a little humiliating, but that wasn't my fault. I started going over it, wishing I had said something different; behaved differently. Emma would've been cool, calm and collected if it had happened to her.

I huffed loudly and stomped into the kitchen, switching on the kettle. There was no point in replaying the entire episode. What was done, was done. We don't get a second chance to make a good first impression.

Why did I even care about making a good first impression? Aaron meant nothing to me. After this morning, I would try to avoid bumping into him while I was at Emma's. We might be neighbours for the next four weeks, but that didn't mean we would have to be friends.

I made myself a mug of coffee in one of Emma's Christmas themed mugs, which had three cute, drunk looking penguins on it, before searching Emma's cupboards once again.

I'm not sure why I did that. Did I really think some of Santa's elves had stocked them for me while I'd been outside or something? Did I expect to find candy canes and mince pies hidden away somewhere?

Wishful thinking and hope are funny things, aren't they? Even though we know something is impossible we still believe there is just a teensy-tiny chance it might be possible after all.

Damn it! Why did I have to have a sister who didn't buy biscuits, sweets or cakes? It just wasn't normal. Who doesn't have biscuits and cakes in their cupboard, especially at this time of year? Who doesn't have at least one bar of chocolate? I had several at home.

Home.

I no longer had a home.

I let out another sigh, this time one of sorrow and self-pity and I slammed the cupboard doors closed. I hugged my mug of coffee to my chest. I thought I might start to cry, but all I could think of was chocolate.

And biscuits. Gingerbread biscuits. And mince pies. They all danced before my eyes like the characters in *The Nutcracker*.

With renewed determination I put down my mug and strode into the hall. I had to go and buy myself some chocolate.

Nine

'You did what!'

After her initial surprise, Meg could not stop laughing when Aaron video called her to tell her what had happened.

'How was I supposed to know who she was?' Aaron defended his actions. 'I saw a complete stranger walking down the road with my dog. Dog-napping is a big thing now, you know. I panicked. I reacted as any dog owner would. Let's not forget, if you had texted me straight away, none of this would've happened.'

'Oh, Aaron. Only you could've behaved like that.' Meg was laughing hysterically.

Aaron frowned at her. 'I'm glad you find it so amusing. I could've broken her arm. Or worse. Mind you, I didn't exactly get off scot-free. The woman could've broken my nose. Luckily for me, she caught me on the chin instead. But I bit my tongue.'

'You poor baby. Will you live? You deserved it. You knew Ember had been with me and you know I would never let anything happen to him. Didn't it occur to you, even for a second, that I might've asked a friend to look after him? You know how crazy my work gets sometimes. That I often have to dash away at a moment's notice. I'm fully aware that *The Weekly Conqueror* isn't *The Times*, but news is news wherever it happens and even local newspapers have deadlines. I realise my job isn't as intense as yours, but even so, Aaron. All you had to do was stop and think. Why couldn't you have simply run up to her and asked who she was?'

Aaron sighed and ran a hand through his hair. 'That's exactly what she said.'

Meg sniggered. 'Sensible woman. I liked her the moment I met her. I assume you'll be getting her some flowers. Or chocolates. Although I think perhaps this situation calls for both.'

Aaron's eyes shot wide open like a startled reindeer caught in the headlights.

'Why? I said I was sorry.'

'And you think sorry is enough?' Meg shook her head at him. 'What's wrong with you, Aaron? I apologise,' she hastily added, looking contrite. 'No need to answer that. But you know what I mean. Katie was doing both you and me a favour. I didn't ask her to look after Ember. She offered. She was being kind and thoughtful. And what does she get in return? Shouted at and assaulted. Yep. It's definitely got to be flowers *and* chocolates. And the sooner the better. Go and get them right now.'

'Right now? Do I have to? I'm shattered after last night. I need to get some sleep.'

'You look and sound like a petulant twelve-year-old. Yes, you have to do it right now. Conqueror's Convenience Store is just down the road. It'll take you less than fifteen minutes. And I know I don't need to tell you this because you're always very generous, but make sure it's a large bunch of flowers and a good quality box of chocolates.'

Aaron scowled at her. 'Fine. But next time you feel inclined to hand over my dog to a total stranger, call and tell me right away.'

'Fine. But with that attitude you might find that next time you ask me to look after Ember, I'll be busy.'

Aaron gave a snort of laughter. 'Yeah right. You love Ember as much as I do. You'd never pass up a chance of looking after him.'

Meg tutted and stuck out her tongue at him.

'Now who's behaving like a twelve-year-old?' he added.

'Oh, go away. Not all of us have got the next four days off you know. Some of us have work to do. Go and buy those gifts and apologise to Katie again. I'll see you tomorrow. Love you.'

'I'd like to say I love you too, but right now, you're not on my list of favourite people.'

Aaron's warm smile belied that statement as did the affectionate tone in his voice and Meg blew him a kiss before she rang off and Aaron's screen went blank.

He threw Ember a half smile. 'Come on, boy. It looks as if we've got to go out.'

Ember glanced towards the front door, and then down to his comfy bed where he was currently curled up and made a little whimpering sound as he nuzzled his nose deep into the plump cushion.

Aaron sighed. 'Message received loud and clear. Looks like I'm going on my own then. Fine. I won't be long.' He bent down on his haunches and ruffled Ember's fur. 'You be a good boy while I'm gone.' He smiled wider. 'And don't you go out walking with any pretty strangers. Okay?'

Ember met Aaron's eyes, barked once and let his head drop back down onto his bed.

Ten

Conqueror's Convenience Store was only a short walk away from Emma's but in the snow and icy conditions it had taken me longer than I expected and I was very glad to get inside in the warmth.

The place was like an Aladdin's Cave with aisle after aisle and shelf after shelf stuffed full of anything and everything you could possibly want. I had only come in for something sweet; a couple of packets of biscuits, a cake, and a bar or two of chocolate, but as soon as I stepped inside I knew I would need a trolley.

I wandered slowly along the aisles picking up far more than I needed. Instead of ready-made biscuits and cakes I bought sugar, both white and brown sugar, plus caster sugar and icing sugar. You can never have too much sugar when you're baking. At least I can't.

Two large bags of flour went into the trolley; one plain, one self-raising, to which I added a large bag of wholemeal flour. Bread might not be thought of as sweet but it really depends what other ingredients you add to it. Chuck in a few cranberries and some pecan nuts, and voilà, you've got yourself something very sweet and tasty.

Better still, add dried mixed fruit to plain flour then add candied citrus peel, almonds, a few glacé cherries, pinches of cardamom, mace and cinnamon, followed later with some marzipan, and you've got yourself a Stollen. Believe me, if you haven't tried it, there is nothing as nice as a generous slice of freshly baked Stollen with a large mug of coffee or hot chocolate for breakfast on a cold and frosty morning.

I was on a roll. The home baking aisle was like Christmas had come all at once. I should've got a bigger trolley. I would bake mince pies, a Christmas cake, a Christmas Pudding, gingerbread men, women and reindeers, a Stollen or two, some cinnamon rolls, some sausage rolls. Okay, they aren't sweet but sausage rolls are scrummy. I'd make cheese straws too.

Before I knew it, my trolley was piled high, and then I saw the freezer aisle.

I hastily headed towards it, not really looking where I was going.

I heard the thud and the 'Ugh,' at the same time as I saw the man.

Oh no! This could not be happening. What was he even doing here? And where was Ember?

'I'm so sorry!' I squealed. 'I didn't see you.'

His eyes met mine and recognition dawned. He had opened his mouth, no doubt to shout at the person who had just crashed into him with their trolley, but he quickly closed it when he saw it was me.

'Are you hurt?' I asked, unsure what to do next.

His brows furrowed a fraction. 'Yes. But I'll survive.'

The tiniest hint of a smile tugged at his mouth. Or maybe I imagined it.

My eyes scanned the length of him. Don't ask me why. I couldn't help it.

Then I spotted what was in his basket. A bag of dog biscuits, a bountiful and rather beautiful bouquet of flowers, a bottle of English sparkling wine and a giant box of luxury chocolates. I assumed the dog biscuits were for Ember, but the rest were for a woman. Or maybe a man. They definitely said they were for, 'A date'.

I shivered a little and then I noticed he was studying my trolley as intently as I had studied his basket. Mine said anything but 'A date'. Mine shouted, 'Staying home alone and baking.'

I felt embarrassed and self-conscious, but thank God I'd crashed into him before I made it to the freezer aisle. Three family-sized tubs of Christmas Pudding flavoured ice cream, my favourite flavour at the moment, would've added the words, 'TRULY SAD' in large capital letters. Especially as he knew I was staying on my own at Emma's.

I wondered if she had told him about my recent breakup and now, I also felt pathetic.

'Nan lives in a flat in Conqueror's Court,' I said, louder than I'd meant to. 'Nan is my nan. But her name's Nan, too. Well Nancy, but everyone calls her Nan.' I saw the confused look on his face and hurried on. 'Anyway, I'm going to see her tomorrow so I thought I'd make some tasty treats to take with me. Not just for Nan. Also for her friends. And the other elderly people there. It's Christmas, after all. The season of goodwill and all that.' I coughed in a bid to stop myself rambling.

'That's very kind of you.'

He smiled and all sensible thought escaped me. Although I did have some not so sensible thoughts. But we won't go there.

'Yes. Well. It's that time of year.' I'd already said something along those lines and my eyes flitted about as I tried to find something clever or sophisticated to say. Needless to say, I failed. 'Big date?' I nodded towards his basket.

'What?' He followed the direction of my gaze and emitted a sort of spluttering cough. 'Oh no. Er. These are actually for you.'

'For *me*?'

A few other shoppers glanced over at me so I must've said that louder than I thought.

'Yes. To apologise. Again.'

'Oh. I thought you had a date.'

'No. Definitely not. No way. Just an apology.'

'I didn't mean I thought you were asking me on a date. I meant I...' I let my voice trail off.

'Yes, of course. But I don't date. So I wouldn't.'

'You don't date?' I couldn't hide my surprise.

He looked away into the distance and shook his head. 'No. Not now.'

'They're beautiful,' I said, wanting to bring him back from wherever it was his thoughts had taken him.

'What? Oh, the flowers.' He picked them up and was about to hand them to me, I assume but then he quickly pulled them away and laughed. 'I'd better pay for them before I give them to you, hadn't I?'

I laughed too. 'I suppose that might be a good idea. Although as you haven't yet paid, you can put them all back. There's really no need to buy me flowers, or chocolates, or wine ... or dog biscuits.' I gave him my very best smile.

'Dog...?' he grinned. 'Don't you like dog biscuits? I thought they added an extra something to my gift.'

'Oh they do. But I think Ember would prefer them.'

He laughed. 'Ember knows I've come to the shop. If I go home empty handed, he'll never forgive me. I was going to drop these off to you on the way home.'

'That's very kind, but as I say, unnecessary.'

'That's not what Meg thinks.'

'Meg? Your sister?'

He nodded. 'She told me in no uncertain terms that I must come and get you some flowers and chocolates without delay.'

I bristled. 'So this gift was Meg's idea, not yours?'

His brows drew together. 'Yes. But I realised she was right.' He smiled. 'And the wine was my idea. I wasn't sure what you like so I chose the English sparkling. Most people I know like that.'

'I don't,' I lied, angry for some ridiculous reason that he had come here under duress.

That it hadn't occurred to him to buy me flowers, or chocolates, or anything at all. Not that I had expected him to, but having discovered that he had, I felt deflated when he said he had not done so spontaneously. That he hadn't felt the need to dash out and buy me something so that he could see me again. How stupid was I being? Truly dumb, I know.

Now he was the one to look deflated and I felt guilty.

'Oh. Er. What wine do you like then? I'll put this one back and get you something else.'

'There's honestly no need,' I said.

'I want to.' He met my eyes and held the look.

'No, you don't. Your sister is making you.'

His brows knit tight. 'No, she isn't. Meg can't make me do something I don't want to do.'

'You said it was her idea.'

'It was. But I was tired. I've just got off a long shift and all I wanted to do was go to bed.'

'Don't let me stop you.'

Why was I getting so stroppy?

'I won't. You haven't. Er. Look. I'm not sure how we got to this. Just tell me the wine you like and I'll go and get it.'

'I don't want you to. I don't want the flowers either. Or the chocolates. And if you'll excuse me, I need to finish my shop and get home. Thank you for the thought. Even if it wasn't yours. Pleasant dreams.'

I shoved past him with my trolley and he didn't try to stop me but he did look utterly bemused as I marched by.

I looked over my shoulder when I reached the freezer aisle but he had gone. I wasn't sure if I was relieved or sad but I picked up five tubs of ice cream instead of the three I had planned to buy. For someone who had just lost their job, I was spending far more than I should on things that were considered as luxuries.

I had lost my enthusiasm for shopping so I headed for the till and paid for my goods.

'Someone likes ice cream,' Mr Williams said, and I forced a smile in reply.

As I struggled back to Emma's, carrying more bags than I could sensibly manage, I was annoyed with myself. I shouldn't have snapped at Aaron.

When I turned into the drive and saw the flowers propped against the door, I almost burst into tears. When I got to the door and saw the chocolates were there too, together with a bottle of Bailey's in place of the wine he'd intended to buy, I did burst into tears.

Once inside, I opened the card that was also with them. That hadn't been in his basket. He must have picked that up after our 'chat', for want of a better way to describe it. It wasn't exactly a row. Or perhaps it was.

The card had a picture of one of those cuddly bears on the front holding a bunch of flowers and inside, in a neat handwritten note were the words, 'I'm sorry. Thank you for taking care of Ember. This card is my own idea. Meg didn't suggest it. Best wishes, Aaron.'

I dropped onto the floor and sobbed my heart out.

Eleven

I quickly pulled myself together. Mainly because I remembered I'd bought several tubs of ice cream and they'd melt if I didn't put them in the freezer.

That was my next battle. I shrugged off my coat and scarf, stuffed my gloves into my coat pocket and then hung the lot on the cloakroom doorknob for now. Picking up the bags containing the ice cream I hurried to the kitchen.

I was used to giant-sized fridges and freezers both in my flat and the restaurant. Emma's freezer consisted of two pull out drawers and a chiller section. I was going to have to be creative.

The large tubs wouldn't all fit but a lot of smaller boxes would. I found several plastic food containers in her cupboards and I scooped out some of the ice cream into those. I still had one tub too many though and no matter what I did or how creative I got, there was no way that it, or its contents, were going to fit.

I had no option but to eat it.

Until I realised how cold it was outside. Maybe I could put the tub in the garden and cover it with snow? I'd need to put it inside some more plastic bags though. I didn't want creepy crawlies getting into it. I wasn't sure whether many insects and other garden dwelling creatures were awake and active during winter but it was better to be safe than sorry.

I went back into the hall and retrieved my coat and scarf. Tugging my gloves from the pocket and slipping them on, I pulled six plastic bags from the brightly patterned bag holder hanging on a hook behind the kitchen door. I shoved the remaining tub of ice cream into one after another of those six bags and marched into the garden via the kitchen door.

I would need something to mark where I was going to put my frozen treasure. I suddenly had an idea. I'd watched the kids making snow people earlier, why didn't I make one of those? It would also help to protect the ice cream tub.

I set the bags containing the tub on a garden table that Emma obviously left out no matter what the weather and I went towards her shed. There I found a spade and some bits of wood that might come in handy.

I chose a spot away from the rays of the sun. Not that it was sunny at the time; the sky was promising more snow by the look of it, but I had seen the path of the sun the last time I had stayed. It would be lower now it was December so I took that into account and started shovelling snow in an area that I was sure would remain in constant shade.

I piled snow into a heap and used my hands to shape it where needed. I heard what I thought might be Ember's bark while I was working but the fence was too tall for me to see if he was in the garden. I did wonder if Aaron would be out there with Ember but again, I couldn't see him. Aaron was tall enough to see over the top of the fence, but if he did that, I would see his head, and there wasn't any sign of that, so I continued with my creation.

It took me about an hour all told, partly because I'd got carried away and then remembered I hadn't put the ice cream tub inside the snowman's body, so I had to scoop some of it away and then build that section up again.

I stepped back to admire my work. I'd found two pine cones in the garden so I'd used those for the eyes. A small stick made a nose and two larger sticks, his arms. I found some holly berries on a bush that was overhanging from Aaron's garden, so I pinched a handful of those and shaped a bright red mouth.

I know it sounds ridiculous but the snowman reminded me of Callum, my now ex-boyfriend and looking at him made me feel less lonely somehow, but also more heartbroken. Nevertheless, I recalled seeing a jumper of Cal's in my suitcase. I must've packed it with my things by mistake. It was one that I had bought him last Christmas, so in a roundabout way it sort of belonged to me. I ran indoors, kicked off my boots and raced up to my room. It didn't take me long to find the jumper because I'd put it beside me on the bed the night before.

Sad but true. What can I say?

I hesitated for a moment. If I put the jumper on the snowman, I wouldn't be able to cuddle it tonight.

On the other hand, it would make the snowman even more like Cal. I could look out of the window in the lounge and tell myself that Cal was in the garden.

Sometimes, I'll admit, I'm more like a kid than a woman of thirty-five.

I made a decision and ran back downstairs, sliding my feet into my boots on the way outside. I removed the stick arms and put the jumper carefully over the snowman's head, carefully not to knock off his eyes, mouth and nose and then stuffed each of the sticks in each of the arms and stepped back again to admire it.

It definitely reminded me of Cal. I stepped forward again, wrapped my arms around it and gave it a great big, tearful hug.

'I love you, Cal!' I said, giving 'my man' a kiss on the head.

This time when I heard the bark, I knew for sure it was Ember. I quickly spun around but still could not see Aaron or his dog. And then I looked up and there he was, and the sight of him took my breath away.

He was in one of the rooms upstairs, which, unlike Emma's, had a French window that opened onto a little balcony with just enough room for a chair and a small bistro table. Aaron was standing in front of the open door, bare-chested and wearing a pair of striped pyjama bottoms. He was cradling Ember in his arms but I could see he had a six-pack most men would kill for.

He must've realised I'd seen him but he didn't move away. That's when I realised he might've seen me … kissing and cuddling a snowman! I nearly died on the spot.

'How long have you been there?' I yelled.

He shrugged and smiled. 'Long enough.'

Yep. He'd seen me.

He bent down and gently placed Ember on the balcony floor which only seemed to have a smattering of snow. I thought Aaron would move away from the French doors but he didn't. Ember was snuffling around and Aaron was looking at me.

'It's my boyfriend.' I pointed to the snowman with a jokey smile.

'Really? I thought you'd just broken up.'

So Emma had told him. Great. Thanks for rubbing that in, you heartless git. I didn't say what I felt.

Instead I said, 'We both need time to think. I wouldn't be at all surprised if we're back together by the New Year.'

Was I lying to myself or to him?

Aaron pulled a face as if to say, 'Good luck with that.' What he actually said was, 'He's smaller than I would've expected.' And then he laughed.

'He's the perfect size. He's perfect in every way.'

'Not in every way, surely?'

I nodded. 'Yes. In every way.'

'Well, you'd better get him indoors. He looks frozen solid.'

'Funny. He's protecting my ice cream.'

'Er. Run that by me again.' He furrowed his brows.

He looked rather sexy when he did that. And he seems to do that a lot.

'I bought more ice cream than I planned and I can't fit it all in Emma's freezer.'

He stared at me in disbelief. 'Are you telling me you've got a tub of ice cream inside that snowman?'

I nodded again. 'Yep.'

'Is that wise?'

'It was either that, letting it all melt, or eating it all. I did think about eating it all but ...' I shrugged. 'It's a big tub.'

'It didn't occur to you to, oh I don't know, maybe ask one of your neighbours if they had room in their freezer?'

Damn him. No, it hadn't.

'I don't know any of my neighbours. Other than you. And I didn't really want to ask you for a favour. Which reminds me. Thank you for the flowers. And the chocolates. And the Bailey's. But I told you they were unnecessary. Oh, and the card. That would've been more than enough.'

He shrugged again. We both seemed to be doing that a lot too.

'What flavour?'

'What?'

'The ice cream.'

'Oh. Christmas Pudding flavour.'

'Christmas Pudding flavour? You're kidding, right?'

'Nope. It's my current favourite.'

He made a face as if he were about to be sick and then he grinned at me.

'If you'd said any other flavour I'd have invited you and the ice cream round for coffee, but I loathe the taste of Christmas Pudding.'

Damn it. I should've bought at least one tub of vanilla and chocolate. I hoped I hadn't shown my feeling of disappointment on my face. Though why I should be disappointed about not being invited for coffee was a mystery to me. I didn't even like the man. But I did like the way he looked.

'Excellent!' I said, as cheerfully as I could. 'More for me. And now I know precisely what to get you for a Christmas present.'

'You're getting me a Christmas present? We hardly know one another.'

'I was being facetious.'

'Ah. That's just as well because you're on my naughty list.'

'Really? You have a naughty list?'

That could have all sorts of sexual connotations but he coloured up suddenly. I could see the embarrassment from where I stood and that made me smile.

'Not *that* sort of naughty list. What I meant was, you're not on my nice list. No. That came out wrong. I meant, we didn't get off to a good start, did we? As neighbours. Not as anything else.'

'You should be thankful you're a firefighter,' I said, 'and not in the diplomatic corp. That wouldn't be a good career choice for you.'

'Are you saying I don't get on well with people?'

'Let's review this morning, shall we?' I grinned up at him.

'At least I don't talk to snowmen,' he said, grinning back.

'Perhaps you should. You need the practice. Aren't you cold? I'm freezing out here and I've got a coat, scarf and gloves.'

He glanced down and blushed a little more but his smile was huge.

'Nope. I don't feel the cold. I swim almost every day in the lake in Mulberry Park.'

'The lake? You mean the duck pond?'

'It's a lake. It's deeper than it looks.'

'It's got delusions of grandeur if it thinks it's a lake.'

'Try to wade across it. You'll soon discover it's a lake. Actually, don't do that. I'd have to come and rescue you.'

A spurt of laughter escaped me. 'I wouldn't need rescuing, thanks very much. I can swim.'

'In a lake? It's very different than swimming in a pool or in the sea.'

'It's a pond. And yes. I could swim in it.'

His eyes lit up.

'Would you like to bet on that?'

'Are you proposing a challenge?'

'I am. Although I suppose it's unfair of me to do so. As I said, I swim every day if I can. I'm used to freezing water. You said you're freezing, wearing all your clothes and a coat, scarf and gloves.'

I couldn't argue with that. But it didn't stop me.

'We could wait until the summer. Or until the water warms up.'

'Are you going to be here in the summer?'

I hadn't thought about where I might be.

'I come back and visit Emma and Nan all the time. We could arrange it for one of the weekends I come to stay.'

'It's a deal,' he said.

My mobile phone ringing from the kitchen worktop brought an end to our conversation.

'That's my phone. I've got to get it. It might be...' I didn't say, 'Cal' even though I hoped it was. I merely smiled up at Aaron, gave him a quick wave, and dashed into the house.

Twelve

'How are you, sweetheart?' It wasn't Cal calling, it was Nan. 'Would you like some company today? Emma texted to say she's on the plane.'

I'd phoned Nan to tell her about Cal breaking up with me not long after I'd spoken to Tori and Emma shortly after Cal left. I'd expected a lecture and an, 'I told you so,' but all she had said was how sorry she was that my heart was in pain.

'I'm here if you need me, sweetheart,' she had said then, and today she said the same.

'Thanks, Nan. I know you are. As it happens, I was going to do some baking today and come and see you tomorrow with armfuls of cakes and other delights.'

'Ooh, I like the sound of that. I could always come over to you and we could bake together. Would you like that? I can jump in a cab and be there in no time.'

'I'd love you to join me, Nan. But I'll come and get you, there's no need for a cab. It is a bit icy out though so I'm a little worried you might fall. I wouldn't want that.'

'Pah! You think I'm too old and frail to walk?'

'No. I fell over myself this morning and landed on my bottom. It hurt.'

I heard Nan snigger. 'Oh deary me. You're all right though, aren't you?'

'Yes. Emma's neighbour's sister arrived and helped me up. But that's another story.'

'Emma's neighbour's sister? You mean that lovely young Meg? I like her. She writes a column in the local paper. It's got something to do with marriage. It's a well-known saying. Oh goodness me. I can't think what it's called. Oh well. It'll come back to me. Have you met the gorgeous Aaron? Emma told me you hadn't the last two times you were here.'

'Yes. We've met.'

'Is that it? "Yes. We've met." No, and I agree he is gorgeous?'

I sighed. 'He's good to look at, and sometimes he seems nice, but he's also extremely annoying.'

'I'll alter him!' Nan shrieked.

'Good luck with that,' I said.

She laughed. 'No, sweetheart, not, I'll alter him. It's 'Aisle, Altar, Hymn'. That's the name of Meg's column. She gives humorous advice to brides to be. She also gives some sensible and useful tips, but it's mainly a fun column, as the name of it suggests.'

'Really? She told me she's a photojournalist. At least I think she did. I'll have to buy a local paper and read it.'

'No need to buy one. There're plenty here you can read. I'll save you one. Oh goodness. It's snowing again. And it's really coming down hard. Perhaps you're right, sweetheart. Maybe I should stay here in the warm and dry and let you come to me.'

I peered out of the window. Nan wasn't kidding. It was snowing so heavily that I couldn't see the end of the road.

'Er. If it carries on like this, I might leave it until tomorrow. If that's okay with you. It's blizzard-like out there. I'm not sure I want to drive in this and I know it's only a ten-minute walk if I cut through Mulberry Park, but in these conditions I could get lost! I might end up going round and round in circles.'

I laughed but I was only partially joking. And as much as I love Nan, going out in a blizzard didn't really appeal to me.

'No, no. You stay home in the warm as well. I wouldn't want to think of you driving around in this. Or walking. We can see one another tomorrow, assuming it's better weather.'

'I love the snow but I can't recall the last time it was like this. I might have to dig my way out.'

Nan chuckled. 'Don't forget you've got a gorgeous firefighter next door. Get him to come and dig you out.'

'I won't be doing that anytime soon.'

There was a momentary silence but I could hear Nan's breathing.

'I won't mention you know who,' she said, her care and concern evident in her tone,' but you are all right, aren't you, Katie, love?'

I sucked in a breath and nodded even though Nan couldn't see me.

'Yes and no. I'm heartbroken, lost and … a little lonely.' I tried to sound more cheerful. 'But I've built a snowman in the garden and it looks just like him. I can sit and look at it. Or, when I'm feeling cross, I can throw things at it and pretend it's really him.'

'That's my girl! Call me if you need me. Or if you just want a chat. Or a good rant.'

'Thanks, Nan. I'll do some baking and that'll cheer me up. Look after yourself. See you tomorrow.'

Thirteen

I sat by the window for several minutes after speaking with Nan, and watched the snow fall onto my snowman. It was really coming down and the weight of it soon made his stick arms droop.

My phone rang again and this time I saw right away that it was Tori calling, so I didn't have time to hope it might be Cal. It was a video call and I could see the walls of her small office but not the window.

'Is it still snowing in London?' I asked.

'Good morning to you, too!' Tori didn't hide her sarcasm and she added to it by pulling a face.

I laughed. 'Good morning. Well, is it? The heavens have opened down here. It's virtually blizzard conditions. Look.' I turned my phone so that she could see outside.

'Wow. That's crazy. And nope. We've had everything but snow so far today. Hail when I got up, which turned to sleet and then heavy rain on my journey to work. The sun came out for about ten seconds and now it's a sort of sleety drizzle with the occasional lump of hail.' Now she briefly turned her phone so that I could see out of her window. It just looked grey but there were trickles of water running down the glass. 'Perhaps we'll get some more snow later. The blizzard will no doubt arrive as I'm about to leave for home. So how's things?'

'Emma's gone.'

Tori furrowed her perfect blonde brows. 'Er. We knew she was going.'

I shrugged. 'Yeah, I know. But it still feels weird.' I gave a sort of laugh. 'I made a snowman just now because I was feeling a little lonely. It looks a bit like Cal. It's even wearing the jumper I got him last Christmas, which seems to have accidentally fallen into my suitcase.'

She quirked a brow. 'Accidentally? Hmmm. Wait. Are you serious? About building a snowman, I mean.'

'Yep. I'd show you, but you can't see it at the moment because of this blizzard and I'm not going outside in this. I needed somewhere to put an extra tub of ice cream that wouldn't fit in Emma's freezer.'

'So you built a snowman? On your own?'

'Yep. Oh, but Aaron, Emma's gorgeous neighbour, saw me kiss it and hug it, so that was somewhat embarrassing.'

'You kissed and hugged a snowman? In front of a witness?'

'I didn't know he was watching me. I must admit he's hot. He was only wearing pyjama bottoms and his chest was bare so I got an eyeful. If I weren't in love with Cal, I might be interested.'

Tori coughed and glanced away and I knew immediately that something was wrong.

'Tori? What's happened?'

'What? Nothing. Just the same old, same old. Remind me again why I wanted to work in the music business.'

'Because you love it. What's wrong?'

'Nothing's wrong. Apart from the fact that I'm missing my best friend. How crazy is that?'

'Please tell me. Is it … is it something to do with Cal? I can see it in your eyes, Tori. You know something and you're not sure whether you should tell me or hide it from me.'

Her eyes opened wide. 'You can see that in my eyes?' She quickly shut them tight. 'What about now? If I say nothing's wrong, will you believe me?'

'Tori. Please. Whatever it is I'd rather know.'

I braced myself for what I was about to hear. I'd known Tori all my life. We didn't keep secrets from each other and we always told the truth, no matter how bad it might be.

'Callum Blake is a git. You're better off without him.'

'And?'

She sucked in a breath and let it out as a heavy sigh.

'He was in The Fulcrum last night. Having dinner with Felicia Tomlinson.'

She looked straight at me when she said it but it took a moment for the news to sink in. The Fulcrum was the new 'place to be seen' in London right now. One of those uber-trendy places that's frequented by the rich celebrities and wannabes. There was a bar on one side and an exclusive restaurant on the other.

Getting a table at The Fulcrum was like winning the Lottery Jackpot. And Felicia Tomlinson had just done that. Figuratively speaking. She'd been on one of those reality TV shows to find the next singing superstar – and a few months ago, she'd won. But prior to that, she'd been a waitress in one of the restaurants Cal had worked in.

She sometimes came for drinks with Tori, Cal and me, and some others from our work, but I never really liked her and neither did Tori. She was always flirting with Tori's colleagues. It was obvious she liked Cal but he told me he wasn't interested and she was far too young. She was only nineteen at the time. She'd left to 'pursue her dream' but oddly enough, she had stayed in touch with Cal. He'd even suggested she might like to come and work in our restaurant – Cal's restaurant, but thankfully, she'd felt that Lewisham was 'too far out to be seen'. I wasn't sure who, exactly, she expected to be seen by but I was grateful that was how she felt.

I coughed to clear my mouth of the sick feeling that was building there and took a deep and calming breath.

'When you say, 'with' do you mean two former work colleagues catching up, or two people on a date?'

Tori paled before my eyes. 'They were holding hands across the table, Katie. I was there with my boss and a couple of others from work, celebrating a deal my boss has just signed and I couldn't believe it when I saw them come in. I'm only telling you because there're photos of them together on social media today. You can't see Cal that clearly, and they call him "a mystery man".' She snorted derisively. 'That'll irritate Cal. But you'll know it's him if you see the photos.'

Photographers aren't allowed in the restaurant at The Fulcrum so if there were photos on social media, they must've been taken by someone inside.

'Did you see them holding hands?'

Tori nodded, a sad expression on her face. 'I did.'

'Did Cal see you?'

Tori furrowed her brows. 'I'm ... I'm not sure. I was going to say something to him. Call him a git or something more unpleasant, but my boss was there, so ...' She shrugged and I understood completely.

'And Cal only had eyes for her?' I knew exactly what that felt like. Cal could make it seem as if there was no one else on the planet, just you and him.

Tori nodded slowly. 'It could be nothing. It probably is. I'm not being funny or anything but Cal is thirty-five and Felicia's what? About twenty-three now?'

'Yes. About that.' I couldn't take this in.

'But it's even weirder than that. I mean, her star is on the rise and Cal's ... well, his isn't.'

'So why were they together?'

'My point exactly.' Tori looked confused. 'He hasn't ...?'

She didn't need to say it. I knew what she was thinking.

'Has he been seeing her behind my back? Is that what you're wondering?'

'Yeah. Except when would they find the time? He's been working with you every day at the restaurant and she's been ... doing whatever it is people on TV talent shows do.' She leant forward, closer to her phone camera. 'Are you okay, Katie? Should I have kept this from you?'

'No. Don't ever keep anything from me. We agreed we'd never do that. And yes. I'm okay. Well, as okay as I can be, knowing my boyfriend might've been cheating on me. It would explain why he doesn't love me anymore, wouldn't it?'

She shrugged her shoulders high. 'I suppose it might.' She glanced towards her office door and I could hear her name being called. 'Oh bloody hell. I'm really, truly sorry, Katie, but I've got to go. Are you sure you're okay? I'll call you back as soon as I get a chance.'

'I'm fine. You go.'

'Love you,' she said. 'Hang in there. Everything will work out for the best.'

'Love you too.'

After Tori rang off, I sat in numbed silence, and then I scrolled through every social media account I was on to find the photos. Tori was right, you couldn't really see Cal that clearly, but it was definitely him.

I've never been a fan of social media, to be honest. It sucks so much time from your life. And everyone on it seems to have fabulous lives. Or no lives at all. Plus I was always too busy working to be able to spend hours scrolling through anyone else's day.

Foolishly, I tried to call Cal but his phone went straight to voicemail and I didn't want to leave a message.

I tossed my phone to the side and got to my feet. It was definitely time to bake.

I don't know how many hours I was in the kitchen but the worktop was now covered in plates bearing cakes, biscuits, chocolates and candy canes and I was exhausted from being on my feet.

I had done everything I could to stop myself from thinking about Cal, but I couldn't stop myself from calling him another couple of times. I got his voicemail every time.

I turned on the radio but that hadn't helped, so I told Emma's home-hub to play Christmas music, hoping that would cheer me up. For a time it had but now, as I stood in the kitchen surveying my baking, a wave of gloom swept over me. It was then that I saw the bottle of Bailey's Aaron had given me.

I don't drink much, or that often, but right at that moment, drowning my sorrows seemed like a great idea.

I didn't even bother with a glass. I drank straight from the bottle. Several large gulps. It went down like melted ice cream, or a very tasty milk shake. The alcohol didn't even seem to touch my sides.

Until suddenly it did.

And I'm not sure exactly what happened after that.

Fourteen

Aaron awoke with a start. What was that awful noise?

It almost sounded like someone was singing along to very loud music. Christmas music. Was he dreaming? Or had he woken up to some sort of Christmas disco going on at his neighbour's? Now Ember was howling by his side, no doubt trying to join in with the awful din.

And then he remembered Emma was away and her sister was staying next door.

Aaron went to his bedroom window and peered out.

And there she was. Emma's sister, Katie. Dancing around the snowman she'd built in the garden, seemingly untroubled by the heavy snow falling all around her. He could only just make her out through the curtain of white. The earlier blizzard that had started when he went to bed seemed to have blown itself out and now snow was coming down in straight lines as if it was falling from a massive sieve in the sky.

What on Earth was the woman doing? She wasn't even wearing a coat. She'd catch her death of cold.

He watched her tip a bottle to her mouth. And then she stumbled over, crashing into the snowman, her arms flying up in the air. She held her grip on the bottle though and burst out laughing as she hugged it to her, still leaning against the snowman.

Oh hell. The woman was clearly drunk. She seemed unable to stand upright now and was tipping first one way and then the next. She appeared to be trying to get herself together and then she made a valiant attempt to push herself upright. And she did. Until she fell forward, landing head first in the snow.

Instinctively, Aaron reacted. He raced downstairs, grabbed his coat from the rack and stepped into his boots, dashing outside and around to the gate at the side of Emma's house. He had it open in a second and ran into the garden as fast as he could.

To his relief and utter amazement, Katie was lying on her back in the snow, laughing loudly, making snow angels with her legs and arms while still holding the bottle tight. The bottle he now saw was a bottle of Bailey's.

Possibly the one he'd bought for her that very morning.

He tried to pull her to her feet but her legs didn't seem to want to hold her up so he swept her up in his arms and carried her into Emma's kitchen. He placed her gently on one of the kitchen chairs that he pulled out with his foot and, holding her with his hands, let her head and body gently flop over onto the kitchen table.

He had to get her out of those wet clothes. And he had to do it quickly. There was only one thing for it. He knew exactly what he had to do.

Fifteen

Someone was carrying out cranial surgery on my head without an anaesthetic.

Either that, or I had the hangover from hell.

I tried to move but my body wouldn't let me. Every bone, every nerve, every cell, every fibre of my being throbbed. And not in a good way.

I looked around but my eyes seemed to be having trouble focussing. I recognised the framed photo on the wall though. It was one of me and Emma, taken on her birthday in October. I was in the guest bedroom at Emma's.

But what was I doing in bed and how did I get here? The last thing I remember was baking in the kitchen.

Oh God.

And then opening the bottle of Bailey's.

I heard footsteps and panic rushed through me. Someone else was in the house.

I tried to slide further under the duvet as the bedroom door creaked open.

Well, maybe not creaked, exactly, but it did open slowly.

'You're awake! Finally.'

'Nan?' She was carrying a tray bearing a steaming mug of what smelt like coffee. At least my sense of smell still worked. But the plate of toast that accompanied the coffee made me want to heave. Thankfully, I didn't. 'What are you doing here? What time is it? Why am I in bed?'

'Where would you like me to start?' She grinned at me and placed the tray on the bedside table, before clasping her hands together and resting them on her ribcage. 'You got drunk. You tried to give yourself hypothermia. It's about five p.m. and you're in bed to sleep it off. I think that just about covers it.'

'Er.' I tried to remember but I couldn't. 'But how did you know? How did you get here?' It was then that I realised I was wearing my pyjamas. 'Who undressed me? Did I do that?'

She shook her head and chuckled.

'I don't know why I'm laughing. It's really not funny. You could've done yourself an injury. If it hadn't been for that lovely young man, Aaron, you might well have done.'

'Aaron! What ... what's he got to do with this?'

She raised her brows. 'He rescued you. And you make sure you thank him when you see him.'

A vague recollection of someone carrying me into the house began to filter through the haze of my memory. I gripped the duvet and lifted it, looking down at my PJs

'Oh God! He didn't...? He wasn't the one who...?' I couldn't bring myself to ask the questions racing around in my head.

Nan laughed. 'No, sweetheart. He didn't undress you and put you into your pyjamas. That was his mum.'

'His ... his mum?' Somehow that seemed worse. 'How did his mum get here?'

'His father brought her, I believe.'

I tried to sit up but only made it halfway and I fell back against the pillows.

'What I meant was, what was his mum doing here in the first place?'

'Well, sweetheart, as I understand it, you were singing and dancing in the garden. Without a coat, I might add. Aaron heard and saw you and when you fell head first into the snow, he dashed round to help. He brought you inside and, as he knows about these things, he removed as much of your wet clothing as he felt he could, whilst calling his

147

mum via his speakerphone. His parents live a few minutes' drive away and by the time he'd dried you with the hand towels from the kitchen, which was all he could find in a hurry, and wrapped you in the throw from the back of Emma's sofa, they had arrived. He carried you upstairs and his mum put you in the shower, then got you into your PJs and Aaron helped you into bed.' She sniggered. 'He told his mum that he didn't feel right about undressing you but if you'd been a total stranger it wouldn't have bothered him one bit. The sweet young man was embarrassed. That is so delightful, don't you think? He wanted to spare your blushes. Now that, my love, is a nice man.'

He hadn't 'spared my blushes'. I couldn't have felt more embarrassed if I'd been naked in front of him. Okay, maybe I could.

'But how did you get here?'

'His mum, Daphne, called me. She's a lovely woman too. She saw my number on that list Emma keeps on the fridge. Aaron came to get me and here I am. Now drink that coffee before it gets cold and eat some toast. It'll make you feel better. I'll be back in just a minute. Daphne and Roger are about to leave, so I must go and say goodbye.'

This was all so surreal.

'Nan!'

She turned at the door to look back at me. 'Yes, sweetheart?'

'Say thank you to his mum and dad for me, please. And ask them to thank Aaron, too.'

'You can do that yourself. He's still downstairs. That little dog of his is precious, isn't it? Although he did pee on the Christmas tree you seem to have ... struggled to put up. But we won't mention that to anyone, will we?'

'Christmas tree? What Christmas tree?'

But Nan was gone.

That was very odd. I didn't even know Emma had a Christmas tree. But I must've got it from somewhere.

It seemed a lot had happened in the last few hours and I couldn't recall any of it.

Sixteen

The coffee helped a little – the toast not so much. My stomach was growling like a grizzly bear and gurgling like a flooded river about to burst its banks. I might never be able to eat again.

Despite my pounding head, I struggled out of bed, groaning once more at the sight of my reindeer-patterned pyjamas and the reminder that Aaron's mum – *his mum!* – had undressed me and put me to bed. The last time anyone had done that (in a non-sexual way) was when I was about five, I think.

How humiliating!

I considered, for a nanosecond, getting dressed before attempting to go downstairs, but I realised I had neither the strength nor the enthusiasm, so I pulled on my dressing gown with some effort I should add and trudged along the hall.

Each step seemed to reverberate through me and around me as if I were marching to a beating drum and when I arrived at the top of the stairs, I had to reach out for the handrail and hold on tight as I swayed back and forth. The ground floor appeared to be a very, very long way down.

'Need a hand?'

I almost toppled over at the sound of Aaron's voice as he appeared at the foot of the stairs. The undertone of amusement was evident, even in my present state of discombobulation. It took me a second or two to focus on his face.

'Thank you. But no.'

'Stomach pump?'

I glowered at him as the corners of his mouth quirked.

'You're so funny. But I'm not in the mood.'

'Paracetamol?'

'Several.' At last he'd made a sensible suggestion. 'Please.'

I slowly took my first step down, tightly clutching the handrail as Aaron stood and watched me with undisguised apprehension.

It wasn't as difficult as I'd thought it might be, so I took another step, followed by another and another. But I was over confident and as I smiled triumphantly, I tripped on the hem of my dressing gown.

How he caught me I have no idea, but annoyingly, he did.

I say, "annoyingly" because it was as if he had expected me to fall. He was up the first few stairs in a flash and, even though my body thumped against his as I was rapidly on my way down, he managed to retain his footing and save us both from landing in a heap at the bottom.

Even more irritating than that, he swept me into his arms and proceeded to carry me down the final few stairs before gently depositing me on my feet and holding me upright until I had regained my equilibrium ... which, let me tell you, isn't the easiest thing to do when you're hung over and have just been rescued, for a second time apparently, by a hunky and handsome man. Especially one who smelt of sandalwood and ... pine trees.

'How did you do that?' I gazed up into his eyes. And momentarily got lost in them.

His dark brows slowly knit together and he whispered the words, 'You're welcome.'

'What? Oh. Er. Thank you.'

'I wasn't asking for thanks.'

'O-kay.' Then why had he said, "You're welcome" instead of answering my question? 'But how did you do it? How come we didn't both land in a heap on the floor?'

'I'm a firefighter.'

He shrugged as if that did provide me with the answer.'

'And?'

Confusion deepened in his eyes. 'That's what we do. We train for it.'

'For people throwing themselves at you down a flight of stairs?' I threw him a doubtful look before realising that hadn't come out in quite the way I'd meant it to. 'Not that I threw myself at you. Obviously. I'd never do that.'

He gazed at me for a second as if he was searching for some answers of his own.

'Obviously,' he replied. 'Neither of us would want that.' He coughed and seemed to stand taller somehow, and as he stepped back from me, it felt like he was putting a wall up between us. 'We train for all sorts of situations. Now, if you're okay, I'd better take Ember for a walk.' He turned away but briefly stopped and glanced back at me. 'Oh, and I'm sorry about him peeing on your Christmas tree. He does that sometimes when he's nervous. I'll pay for any damage.'

'Damage? To a Christmas tree?'

I'm not sure why I smirked.

'To the floor.'

'The floor?'

I must've sounded like a moron, but now I was panicking.

I had no recollection of this Christmas tree both he and Nan had mentioned but clearly there was one. And one that Aaron's dog had peed on. Which meant that Emma's gorgeous wooden floor might now be ruined and if so, it was because of me.

And because of Ember, of course.

I dashed from the hall into the living room, my hangover all but completely forgotten, and stopped in my tracks when I saw it.

That was the Christmas tree they were talking about?

Now, I burst out laughing.

In a corner of the living room area, close to the front window, stood a tall, metal planter, more rust-coloured than grey, with what appeared to be my favourite red-checked, kilt-like, mini skirt hanging loosely around the top of it. Sticking out from the planter, at various – and somewhat precarious – angles, were several long branches that I recognised as having come from a selection of trees like the ones in Emma's garden. Dangling by their handles, from those branches, were some of the Christmas-themed mugs that I'd bought for Emma over the years, together with a variety of Emma's cutlery, tied on with string, no doubt from the roll I'd seen in one of Emma's kitchen drawers. In addition to all that, I'd draped my scarf and two of Emma's, taken from her cloakroom, around this work of art and crowned the tallest branch in the middle with my bobble hat.

'Did Tate Britain call to say when they'd be coming to collect this masterpiece?'

I was only half joking. I bet some people would've paid a fortune for it. Although by peeing on it, Ember had been the only one so far to leave me his 'review'.

'I'm hoping you did that after you got drunk,' Aaron said, with that annoyingly sexy smile tugging at his mouth.

'It's for you,' I replied, beaming at him as he pulled a lead from the pocket of the jacket he had just put on.

He raised his brows and called for Ember to come to him. Both Nan and the dog appeared from the kitchen; Nan was smiling warmly, and oddly enough, so was the dog. At least it looked as if he were smiling. It might've been a sort of growl.

'That's exceedingly kind,' Aaron said, bending to attach Ember's lead, 'but sadly I don't have room for it. And I may be wrong, but I think you might be needing those mugs and the cutlery. Plus, it would be wise to wear at least one of the scarves and the hat when you go outside, in future, not to mention a coat.'

'But I made it just for you,' I lied as he straightened up. I think it was a lie. I don't know what was going on in my head when I made it, and I still couldn't remember doing so. 'You bought me a gift after I did you a favour, so the least I can do is give you something in return after you saved me. Twice.'

He looked me directly in the eye and held my gaze. 'I happen to know that's not quite true. For a start, I hadn't "saved you" even once when you made it. But more importantly, you told me when I brought you inside from your little adventure in the snow, that you wanted the love of your life to have your tree. And that, I know for a fact because you told me several times, is someone called Callum Blake, not me.'

'Oh,' I said, feeling like I'd been told off and desperately trying to recall what else I might've told him.

A chill wind hit me when he opened the front door, and snow swirled onto the mat.

'I'll be next door if you need me,' Aaron said, more to Nan than to me. 'Feel better soon,' he added for me, and quickly closed the door behind him and Ember.

Something suddenly came back to me and, don't ask me why, but I yanked the front door open and yelled after him.

'I don't know why I told you that. Callum's clearly not the love of my life. He's dating someone else and he might've been seeing her before he dumped me!'

I'm not sure if Aaron heard me because he was already halfway down the drive and the weather was blizzard-like out there. Either way, he didn't react. He and Ember just kept walking.

Nan came and stood beside me, eased me into her arms and closed the front door once again.

'Let's have a nice cup of tea and a chat, sweetheart. And maybe one or two of those delicious cakes you spent several hours baking today.' We walked towards the kitchen, her right arm still wrapped around me. 'I gave a selection to Daphne and Roger before they left. I knew you wouldn't mind.'

'No. That's fine. I don't mind at all.'

'We should've given some to Aaron. He did have a mince pie with his cup of tea earlier and he said it was the best he'd ever tasted.'

'He did?' That surprised me for some reason, even though I know my baking's pretty good. 'I'll drop some round to him.'

'That's my girl. He's such a lovely young man.'

I couldn't help but notice the twinkle in her eyes.

'Don't get any ideas, Nan. You're as bad as Emma. I know I just said Cal's not the love of my life, but that's only because I'm clearly not his! I still love him, Nan. I can't help it. And I know what Tori said, but I don't think Cal was cheating on me. I'm sure I would've known.'

'What, exactly did Tori say?' Nan asked, easing me down on a chair and walking towards the kettle on the worktop. 'And when? I realise it must've been today and I'm assuming it was after we chatted.'

'It was.' I nodded and told her what I could remember Tori saying, which actually wasn't that much. My head still felt as though it were trapped in a washing machine, on a slow cycle.

'This Felicia Tomlinson's much too young for Callum.' Nan said it as if that would be the end of that. She made a pot of tea and brought it to the table along with two of Emma's best tea cups and saucers. The ones Emma only used for special occasions. 'But that doesn't mean you should take him back.' Nan wagged a finger at me and gave me a serious look.

I smiled at her and nodded. 'I know. But I'm not sure I'll have the chance. Felicia may be young but she's famous, and if she's not already rich from doing that stupid show, she soon will be.' I watched Nan pour the tea.

'She might be able to help Cal get back on his feet. Which is something I can't do.'

'Nor should you after the way the man's behaved. Who's going to help you get back on your feet, Katie love? That's all that matters to me. And I don't think that's going to be Callum Blake. Now drink your tea and have a cake and then we'll decide what we're going to have for supper. I'm sure Emma won't mind if I sleep in her bed tonight. Aaron did say he'd take me back home later, but it's getting worse out there, and now I'm here, I might as well stay till tomorrow. If that's all right with you.'

She winked at me and I grinned.

'Of course, it's all right with me. You know it is. You also know Em won't mind a bit. To be honest, I'd be happy to have some company, and there's no better company than yours.'

'Ditto.' Nan blew me a little kiss and then she glanced towards the living room. 'Fortunately, I can't see it from here, but as much as I love you, sweetheart, we need to do something with that awful Christmas tree of yours.'

It took us longer than expected to remove every item of cutlery, crockery and clothing from the tree, and several trips to the garden and back to dispose of all the branches and the rusty planter. How I'd managed to do all that designing and decorating, including obtaining everything, on my own, whilst drunk, is still a mystery to me.

Nan took a couple of photos of it on her phone to show her friends back at Conqueror's Court and I took some to send to Tori, who called me later to tell me to remind her never to ask me to help her with her Christmas decorations. But we did have a good laugh about it.

I'll admit I sent one to Cal but he didn't acknowledge receipt so I don't know if he got it.

Luckily, Aaron had mopped up Ember's pee and his mum, Daphne had sent him back to his house to get some of her 'special cleaning solution', consisting of white vinegar and grapefruit oil, or so Nan told me. He'd used that on the small area of floor on which the pee had landed and we couldn't smell anything other than a hint of grapefruit by the time the tree was gone. My favourite skirt had escaped Ember's soaking, thankfully, mainly due to the fact that the dog was small and my kilt-like mini skirt was mainly draped around the top part of the tall planter.

'Why did he bring the dog with him?' I queried, wiping the wood with a soft, dry cloth which Daphne had told Nan we should do.

'He was rushing to get to you, sweetheart, and he didn't close his front door properly. Naturally, Ember followed him, as dogs do. He said that he didn't realise Ember was there until it was too late. I suppose the poor little thing got scared when Aaron was racing around after you. Daphne told me that by the time Aaron came to get me, Ember was fast asleep in the kitchen and they didn't have the heart to disturb him.'

'I think that dog rules the roost,' I said. 'But I'll admit he is rather cute. And it seems there's no permanent harm done to the floor. Which is good because it means Emma won't kill me.'

'We could always put a plant there if there is.' Nan winked at me. 'But I've sent her a photo of your tree, so I'm sure she'll see the funny side.'

'She might not see the funny side of me using her scarves as tinsel or ribbons.'

But as it happened, Emma did.

I was almost asleep when she phoned me, wanting to hear all about it. It was eleven p.m. here and she'd video-called me, rightly assuming Nan would now be fast asleep but incorrectly assuming I wouldn't.

'I'd forgotten New York is five hours behind us,' I said, trying to stifle a yawn.

'Sorry. Did I wake you up?'

'Sort of. But don't worry. It's lovely to see your face. How're things in the Big Apple?'

'Much the same as there if all the photos Nan sent of the snow are anything to go by. It's been snowing here all day too.'

'I meant work-wise, Em. How're the new clients? How's the hotel? Met any dishy men?'

Emma laughed. 'And you moan at me for trying to fix you up with guys! Everything's good, thanks. I've had meetings since about an hour after I arrived, but everybody's been great. And that's all I'm going to say for now because you look absolutely shattered, Katie. You need to get some beauty sleep.'

'Thanks a lot. If you knew the day I've had, you'd understand.'

'You can tell me all about it tomorrow. I particularly want to hear about the tree. Oh, and how Aaron rescued you. But it's unlike you to get drunk.' She gave me her motherly look, which, bearing in mind she's five years my junior, always makes me smile. 'I have to ask though, are you doing okay?'

'Yes. Don't worry about me. It's nothing really. Tori gave me some news about Cal, and it's something I didn't want to hear. Let's just say that the drink helped me to get it out of my system. I'll tell you about that tomorrow too. But honestly, I'm fine. Nan's staying the night, which she probably mentioned when she sent you the photos, and we had a really long chat this evening.'

'That's good. And yes, she did mention it. But call me if you want to talk tonight. No matter what time it is. I've got meetings all day tomorrow but I'll give you a call at lunchtime. That's about one p.m. here, so around six p.m. your time.'

'That's perfect,' I said, yawning again. 'Have a good evening and don't do anything I wouldn't do.'

'What? Like make a Christmas tree out of branches and other people's belongings, you mean?'

She laughed, blew me a kiss, gave me a wave, and vanished from my screen.

Seventeen

I felt so much better after a good night's sleep, but I had woken once or twice from some rather disturbing dreams. I can't recall the exact details but I do remember being rescued – yet again, by Aaron. And I remember kissing him and being disappointed when he pulled away. I can't say what the kiss felt like but I can remember not wanting it to stop. Cal also made an appearance, and I know the dream-me was thrilled to see him, but when I awoke, the real me wasn't quite so pleased he'd popped up in my dreams. Or about that kiss with Aaron.

After showering and getting dressed, I hurried downstairs to find Nan in the kitchen drinking coffee, and a steaming mug was already waiting on the kitchen table for me. Cal had never had my coffee waiting.

'Thanks, Nan. You're a life saver.' I kissed her on the cheek and took the seat opposite her. 'It's stopped snowing, I see. So what's the plan for today? Shall we take the cakes and stuff to Conqueror's Court later?'

'As soon as we've had breakfast.' Nan grinned. 'I thought we might walk through the park. I think it'll be beautiful there this morning after all that snow.'

'Are you sure you can manage? It might be deep.'

'I've got my boots.' She slid one foot to the side to prove it.

As I leaned over to see her footwear, I was surprised she was already prepared for outdoors. It was as if she couldn't wait to return to her home.

'Yes. But all the boxes of cakes and treats will be difficult enough to carry, and if it's icy underfoot, we might both end up on our bottoms.'

'Aaron's got a sled.'

'Aaron's got a what? A sled? Why? Isn't he a bit old for that? Oh! Does he have a kid, or kids, from a previous relationship? I'm sure Emma said he was single.' I was irritated that I cared. 'But what's Aaron got to do with it?'

I wasn't fully awake and I certainly wasn't ready to see Aaron after that dream kiss we'd shared. Annoyingly, I couldn't stop myself from wondering if he might have had a dream about me.

Nan laughed. 'Goodness gracious me! What a lot of questions. He is single. I checked. And he has no dependants, just his sister, Meg, who's also single, and his parents. Oh, and Ember. I didn't ask why he had a sled. It just came up in conversation.'

I raised my brows in doubt. 'Really? What were you discussing?'

'We were watching the children having fun with theirs.'

'The children? Here? When?'

'While you were still sound asleep this morning. Like me, and several of the neighbour's children, Aaron's an early riser.'

'Yeah, well, young kids always wake up early. And Aaron spent most of yesterday in bed.'

Now Nan was the one to raise her brows and a smile crept across her mouth.

'You can't blame him for that, sweetheart. He had been working for the last two nights. And, not to criticise or anything, but he didn't get much sleep yesterday, did he? Thanks to a certain someone.'

Unfortunately, I couldn't argue with that, so I decided to ignore it.

'So are you suggesting we borrow Aaron's sled to transport the cakes through Mulberry Park?' I had heard worse ideas.

'No, Katie love. As if I'd suggest we do that!' She tutted loudly and got to her feet.

'Aaron suggested it. He's coming with us and he's going to pull the sled.'

I almost spat my coffee across the table. I love Nan to bits but 'meddlesome' should be her middle name. I knew what was going on. I was just surprised that Aaron didn't. If he had, I'm sure he wouldn't have suggested any such thing.

'Nan!' I tutted even louder than Nan had and when she glanced at me, I rolled my eyes dramatically. 'Don't you dare try to set us up.'

'As if I would. I merely told him we'd be dressing the Christmas tree in the main lounge area of Conqueror's Court first thing this morning, and we could always do with some help. I mentioned there'd be carol singing, hot chocolate and plenty of festive nibbles. I also said the old folks would love to see Ember. You know, as a sort of therapy dog.'

I couldn't help but snigger although this was the first I'd heard about dressing the Christmas tree. Or the carol singing.

'A therapy dog? Ember? They might need therapy after he pees all over them. And when you say, "old folks" I assume you're not including yourself? But I don't recall you mentioning any of this to me, and I can't see Aaron particularly wanting to be involved.'

'It must've slipped my mind.' She placed some slices of wholemeal bread in Emma's toaster. 'I might have also mentioned that you and I might struggle to transport all the delicious cakes you spent most of yesterday making. Which reminds me, don't forget to give him some as a little thank you gift, will you? Now we'd better hurry up and have breakfast. He's calling round in half an hour.'

Don't ask me how, but I knew then that it was going to be yet another one of those days.

Eighteen

Nan was right about Mulberry Park. It was absolutely magical. Oddly enough, it was also practically deserted. Although it was still early as we'd left at just a little after eight-thirty, all the kids seemed to be playing in the street.

Nan, Aaron, Ember and I, together with four other adults, two with dogs and one couple holding hands, were the only ones around.

There was also a gaggle of Canada geese, noisily flapping around the pond – or, lake, as Aaron calls it – when we first arrived, but surprisingly, Ember sent them packing. For such a little dog, he's got a very loud bark and he runs really fast. One of the geese stood its ground for a moment and I thought they might come to blows, but before Aaron could grab hold of Ember, the goose flew off to join the V-shaped formation of the skein. That's

169

what a flock of geese in flight is called, according to Aaron.

'It's like something out of a fairy tale,' I said, admiring the snow-covered trees, some of which were evergreens, so were full and wide and white, and some were like snow-covered skeletons having shed all their leaves in the autumn.

'And it's so peaceful,' Aaron said, before grinning broadly. 'Now that Ember's stopped barking.'

'He's a lively little thing, isn't he?' Nan said. 'Daphne told me you rescued him from a burning building.'

The grin slid from Aaron's face and after a second or two he nodded. 'I did.'

'What happened to his owner?' I asked.

'He died, unfortunately.'

'In the fire? How awful!' I shivered at the thought of it but I noticed Aaron tensed.

'No. He had a heart attack. No one died in that fire.'

'But people have?' I prompted, somewhat ghoulishly. 'I suppose that comes with your job. It must be difficult to deal with.'

He stopped in his tracks. 'Difficult? You have no idea. It's...' His voice trailed off and he ran a hand through his hair, shaking his head as he did so. 'I'd rather not have this conversation.'

'Let's talk about something else,' Nan quickly suggested as we walked on. 'Do you sing, Aaron?'

He didn't answer right away but when he did, he laughed. Except it wasn't a joyful sound and it held a hint of bitterness.

'Sing? Me? No.'

'Neither do I,' I added, trying to lighten the rather dark mood that had suddenly descended. 'Ember probably sounds better than me. Oh. But you heard me singing yesterday, didn't you?' I cringed with embarrassment having remembered, after my good night's sleep, some of the events of the previous day.

A tight smile appeared briefly on his lips but was gone before it was fully formed, and he didn't answer.

We continued in silence for a time, following the outline of the path; both the path and the grass were hidden beneath the deep snow but you could just about make them out, together with the flowerbeds, where the winter plants and bushes poked out from their white blanket.

Conqueror's Court was now in sight and I've never been so glad to see it. It shone out like a multi-coloured beacon in a sea of white, the rows of different coloured fairy lights covering the façade, all twinkling brightly. The huge Christmas tree with its red and gold decorations glistened in the morning sunlight that was peeping through the clouds.

'I could murder a cup of tea,' Nan said, suddenly sprinting forward like a woman half her age.

'Me too.' I quickly followed.

Aaron and Ember fell into step beside us and the sled bounced along on the snow behind us, carrying its cargo of treats for the residents of Conqueror's Court.

I can't say either Nan or I were that surprised when Aaron left shortly after our arrival. Although his phone did ring, so when he said that his sister needed his help, we did believe it might be true and not merely an excuse to get away.

'Well, that was awkward,' I said, watching him and Ember and the sled, hurry back the way we'd come. Although he'd picked up both Ember and the sled and tucked one under each arm before he'd run out into the snow.

'I think we hit a nerve,' Nan said. 'Being a firefighter isn't always a pleasant job, obviously. It's a shame he doesn't have a girlfriend he can talk to.'

'Nan!' I shot her a warning look.

'What, sweetheart? I'm only saying that a man who does such a courageous job should have someone to come home to and relax.'

'He's got Ember. And his sister. And you said his mum and dad are lovely.'

'Yes. But we both know it's not the same as having that special someone, is it? Oh goodness! Listen to me. Let's hand around some cakes, and then we'll get this party started.'

'Party? What party? I thought we were merely decorating a Christmas tree and singing carols.'

I don't know why I was astonished to discover that this was, in fact, an all-day party; one that had been planned since August, so it seemed, with Nan as the head of the Conqueror's Court Christmas Committee. After all these years you would think I'd know Nan inside out, but she still surprises me.

Even Father Christmas joined us, bringing presents to put beneath the magnificent Christmas tree. He'd be returning on Christmas Eve to hand them out and he made everyone promise not to peek until then. As if that promise was ever going to be kept, right?

We started the morning with hot chocolate and mince pies, including mine, and some of my other cakes and treats, just as Nan had told Aaron we would.

It took us all a couple of hours to dress the massive tree, which filled an entire corner of the large lounge housed in the central section of Conqueror's Court. Some of the staff helped, but this was mainly a fun activity for the residents and their families and friends.

The place was packed to bursting and the atmosphere was joyful. It was such a shame Aaron had to leave. I think it would've really cheered him up. I even joined in with the carol singing but thankfully there were plenty of people with great voices loud enough to drown me out.

There was more hot chocolate at eleven, once the tree decorating was finished and that was followed not long after, at twelve o'clock by a Christmas buffet lunch.

That consisted of cold sliced turkey, ham and beef, with potato salad, Christmas coleslaw, pickled red cabbage, mini Scotch eggs, mini pork pies, cocktail sausages warm from the oven along with hot sausage rolls, and both hot and cold vol-au-vents. Basically, everything that was bound to give old people indigestion!

I wasn't surprised to find out Nan had insisted the menu be strictly adhered to. She'd gone as far as raising a petition and getting signatures from all the residents and several of the staff when the manager of the care home had tried to replace it with a healthier but somewhat bland alternative.

'You know Nan!' Daryl, one of the care staff told me, smiling from ear to ear.

'Apparently not as well as I should,' I replied.

And that was a sobering thought. I wish I'd had that yesterday; I could've used some sobering up. But we won't go there.

I'd spent the last five years living in London and the last three, concentrating on making Cal's restaurant a success. In the early days of moving, I came back to visit Nan and Emma often and, no matter what, I always spent Boxing Day with them. I worked on Christmas Eve and often on Christmas Day, so that was my one day off during the festive season. But over the past three years, I hadn't come back nearly as much.

Other than helping Emma move in July and her birthday weekend in October, I'd only returned to Norman Landing in March, and again in May for Nan's birthday. I was only here now because Cal had dumped me and I had nowhere else to go. Apart from Tori's teeny-tiny studio flat.

I had no idea that Conqueror's Court had a Christmas Committee let alone that Nan was the top honcho of the thing.

She said she was certain she'd told me, but that only made it worse. Had she? And had I forgotten? Or had I been so wrapped up in my own dreams and Cal's that I hadn't really listened? I hadn't made my family a priority. I'd put Cal's happiness before theirs. And mine.

That wasn't such a terrible thing. We all put the people we love first, before anyone else, don't we? But the point is, I love Emma and I love Nan, yet I hadn't put them on an equal footing with Cal. I also love Tori. Had I been neglecting her, too?

Things were going to have to change. I was going to have to change.

Nineteen

Either Aaron was out when I called at his house that evening to give him some of my cakes, or he was hiding and ignoring me. I rang the doorbell several times and even peered through the windows but silence reigned, and although his car was in the drive, I assumed he must've walked to his sister's, or wherever it was he had gone. If he'd been in, Ember would've been barking, I was fairly sure of that.

I left the plastic tub of cakes on the doorstep and returned a few minutes later with a note.

It just said, 'I'm still amazed you didn't want my Christmas tree, but I made you these instead. Thank you for saving me. Twice. Merry Christmas from Katie. P.S. I'm the slightly crazy woman staying next door, in case you've forgotten.'

I hoped my attempt at humour would make him smile. Seeing him look so ...

distraught that morning had made me a little unsettled. I couldn't put my finger on it but I got the distinct impression that Nan was right; we had definitely hit a nerve.

But I had an inkling that it went deeper than simply the trauma and stresses of his job. I felt it was something personal. And I couldn't stop wondering what secret hurt or heartache Aaron was keeping hidden.

Whatever it was, I wasn't going to find out that evening. He hadn't returned by the time I went to bed at ten. I had checked every now and then to see if his lights were on. I wanted to stay up till at least eleven; he must be home by then, but I couldn't keep my eyes open any longer. It had been an eventful day.

I had talked with Emma about him when she had called me as agreed, but she said that she had no idea what his secret could possibly be.

'All I know is that, other than the briefest of hellos whenever we saw one another, it took a while for us to have a conversation. And it was Meg who made that happen. I think if Aaron had had his way, we would've still been virtually ignoring one another. I told you he was a bit grumpy, didn't I? I'm sure Nan's right. What he needs is a good woman.'

I regretted telling her what Nan had said. I also regretted the fact that Nan had stayed at Conqueror's Court and hadn't returned with me to Emma's. I don't know what was wrong with me but I was feeling alone once again.

'It's been a wonderful day, but a very long one,' Nan had said. 'I think I need an early night. You're welcome to stay here with us old fogeys for the evening, but didn't Emma say she'd call? And don't forget you owe Aaron some cakes. Why don't you go and see if you can cheer that young man up?'

For once I hadn't been inclined to disagree. The day had definitely been wonderful and I wanted to tell Aaron exactly what he'd missed.

After lunch, we'd all played games, including charades, a less active form of Twister, Monopoly and several different card games. When we'd played passing the balloon between our knees, I'm sure many names were added to the waiting list for hip and knee replacements, but the lounge rang out with laughter and new friendships were made amongst families and friends of the residents during those happy hours.

The tree lighting at four-thirty p.m. just as darkness cloaked the wintry skies was the highlight of the day. I'm surprised the National Grid managed to cope with all those lights coming on at once, not forgetting all the lights outside. Conqueror's Court was probably visible from space.

But instead of talking to Aaron, I had spent the first part of the evening on the phone with Emma, followed by a lengthy and thankfully, funny hour on the phone with Tori.

I sent her some photos of the Conqueror's Court Christmas tree and asked if that was an improvement on the last Christmas tree I'd decorated, to which she had replied that it was.

Not once did she mention Cal, or Felicia, or social media and if it hadn't been for the fact that after Tori and I had said good night I'd felt so alone, I wouldn't have checked my own social media accounts.

I'm very glad I did but I was nonetheless surprised to see a friend request from Aaron's sister, Meg, which made me even more disappointed that there wasn't a friend request from Aaron.

I'll admit I did a search but you'd be amazed how many people named Aaron Holt there actually are. I could've found him via Meg's, once I'd accepted her friend request, but I thought I heard Ember bark and after dashing to the window and seeing it was a completely different dog, I felt even more dejected and that's when I went to bed.

I was frustrated to see Aaron had left early the following morning. His car was gone by the time that I got up, but at least that meant he had returned home at some stage during the night. Or perhaps, earlier that morning.

Had he spent the night somewhere else? Did he have a girlfriend he hadn't mentioned? He'd told me he didn't date, so if that was true, it seemed unlikely. Unless he'd just started dating again. I was cross with myself that I cared.

But did I? Or was I making Aaron the rebound guy after Cal? Or trying to. If that is what this was, so far it was an abject failure.

At least I wouldn't be alone today. I was going back to Nan's and then we were going Christmas shopping in the town.

I showered, and dressed in smart black trousers and a Christmas-themed green jumper, with my long hair tied in a pony tail. Apart from applying moisturiser, a few flicks of my mascara brush and a quick swipe of my dark cherry lip gloss, I didn't bother with make-up. I was going shopping with Nan after all, and I wouldn't be seeing Aaron. Or anyone else who mattered.

Not that Aaron mattered.

I must stop thinking he did.

'This loneliness lark is really getting to you, Katie Barr,' I said to my reflection in the hall mirror.

And now I was talking to myself. Well, wasn't this just great?

I threw on my coat, pulled on my gloves, tugged my scarf around my neck, and quickly had to loosen it so as not to choke myself to death. I yanked open the front door.

Aaron almost thumped me on the nose as he raised his hand to ring Emma's doorbell in the middle of her front door. We both opened our eyes wide in surprise and promptly burst out laughing.

'You're going out?' he queried, still grinning.

'What're you doing here?' I asked at the same time.

That caused us to laugh again.

'I just came to thank you for the cakes,' he said. 'But I don't want to hold you up.'

'I'm only going shopping with Nan,' I replied, wishing I'd taken more care with my make-up. Or lack thereof. 'What time did you get home?' Now I sounded like his mother.

He gave me an odd look, which was understandable.

'When? Last night? Or just now?'

'Er. Whatever.' I'm a firm believer in the saying, "When you're in a hole, stop digging." Sadly, I hadn't quite figured out how to put it into practice. 'I didn't want my cakes – the cakes I'd left for you – to get covered in snow. If it had snowed again last night. Which it didn't. Or this morning.'

A slow smile crept across his mouth and he tilted his head a little to one side. The look in his eyes almost melted me on the spot.

'Were you keeping a lookout for me?'

A maniacal laugh escaped me, which I tried to cover up with a cough, which, in turn, made me choke.

'Of course not,' I croaked. 'I was concerned about the cakes.'

His brows furrowed momentarily. 'The cakes? Of course. Er. I can give you a lift.'

'A lift?' I patted my chest and cleared my throat.

'To Conqueror's Court. That's where you're going, isn't it? Or are you meeting Nan in town? I can drop you wherever. Driving conditions are pretty dicey today.'

'What? And you think I can't handle them? I can drive in the snow, you know.'

'I didn't say you couldn't. I simply thought you might not want to.' The look in his eyes had cooled.

'I'm not. But not because I can't. I can.'

'So you said. I'll leave you to it then.' He turned to walk away.

'You missed a really good day yesterday.' I hadn't meant to raise my voice, or for that to sound like a reprimand.

He half turned and seemed to sigh. 'Yes. I expect I did.'

'It's such a pity you had to dash off like that.'

'I didn't want to.' He shook his head. 'I didn't really have a choice.'

I stuck my chin out. 'We always have a choice. And you didn't seem in any great hurry to stay.'

He glared at me as he turned fully to face me.

'What are you trying to say? That I made up an excuse to go?'

'Well, did you?'

'No! I don't know why you would think I would. If I hadn't wanted to be there, I wouldn't have gone in the first place.'

'You didn't want to be there. You made that pretty obvious.' His mouth dropped open but quickly snapped shut as I continued: 'Nan made you come.'

'Don't be ridiculous.' He glowered. 'No one can make me do something I don't want to do. Not Nan. Not my parents. Not my sister. Not even you. I mean...' He seemed flustered. 'Actually, that's not entirely true. Meg did make me leave yesterday, so in a way, she did make me do something I didn't want to do, I suppose. But she needed my help, and Meg means the world to me.'

'Hah! Meg made you leave! What could've been so urgent that you had to dash off that very second?'

I don't know why I was being such a bitch but I couldn't seem to stop myself.

'A chip pan in her neighbour's kitchen caught fire and the poor woman foolishly threw water on the flames. Meg called 999, but she also called me because, apart from me being her brother and a firefighter, she knew I would be furious if I'd heard about it from someone else. And I would've heard about it. She didn't want me to worry. And she needed me to be there as much as I needed to be there with her.'

Okay. That was fairly serious.

'Oh my God! I'm sorry. But the fire wasn't in Meg's kitchen? It was in her neighbour's?'

I'd only queried that in case I hadn't heard it correctly, but Aaron seemed to think I was downplaying the event, and before I had a chance to ask if everyone was all right, he vented his annoyance.

'A fire is a fire! They're unpredictable, they're dangerous, and they can kill people in a matter of minutes. Sometimes, in a matter of seconds in extremes. You never dismiss a fire as a minor occurrence unless you know

185

what you are doing, and even then, unexpected things can happen. A chip pan fire may seem small to you, but putting water on burning oil causes it to explode and the resulting fireball went up and over her head and caught the ceiling alight. If Meg hadn't been there and grabbed her and pulled her away the moment she saw the woman throw the water, that woman could've...' He shook his head and took a breath. 'She could've been seriously injured, or worse. If there's a fire in your home, or a neighbour's, no matter how small it may appear, the first thing you do, even before you dial 999, is to get the hell out and stay out. And then you call the emergency services.'

'Shouldn't you at least try to put it out? I thought you were supposed to cover chip pan fires with damp tea towels?'

'No. That might be possible if the flames haven't taken hold and you're absolutely sure it's safe to turn off the stove, and do so, but I'd always advise against it. We all would. And never, ever use just water.'

'I'll bear that in mind if I ever have a fire.'

'Don't joke about it, Katie. Don't make light of this. Fires kill. You never, ever take a risk if there's a fire.'

'Okay. I'm sorry. And I wasn't making light of it. Is Meg okay? Is her neighbour?'

'Yes. But the kitchen's a total mess. She was so lucky Meg was there. I dread to think what might've happened.'

He hung his head and I should've known not to ask any more questions.

'Did you lose someone, Aaron? In a fire?'

His head shot up and his eyes burned into me.

'We've all lost someone. As you said yesterday, it comes with the job.' He as good as spat the words at me.

'I didn't mean that dismissively, either.' I felt the need to defend myself. 'I know it's probably none of my business, but was it someone close to you?'

'No, it isn't. You're right.'

He turned and walked away and I shouted after him.

'There's no need to be so stroppy. I was only asking because I care.'

He moved like lightning and was right in front of me before I knew it.

'Care? About me?' He gave a snort of derision. 'If you cared about me you wouldn't push with all the questions. Not that you could possibly care. We've only known one another for about a day and a half. And a large part of that was spent with you, in a drunken state, telling me how much you loved your ex. An ex who seems to have cheated on you before he dumped you. And

187

yet you're still crazy about the guy. Not that that's any of my business, either.'

'Perhaps we should both mind our own business,' I snapped, angry with myself as well as him.

'I couldn't agree more.'

'Fine. I'll never ask you anything ever again.'

'That sounds good to me.' He turned away but quickly turned back, holding his hand up to stop me from slamming the front door. 'I'm sorry. I shouldn't have said that about you and your ex. Are you okay?'

'What part of mind your own business did you not understand?'

He tensed and narrowed his eyes but he stood his ground. 'I understood every word.'

'And yet you're still here.'

'I'm leaving now.'

'Good riddance!'

Now, he did walk away.

'And don't bother saving me ever again,' I shouted after him, feeling I hadn't said quite enough.

'I won't,' he shouted back, still marching away.

I yelled louder. 'I don't need you. I don't need anyone. I am perfectly capable of saving myself.'

He continued on his way, but he gave me a sort of thumbs up. At least I think that's what it was.

'Good luck with that.'

They were the last words he said as he rounded the end of the drive, got into his car, and sped away down the road. Luckily, all the kids were indoors, otherwise they might have needed to dive out of his path.

I slammed the door in fury, only then remembering I was on my way out when he had arrived on the doorstep.

The last thing I felt like doing was Christmas shopping with Nan.

Twenty

Despite the awful start, the day improved.

I phoned Tori to give her a quick update on my latest clash with Aaron. We didn't speak for long because her boss was leaving on business and she had a lot to do, but just hearing her voice cheered me up.

The walk to Conqueror's Court via Mulberry Park reminded me how beautiful nature could be. The geese were back and without Ember chasing them away, they lived up to the word 'gaggle'. I wondered what they were chatting about. Watching their black tail feathers and bottoms sway as they waddled around the pond made me smile.

I pushed the word lake to the back of my mind. It was a pond, not a lake; Aaron was wrong. But I did, for one second wish that I could drown Aaron bloody Holt in it whether it was a pond or a lake.

And maybe, also Callum bloody Blake.

Men! I was better off without them.

By the time I reached Nan's flat and rang the doorbell, half hidden beneath an incredibly large, festive wreath, I was in a much better mood.

The flats in Conqueror's Court had a separate entrance at one side, although they could be accessed via the main, portico entrance at the front of the once grand stately home. A long corridor led you from the main entrance to the wing of the property that had been converted long ago, into individual flats.

Nan's flat was on the ground floor, at the back, and she had a small, private area of garden, large enough for two or three chairs in the summer months, but now only the bird table and the bird bath remained in situ.

'Come in, sweetheart,' Nan called out, loud enough for me to hear. 'The door is unlocked.'

I stepped inside to find her filling up the bird feeder.

'I could've been an axe murderer, you know.'

'You're right.' She grinned at me and winked. 'We get a lot of those around here. You're late. Did you oversleep?'

My improved mood ebbed away and I tossed my handbag on a vacant chair and slumped onto the two-seater sofa, shoving

Christmas cushions to one side to make myself more comfortable.

'I wish I had.' I let out a dramatic sigh. 'Aaron came round.'

'Oh how lovely. What did he have to say?'

'A lot. Mostly unpleasant. So you can wipe that hopeful look off your face. Aaron and I shall not be spending any more time with one another. In fact, we may not even be speaking.'

Nan came in and sat down beside me, taking my hand in hers.

'Good gracious, Katie love. What happened?'

'Emma said he was a miserable git and she was right. He called me a drunk and an idiot, and ... I can't remember what else. Oh, a bad driver, for one.'

'He said all that? This morning? How odd.'

'Well, maybe not in those exact words.'

Nan sighed. 'Oh Katie, sweetheart, what did you say to provoke him?'

'Nothing! It wasn't me.' I pouted like a petulant child. 'Okay. Perhaps I did provoke him a little. But I only asked why he had to dash off yesterday.'

Nan shook her head and got to her feet, patting my hand as she stood up.

'I'll put the kettle on and we'll have some tea and you can tell me all about it.'

'I thought we were going Christmas shopping.'

I slumped deeper into the sofa as Nan switched on the kettle and took two Christmassy mugs from a rack.

'We are. The shops will be open till late tonight, so we'll have lots of time. It's not even eleven yet, and this won't take all day.' She stopped what she was doing and turned to look at me. 'Or will it?'

'Nope. The less said about Aaron Holt, or about Callum Blake, the better!'

'Callum? What's Callum got to do with this?'

I shrugged dramatically. 'Quite a lot, as it happens.'

I told Nan everything I could remember and she tutted at me more times than I believed were warranted. It was almost as if she felt I was mainly to blame for Aaron and me falling out. I couldn't see that at all, so we agreed to differ.

Luckily, it didn't stop her wanting to go Christmas shopping with me.

We had a delicious lunch in our favourite Italian restaurant, Alberto's. It was still there but Alberto had retired last year – an event I had returned for, as had Cal and Tori. Now his son was running it but nothing had changed at all. It was still the wonderful, friendly place it had been when Tori and I had worked there.

I only had one small glass of wine. Aaron's words still hurt. I wanted to send him a text telling him I hardly ever drank, but I didn't have his number. I did have Meg's but I wasn't going to get her involved in our row. Assuming she would still be talking to me once Aaron told her what had happened between us. It was like being back at school and I told myself off for being so silly.

Afterwards, Nan and I wandered happily around the shops for several hours and once again, I spent more money than I should have.

But there was light at the end of my financial tunnel. Alberto's son, Silvio had asked how long I was staying and when I said until the New Year, possibly, he told me we should have a chat. One of his waiting staff had handed in her notice unexpectedly and there might be a job if I was interested.

It would be a backward step, but as Nan says, "Beggars can't be choosers". The money would come in handy, and perhaps being out of the house and working in a fun environment would stop me from feeling lonely. It might even stop me from behaving like a raving looney. Which was what I was beginning to realise, I was rapidly turning into. The more I thought about the row with

Aaron, the more I acknowledged it was mostly my fault. Nan was right, as she so often is.

That's another thing that's annoying. That ... and the truth.

Twenty-one

I had planned to apologise to Aaron as soon as I got home to Emma's, but it now seemed he was avoiding me. His car was gone and the lights were out, and Ember didn't bark on either of the occasions I rang Aaron's doorbell.

He wasn't there the following morning and he didn't return all day. I had actually started to worry and considered texting Meg to see if he was okay. But I thought better of it.

I knew that he hadn't come home because I spent the day putting up decorations at Emma's. Her decorations that I had found in the loft were exactly where she had told me they would be. She didn't have a tree; she said she always bought a real one.

We had always had a real tree when Mum was alive, and we did the first Christmas after she passed away, but once the house was sold, and Cal, Tori and I had moved to London, we had an artificial tree.

When Cal and I moved in together in the flat above the restaurant, we'd also had an artificial tree, and the two trees in the restaurant, one near the front door and one near the back, were artificial too, but more expensive and more realistic-looking.

I'm not sure what happened to those trees. I suppose Cal must've taken them, or maybe they were still there. Christmas trees, artificial or otherwise had been the last things on my mind when I had packed and left in such a hurry, thanks to Cal.

I would have a real tree this year, just as Emma would've done. I wasn't sure where to buy one. I hadn't spotted any on my shopping trip with Nan. But Nan would know. Or, maybe if Aaron did return at some stage in the next few days, I could use that as an ice-breaker, by asking him if he knew the best place to buy one. Or I could simply ask Emma where she got her tree each year.

Once the decorations were up, I sat by the front window and watched as more snow slowly began to fall. It hadn't snowed since that blizzard but the roads, pavements and the park were still blanketed in white.

I'd have liked to have sat and watched it, but now I had a job to go to, having taken

Silvio up on his offer of the waitress position at Alberto's.

I thought Tori might confirm my fear that it was a backward step, but when I called to tell her about it, she couldn't have been more thrilled.

'Oh how I envy you! It's just what you need right now. You'll have a fantastic time and be earning money too. The tips were always great and the people were all so lovely.'

'It doesn't seem to have changed one bit,' I told her, delighted that she was genuinely pleased for me. 'Apart from Silvio having taken over.'

Emma had been equally enthusiastic.

'It'll mean I can pay you some rent,' I said.

'Don't you dare!' She scolded. 'You keep that money and make yourself some new dreams. But don't forget to have some fun too. You deserve it.'

I glanced at the clock; it was time for me to leave. My shift was starting at six-thirty and I wanted to be there in plenty of time.

It wouldn't take me long to walk there, especially if I cut through Mulberry Park. It might be dark out but there were old fashioned lampposts dotted throughout the park and they had those ornate, lantern lamps that looked so warm and festive. They were each hung with wreaths, and fairy lights were draped between them, making it even brighter in the park and made the whole place seem as if Charles Dickens or even Scrooge himself might stroll by at any minute.

The main town was split into two, and had been since the day it was built, so the story goes. Both sides had residential dwellings but only one side had shops and other commercial buildings. That was, of course, the largest area and it ran from the former boundaries of Conqueror's Court, or the once grand stately home it had been all those centuries ago, and continued down towards the sea. The smaller residential-only area was built amongst the hills and fields sat between it and the sea.

Conqueror's Court sat slap bang in the middle of its former large estate, with hills rising up on either side. Mulberry Park had once been a part of that estate but now it sat between Conqueror's Court and the main town of Norman Landing.

The new part of the town had sprung up in the 1970s, and like the smaller area of the main town, this was only residential. Emma's house was here, nestled amongst several others, all very similar, and all far enough from the main town to feel as if they were in the countryside, but close enough not to feel isolated.

I smiled as I reached the part of Mulberry Park from where you could see Conqueror's Court. All its festive lights were ablaze and I wished I'd given myself more time so that I could pop in and see Nan, despite the fact that I'd seen her for coffee that morning. I had asked if she wanted to come back to Emma's with me and help me decorate but she said she was a little tired after our shopping trip of the previous day. Sometimes, I forgot that Nan was in her eighties. She was always so full of life.

I arrived at Alberto's with plenty of time to spare and I spent a delightful ten minutes re-acquainting myself with the place I'd loved so much. But now I had mixed feelings. This was also the place I'd met Cal – that Christmas Eve, almost six years ago. How strange to think I'd be working here again this Christmas Eve.

I was nervous on my first shift, but I needn't have worried. Even though I was officially front of house at Blake's, Cal's restaurant, I often worked as a waitress, especially when we had been short-staffed.

One thing I'd forgotten was that at Alberto's we could keep all the tips we made from the tables we waited on. That was a welcome surprise. It was good to be earning money again, no matter how long I worked there. I hadn't yet given any thought to where I would live after New Year when Emma returned from the States. She had said that I was welcome to stay for as long as I liked and although it was great to know I wouldn't be homeless, I was thirty-five and I needed a place of my own. I just wasn't sure yet where that place might be.

One of the other staff, a lovely woman called Gertie, who had told me she was sixty-five but looked more like forty-five to me, offered me a lift home, but for some reason I wanted to walk. I didn't feel at all tired and the snow clouds had made way for the moon and the stars tonight.

It was one of those stunningly beautiful nights when the cold, frosty air took your breath away and yet made you feel it was wonderful to be alive. Snow crunched beneath my feet and silence was all I could hear as I left the main part of town and headed towards the grounds of Conqueror's Court.

I'm not sure when I noticed a slight change in the air but it was as I closed in on the rear of the grand old building. There was a public footpath to one side and that was the route I was taking. I heard a crackling sound, like twigs being stepped on, or something similar to that, but I couldn't quite make it out and I pricked my ears to listen more intently.

It was only when I rounded the front of the building that I saw and smelt the fire. Tiny flames were licking at the attic windows but the rest of the building looked exactly as it had done when I'd walked right past it earlier. The lights were still blazing although some near the attic rooms appeared to have gone out.

I think it took me two seconds to react. My first thought was of dashing in and rescuing Nan and everyone else I could, but even as I ran towards the front door, yelling 'Fire! Wake up! Get out! Fire!', I remembered Aaron's words and I dialled 999.

As soon as I'd spoken to the Fire and Rescue call handler, I had called Nan's mobile to tell her to get out, but it went straight to her voicemail.

Would Aaron have told me to remain outside? I thought he probably might, but I couldn't wait and watch and worry while the attic of Nan's building burned.

I raced towards the building and banged on the locked doors, yelling at the top of my voice before peering through one of the front windows to the side of the main doors.

They had a security guard, and a night shift worked through the night. Where were those people now? Why hadn't they opened the front doors? The door to the flats was made of heavy steel so I knew I had to get to Nan via the main front entrance.

I frantically scanned the snow-covered ground around me, looking for something I could use to break in. I remembered there were large, ornamental rocks surrounding some of the flowerbeds and I fell to my knees and groped around until my fingers found one.

The first one was far too small but the second one was perfect. It was heavier than I thought and it took both my hands to lift it so I was sure it would do the job. I threw it against the window with all my might and as the glass smashed, an alarm rang out. That must be the burglar alarm. Why hadn't the fire alarm been ringing too?

I couldn't concern myself with that right now. I had to get to Nan. I used the smaller rock to smash away some more of the glass and I brushed the broken pieces out of my direct path as much as possible, with my gloves. If I slashed my wrists, or arms and legs on broken glass, I wouldn't be much use to Nan or anyone else.

I pulled myself up and as I hurled myself through the window and tumbled to the floor, I heard shouts and screams circling around.

'Fire!' I yelled. 'Get out.'

I tried to open the front doors but they were locked with a key; a key I didn't have time to find right now. I had to get to Nan. I knew the emergency services would be here at any moment and they would break down the doors if need be.

I wasn't sure how bad the fire was and I didn't have time to wait. I raced along the corridor thumping on every door and yelling, 'Fire. Get out!' as loud as I possibly could. My yells, together with the alarm had woken people up and now the corridor I was racing down was quickly filling up.

'Move!' I screamed. 'Get to the doors. Get out of the building as fast as you can.'

It didn't occur to me for one second that the fire might not be that bad and that it might even be under control by now. I remembered Aaron saying fires were unpredictable and dangerous unless you knew what you were doing, and even then, unexpected things could happen. I would rather everyone stood outside in the cold for half an hour or so than take the risk of something more serious occurring.

And I didn't think this fire was under control. If anything, the opposite was happening. The smell of smoke and burning wood and materials was stronger than it had been. The noises I had heard were louder but were now muffled by the shouts and screams.

I eventually reached Nan's door and I rang the bell and banged on it as hard as I possibly could. Some of her neighbours were filtering out and I told them what was happening. I had never seen elderly people move so fast but I was thankful that they did.

'Where's the nearest exit?' one of the women asked.

'I don't know,' I replied, horrified that she had no idea. 'Maybe one of the others knows. I've got to get Nan out.'

The woman looked at me aghast as she hurried along the corridor. 'Nan's not in there.'

She was gone from sight before her words registered. Of course Nan was in her flat. Where else would she be at several minutes after midnight?

Unless she'd gone to Emma's? But she would've told me if she had. And she knew I was working tonight.

I didn't know what to do next. Nan's door was solid wood and I couldn't break it down. In desperation, I phoned Meg.

'Meg? It's Katie. Do you know where Aaron is, or can you text me his number? There's a fire at Conqueror's Court and I can't find Nan! I can't find Nan!' I repeated, half mad with worry and fear. 'I don't know what to do!'

'You're inside the building?' Meg sounded as concerned as me. 'Katie, get out of there right now. I know about the fire. I'm just arriving myself. I can see the Fire and Rescue trucks. I think Aaron's here. He had to cover for someone tonight. I'll try to find him, but please get out of there, Katie. The central section's in flames. Get out of there right now!'

Twenty-two

The thought that Aaron might be here made me a little calmer somehow. My racing heart stopped pounding quite as badly and my frantic breathing slowed. But an acrid smell pervaded my nostrils as I made my way back in the direction I had come. And then what Meg had said sank in.

"The central section's in flames."

Those were her exact words and that only meant one thing. I couldn't get out the way I had come in.

So where could I get out? I'd never paid attention to the placement of the fire exits; it hadn't seemed to matter. I didn't know the building well. The only parts I'd visited were Nan's corridor, the main lounge, the central hall and the ladies loo just along the corridor from there. That was the extent of my knowledge of Conqueror's Court.

I could hear shouting but I couldn't see any people. That meant Nan's neighbours must've gone somewhere.

'Hello!' I shouted. 'Can anyone hear me?'

It was as if a fog was creeping along the corridor towards me. Was that smoke? Was the fire closer than I thought?

'Help! Is anyone there?'

I peered into the hazy darkness as I stumbled forward. The main lights and the Christmas lights had all gone out and only the emergency lighting was working. But thank God it was. The fire alarm certainly hadn't, and nor had the sprinklers, it seemed.

I made progress forward but I caught my foot on something and I felt my ankle twist beneath me and I fell against the wall.

And then, just like the heroes do in all those disaster movies, a tall man in the gold and yellow firefighter's turnout gear, his helmet and visor covering his face, came striding towards me through that smoke.

'You're safe,' he said, and I thought I recognised his voice. 'Let's get out of here, shall we?'

I nodded, spluttered and coughed. My throat was suddenly parched, no doubt from all that shouting and running but I managed to get the words out, 'I think I've hurt my ankle and I can't find Nan. My nan. She should–'

'She's safe too,' my saviour said. 'She and her friend are with my colleagues.'

He swept me into his arms and carried me almost at a run and I saw he wasn't alone. Another firefighter had been close behind him and another met us a few paces ahead.

'Everyone's out,' the man said.

'Except us,' I almost added, but this wasn't the time for such comments.

My head was buried against my rescuer's jacket and although I wanted to look, he told me not to. I think that was in case I panicked. I closed my eyes and didn't open them again until I felt the chill of the cold night air against my skin. Then I did glance over his shoulder and I couldn't believe my eyes.

Whilst flames danced against the backdrop of a starry, winter night sky, large powerful lights situated on the top of the fire engine illuminated the building like a stage, as did more lights on the ground. It made it all seem slightly surreal as if I was watching it all on a huge TV screen.

The main entrance and the window I climbed through were hidden by the flames and more were licking the floor above. Flames devoured the roof. But only the main, central section of the building appeared to be on fire. The wing containing the flats and the wing on the opposite side where most of the care home residents lived, seemed to have escaped the flames. So far, at least.

Firefighters on the ground drowned the fire with their hoses and more firefighters on the raised platform ladder, fought the flames from there.

'We'll soon have this under control,' I heard one of the other firefighters say as we passed him.

From where I was perched, I found that optimistic.

'Take special care of this one, please, Lou,' my saviour said. 'And check out her ankle. It might be injured.'

I turned to face a stunning paramedic with the warmest smile and the brightest blue eyes, standing at the rear of an ambulance, the doors of which she had clearly just opened, ready to administer medical assistance to those who required it.

'Will do, Aaron,' Lou replied.

'Aaron?' My head zipped round and I stared up into his eyes; the only part of his face that was visible, as he sat me down on the edge of the box area of the ambulance.

He removed his helmet, swept his hair back from his forehead and gave me an odd sort of smile.

'I know you told me not to save you ever again, but I'm afraid it's part of my job.'

I wasn't sure if that was a joke, sarcasm, or if he was actually being serious.

Meg came running towards us while Lou asked me if my ankle hurt.

'No,' I said, feeling surprised it didn't.

'You're safe!' Meg gasped, reaching out and squeezing my hand. 'I was so worried about you, Katie. But I knew Aaron would find you.'

'I'm fine too, thanks,' said Aaron.

'I'm glad.' Meg beamed at him. 'I'm sorry but I need to get more photos for the paper. I'll call you later, Katie.' She dashed off the way she had come, glancing briefly back and waving at Aaron. 'I'll call you later, too, big brother.'

'Stay a safe distance from the fire!' he shouted after her and then he glanced at me. 'You know she'll want to interview you, don't you?'

'Me? Why?'

He quirked a brow. 'You did just help to save several people. And this could be a big story. Questions will be asked about why the fire safety equipment wasn't...' His voice trailed off, and then he added, 'I'd better get back to work. I'll leave you to it.'

He smiled at Lou and she returned his smile.

I suddenly felt nauseous.

'Thank you,' I shouted after him.

He simply waved his hand but he didn't smile at me as he had smiled at Lou. I decided I didn't like her, but I knew I had to ask.

'Have you known him long?'

Lou gave me a curious look and an even more curious smile.

'Who? Aaron?'

No, Father bloody Christmas, I was tempted to say, but instead I simply nodded.

'Years. Don't ask me how many. I was best friends with his...' She darted a look at me. 'How long have you known him?'

'Er. I don't remember,' I lied. 'Not that long. My sister lives next door.'

'Your sister? You mean, Emma?'

'Yep. I'm staying at her place for a while. Wait! Where's Nan?'

I leapt down onto the ground almost knocking Lou off her feet. How had I forgotten about Nan? I know Aaron told me she was safe, but I wanted to see her with my own eyes.

I searched the crowds of people. There were firefighters, paramedics, Meg, and others taking photos. There were people who had obviously come to gawp. There were four other ambulances that I could see, a couple of Rescue Service cars and lots of elderly people, but I couldn't see Nan.

'You need to sit down,' Lou said. 'I'll ask someone to look for your nan.'

It was at that moment that I spotted her and my sigh of relief would've been audible from Scotland.

'Nan!' I yelled, waving frantically.

To my utter delight, she waved back. There was an elderly gentleman with her and as they came towards me, I ignored Lou's protestations and I rushed into Nan's arms.

'Hello, sweetheart,' she said, stroking my hair and kissing my forehead. 'I hear we all owe you and these brave firefighters our lives.'

'Not me,' I said. 'I couldn't find you. I looked for you but you weren't in your flat. I thought I'd lost you, Nan. I thought...' I sobbed into her shoulder.

'There, there, sweetheart. We're all safe and sound. Everyone got out and there are only a couple of people with minor injuries, so one of the paramedics told me. That's thanks in no small part to you, whatever you may say. I'm so sorry you were worried. But how are you? Are you hurt?' She eased me away and scanned my body from head to foot.

I shook my head and smiled. 'I'm fine. I thought I'd twisted my ankle but it seems to be okay now. Where were you, Nan? It's way past midnight.'

213

She gave a little cough and looked me directly in the eye. 'I was with a friend. This friend.' She held out a hand to the elderly man. 'Katie love, this is Donald. Donald, this is my eldest granddaughter and I love her very much.'

It was as if all the mayhem going on around us wasn't happening.

'Hello, Donald,' I said, slightly bemused that Nan would choose that particular moment to introduce us.

'Hello, Katie.' He gave me a friendly smile. 'Nan's told me all about you and it's so good to finally meet you. I was sorry to miss you at the Christmas tree lighting the other day, but I only got back from my son's last night. He lives in Bristol.'

And then the penny dropped. Nan had spent the night with Donald, or at least she had before the fire disturbed them. Donald was more than just a friend and Nan wanted me to know that.

'Do either of you need my services?' Lou asked.

'No thank you,' said Nan. 'We've been given the all-clear by the paramedics in that ambulance over there, and told to call our doctor or go to the hospital if we should feel unwell later.'

'Katie?' Lou gave me a smile. 'I'm supposed to be taking care of you.'

'Sorry,' I said. 'But I think I'm good.'

'Why don't we let me be the judge of that? You have just been rescued from a burning building. I really should check you out.'

'She's right,' Nan said. 'You might have smoke inhalation. Let this young lady do her job. We'll wait for you over there. I'm dying for a cup of tea.'

'There's tea?'

I couldn't believe what was happening. But Nan was safe and well, and so it seemed, were all the others. That's all that really mattered.

Twenty-three

Getting information from Lou about Aaron was like getting blood from a stone. Every time I asked her a question, she turned it back on me.

'How did you say you met Aaron?' I asked as soon as Nan and Donald were out of earshot.

'I don't think I did say, did I?' She wrapped an inflatable sleeve around my arm to take my blood pressure.

'Was it through work? I thought you mentioned something about a best friend.'

'Did I?' She shrugged. 'We often meet up through our jobs. Your blood pressure's fine, which is good, especially after what you've been through. What do you do for a living, Katie?'

'Er. I ran a restaurant in London with my boyfriend until recently. My ex-boyfriend, I should say. We broke up.'

'Oh I'm sorry. Is that why you're staying with Emma?'

She took my temperature so I couldn't reply right away. Apparently, my temperature was also fine.

'Yes,' I said. 'Do you know Emma via Aaron? Did he introduce you?'

'I've never actually met her. I just know she lives next door. Slip off your boot and let me look at that ankle.'

'It doesn't hurt now. I'm sure my ankle's fine too.'

She gave me the sort of look that parents give to tiresome children, so I took off my boot and laughed when I realised I'd removed the wrong one. Now she no doubt thought I was stupid.

Once she'd confirmed that I was okay – although she did say the same as the paramedic had said to Nan, that if I felt unwell at any stage within the next twenty-four hours, I should see a doctor – I went in search of Nan. It was clear Lou had no intention of telling me anything and it was around one a.m. now; I seriously needed sleep.

Nan and Donald were wrapped in blankets, speaking with a firefighter, and even with his back to me, I knew it was Aaron. I was about to make my presence known when a police officer appeared beside me.

'Excuse me,' the officer said. 'Are you Miss Barr? Miss Katie Barr?'

'I am. Oh. Is this about the window? About me breaking in?' That probably wasn't the best thing to say to the police, but I was exhausted and I wasn't thinking clearly. Now I was panicking. 'I didn't have a choice. The doors were locked and I couldn't–'

'It's okay, Katie,' Aaron said, turning and nodding at the policeman. 'The officer knows what happened. Someone saw you. You're not in any trouble. Quite the opposite, in fact.'

As he gave me a reassuring smile, my heart skipped a beat. That must've been an after effect of the fire.

'That's right, Miss Barr.' The officer's smile was brief and less reassuring. 'Although the owners of the building might think differently, but considering the events of tonight, I doubt it. I just need to take a statement from you to get a clearer picture.'

'Does it have to be right now, Tony?' Aaron asked, grabbing a blanket from a pile in the back of a nearby Fire and Rescue vehicle, and wrapping it around me. 'Can't it wait till later? I think Katie needs to get some sleep and she's probably still in shock. Plus it's freezing out here.'

Oddly enough I hadn't felt cold until I was wrapped in that blanket. Only then did I realise that my teeth were chattering and I was shivering, but now I was beginning to warm up.

The officer didn't look particularly pleased but he nodded and tapped Aaron on the arm in a friendly gesture.

'Of course, it can. I'll just need your address and contact number, Miss Barr. This can wait until tomorrow. Or I should say, later today.'

'Thank you,' I said, before giving him my details.

He wished us all a good night and was gone as quickly as he had appeared.

'As if the owners would dare to suggest you shouldn't have broken in,' Donald said, angrily. 'The police should be investigating them.'

'They are,' said Aaron. 'That's why they need Katie's statement. It'll be a joint investigation with us, and the insurers will be involved. They'll be interviewing everyone.' He sighed. 'As will my sister.'

Meg was taking photos of some of the residents of Conqueror's Court and would, no doubt, be heading in our direction.

'I think it's time we went home,' I said. 'As much as I like Meg, I'm not in the mood to be photographed and questioned, especially not for the local newspaper.'

'I don't blame you,' Aaron said, glancing at my hair.

My hand shot up instinctively. 'Is there something wrong with my hair?' I tried to comb it with my hand.

'Your hair's fine,' he said, grinning suddenly. 'I just hadn't realised it was ... such a pretty colour.'

'Oh!'

I didn't know what else to say. He looked sincere. And a bit embarrassed. But when he met my eyes and held them, it was me who went bright red. I could feel the heat sweep across my face.

'We've been told we can't go back inside,' Nan said.

She sounded a little despondent, which was unlike her, and I dragged my gaze from Aaron.

'I wouldn't think you'd want to, even if you could.' I was astonished and didn't try to hide it. 'That place is a death trap.'

'But it's our home,' Donald added, as equally downhearted as Nan.

'Not right now, it's not. You're coming back with me, Nan. Do you have somewhere else to go, Donald? If not you're welcome to stay with us. I'm sure Emma won't mind.'

Nan and Donald exchanged brief glances and then he smiled gratefully.

'That's very kind of you, but I've called my daughter. She doesn't live that far away and she's coming to get me. She should be here any minute and we can give you two a lift.'

That was good news on two counts. Firstly, I had nothing against Donald, and I knew Emma wouldn't have minded if he'd stayed with us, but I didn't relish the thought of him and Nan sleeping together, so I'd intended to offer him the sofa. Being able to avoid an awkward situation was good. And secondly I didn't fancy walking home and I wasn't sure we'd be able to get a minicab, so the prospect of a lift was bliss.

'I'd better get on,' Aaron said, clearing his throat and avoiding my eyes. 'Don't forget. If you feel unwell, any of you, call for an ambulance. It's better to be safe than sorry.'

He held up a hand to say goodbye and turned to leave but I reached out and grabbed his sleeve to stop him.

'Aaron?'

'Yes?'

I waited until he looked me in the eyes.

'Thank you for saving my life. Yet again.'

He smiled. 'I think it's becoming a habit. But you're welcome.'

'Stay safe,' I added.

'You too.'

A strange sort of explosion sent new flames shooting into the air and before I could say another word, Aaron was racing back towards Conqueror's Court and the fire.

Twenty-four

Sleep is a wonderful thing, especially when you're exhausted. But how I slept that night, is a mystery to me.

Only seconds after that explosion, Donald's daughter, Mary arrived – which was just as well because the police were already putting up new barriers and stopping anyone other than emergency service personnel from entering the vicinity.

I desperately wanted to stay. The thought that something might happen to Aaron terrified me. But we were all told to leave, and the remaining two ambulances and the other rescue vehicles were moving further away, despite being – what had previously been considered – a safe distance from the fire.

Aaron had told me that fires could be unpredictable. This fire was certainly being that. And then some!

I spotted Tony, the police officer who'd spoken to me earlier, and I ran up to him.

'Can I stay?' I pleaded. 'I'm worried about Aaron.'

He gave me the strangest look before shaking his head.

'Aaron will be fine. He knows what he's doing. The best thing you can do for him right now, is to go.'

'But I...' I let my voice trail off. Tony had already moved on.

And then I saw Meg, who was also being moved away from the area, and was protesting about it.

'Oh, come on!' she was saying. 'You know it's my job.'

'Out!' the male officer with her said, lifting the tape and ushering her to the other side.

'Fine,' she grumbled. 'But don't expect me to buy you a drink anytime soon.'

'Katie!' Nan called to me from beside Mary's car. 'We need to go.'

'Just a second, Nan.' I dashed to Meg. 'Are you staying?' She seemed surprised to see me.

'I thought you'd left! Er. Yeah, I'm staying.' She held up her press lanyard. 'I've got a magic key.'

She didn't seem very concerned about Aaron.

'Aaron's gone back to fight that!' I pointed at the flames shooting skywards.

'I know. I've got a great shot of him and Steve on the ladder. Oh, don't worry.' She squeezed my arm. 'He'll be fine. He'd worry about you if he knew you were still here. These guys know what they're doing, Katie. You go home. I'll tell you what. I'll call you if anything happens to him. Okay? But it won't.'

I wish I'd had her certainty.

As it happens, she was right. Aaron was fine. I saw him arrive home shortly after nine a.m., and I will admit, I had a peculiar desire to run outside and hug him.

Thankfully, I managed to stop myself. But I did bang on the window and wave at him. Somewhat maniacally, I might add. To my disappointment, he gave me the smallest, briefest wave possible in return.

Had I done something else to annoy him? We'd been on fairly good terms when we said goodbye last night.

Perhaps something awful happened after I had left. But wouldn't Meg have phoned to tell me? Or texted me at least?

'Nan?' I called to her from the kitchen while watching Aaron walk to his front door and let himself in. Nan was sitting by the fire in the living room, reading a magazine. 'Does the local paper have a website? Or a digital copy on line?'

'Good gracious, sweetheart, I don't know. I prefer my news on real paper. Or via the radio. Not that the local paper is on the radio. And we still don't have a local radio station either. The paper comes out once a week. On Saturday.'

I dried my hands on a snowflake-patterned hand towel. I'd been washing up a couple of mugs that weren't dishwasher-safe.

'It's Saturday today!' I walked into the living room. 'I suppose that means it won't have any news about the fire. It was gone 1 a.m. when we left and Meg was still taking photos. There's no way a small, local newspaper would've had time to change the print run and still get the paper out in time this morning. They're in the shops by five or six a.m. I believe. Wait! He didn't have Ember with him! Oh God. I hope nothing's happened to Ember.'

'Who, sweetheart? Aaron? When? You've lost me. Weren't we discussing the paper?'

'We were.' I hurried to the front door, kicked off my slippers and pulled on my boots. 'But Aaron came home a minute ago, looking miserable and I've just realised he didn't have Ember with him.'

I yanked open the door and rushed round to Aaron's, so I didn't hear what else Nan might have said. It was probably that I should put on my coat. And I should have. It was absolutely freezing out this morning.

'Katie?'

Aaron looked half asleep. He *was* half undressed. Although he was struggling to put on a jumper to cover his bare chest. I was so tempted to help him, mainly in the hope that I could touch that super fit body of his.

I almost forgot why I was there.

'Is Ember okay?'

He looked bemused as his brows knit together.

'Ember? What? As far as I know, yes. He's with Mum and Dad. Why?'

I let out a sigh of genuine relief.

'Thank goodness. Then … has something else dreadful happened?'

He scratched his head and yawned.

'What? Why? What's going on?'

'You look miserable.'

He blinked at least twice.

'Er. Thanks.' He looked me up and down. 'Don't you ever wear a coat? It's freezing this morning.'

I laughed. 'Tell me about it.'

He sighed heavily and opened the door wide, stepping to one side.

'You'd better come in. I was just about to go to bed.'

'Ooh! Is that an offer?'

Don't ask me why I said that as I stepped into the hall. I never say things like that. Ever. And I soon wished I hadn't.

'No!'

If he'd slapped my face, it couldn't have stung more. One little word but so decisive. So final. And the expression of abject horror on his face didn't help. I know I'm not beautiful but surely I'm not that repulsive? Cal thought I was pretty, and he was just as good looking as Aaron.

'I was joking.' I shouldn't have snapped at him.

'Sorry. I'm too tired for jokes. You might have forgotten but I have just come off a night shift. A busy night shift. On what should've been one of my four days off. We're so short-staffed right now, it's crazy.'

'Well excuse me for caring! At first I thought I'd upset you. Again. And then I thought it must be Ember. Now I realise you're just grumpy. I'll let you go to bed. Alone. No doubt as usual.'

I wanted to storm out and not look back, but when a man as broad shouldered and as tall as Aaron is blocking your path and you'd have to squeeze past him to get out, it's a little difficult to make a dramatic exit.

He stared at me for a moment and then he grinned and the light in his eyes sent a completely different sensation shooting through me. One I needed to control.

'Are you going to let me out?' I stood as straight and as tall as I could.

He tilted his head a little to one side and the grin broadened.

'I'm thinking about it.'

His voice was warm and deep and utterly, knee-meltingly sexy.

I had to act fast. I had never thrown myself at a man, and I'd never, ever begged a man to kiss me, but there was a very real possibility that I might do both those things – and more. Since meeting Aaron, I seemed to be doing a lot of things I wouldn't normally. I had to get out of there.

'Oh, for goodness sake!'

I pushed him as hard as I could with both hands and although he didn't fall, or move much at all, to be honest, he did sort of sway a little. Just enough for me to nip past him, grab the front door handle and yank the door open.

I ran down that drive as fast as I could and how I managed not to slip and fall on the ice and snow is beyond me. I think sheer determination kept me upright. Or sheer panic.

But my retreat from Aaron's could not be described as graceful. Or dramatic. And I swear I could hear him sniggering.

On the plus side, I suppose he no longer looked miserable.

But I wasn't going to turn around to check.

Twenty-five

'Everything okay, sweetheart?' Nan asked, as I shut Emma's front door and leant against it, trying to catch my breath.

'Yep,' was all I could manage in reply.

'And Ember's with Daphne and Roger.' That was a statement, not a question.

Damn it! Maybe that's what Nan had called after me when I'd left for Aaron's; not about me wearing a coat at all.

But how did she know that?

As if reading my mind she added, 'Aaron told Donald and me last night that he'd been called in to cover for someone, so Daphne and Roger had Ember. I think he thought we might be worried.'

That might've been almost funny if I hadn't just made a complete and utter fool of myself.

I needed to talk to someone about what had happened, but there was no way I was telling Nan. I loved her to bits but if she got

231

even a hint of the fact that I might be attracted to Aaron, she'd be arranging our wedding before I'd finished the sentence.

Emma would be sound asleep. It was around four a.m. in New York. But I would discuss it with her later. She might be five years younger than me but when it came to men and dating, she was wise beyond her years.

There was only one person I could call, and that was Tori. She would be at work, but she always managed to find time to chat with her friends. Especially her best friend. She might even pretend she was ill and take the day off so we could meet up for lunch somewhere between here and London. Assuming trains were running in this weather.

I could almost hear Emma sarcastically saying that maybe that's why Tori hadn't gone quite as far in the music industry as Tori hoped she might. Emma's work ethic would make a robot on a factory line look lackadaisical. Tori's work ethnic was, let's just say, not a patch on Emma's. Or even mine.

I took a deep breath and popped my head around the living room door.

'I'm nipping upstairs to give Tori a call. I don't want to disturb your reading.'

'You won't disturb me, Katie love. But if you mean you want to talk to Tori about something you don't want me to hear, that's fine. Just remember, I was young once too. Been there, seen it, done it. Several times over, probably. And with bells on.'

'Thanks for that, Nan. Love you.'

I won't tell you the image that had popped into my head, but I did my best to ignore it as I ran upstairs to video call Tori.

I threw myself on the bed and she answered on the first ring.

'Oooh! Look at you,' she said. 'Lazing around on your bed at this time in the morning while some of us have to slave over our desks.' She grabbed a mug of coffee from the desk, in one hand, and with a caramel-iced doughnut in the other, she leant back in the chair and put her feet up on the desk. 'Or should I say, our boss' desk?' She beamed at me. 'When the boss is away, Tori will rule the empire. How's things? How did your first shift go last night at Alberto's? Was it as great as it was when we worked there?'

'Alberto's was brilliant. But other than that things couldn't be any worse! I almost died in a fire and I nearly begged Aaron to have sex with me!'

She spat out the coffee she had quaffed, at the same time dropping the doughnut, which landed icing-side down, half on her dress and half on her cleavage.

'Bugger!' Plonking the mug on the desk, and spilling more coffee in the process, she peeled the doughnut from her chest. 'Are you serious?' She grabbed some tissues and mopped at the coffee slops. 'You nearly died!'

'Okay. That might've been a slight exaggeration. But I could have. Maybe. Probably not. Anyway, annoyingly, Aaron saved me. Yet again!' I sighed dramatically. 'I was completely unharmed.'

'You're definitely okay?' I nodded and Tori tutted. 'Honestly! Doesn't that man have anything better to do?' She grinned at me and licked the icing from her fingers.

'I know! Tell me about it. He's like a bloody superhero. He's definitely got the body of a superhero. He even carried me out of the burning building.'

'The building was on fire? You weren't joking?'

I shook my head. 'I wasn't joking. And I was terrified at the time. I don't know how firefighters do what they do, Tori. But don't worry. Everyone got out and no one was hurt. Just a couple of minor injuries, so I heard.'

'But that's still serious stuff.'

'It might've been if Aaron and the others hadn't turned up as quickly as they did. But as I said, everyone's fine. I'll tell you all about it another time. Right now, I need some advice and it's too early in New York for me to call Emma.'

'So I'm your second choice?' Tori pulled a face. 'Okey dokey. But let me just add, that man must be a superhero if he carried you.' She grinned again. 'I'm still waiting for a photo of him, you know. So is that why you nearly begged him for sex? They say people have strong physical reactions in times of danger and in life-threatening situations.'

'I have a strong physical reaction every time I look at him. I don't know what's the matter with me. I think this might be my way of coping with Cal dumping me.'

'This has nothing to do with that waste of space,' Tori said, emphatically. 'Oh but wait. Didn't I tell you this would happen? Didn't I say you'd meet someone else and fall in love and have five kids? Or something along those lines.'

'I have *not* fallen in love with Aaron!' I rolled over onto my back. 'Even if I had, it wouldn't make any difference. I thought he might be attracted to me. Just a little. But he made it clear just now that he definitely isn't. Yet sometimes, when he looks at me, there's something in his eyes.'

'Smouldering passion, you mean?' Tori giggled.

'Certainly not smouldering. Apart from maybe in the fire last night,' I joked. 'But yeah. Something close to passion. Although it's nicer than that somehow.'

'There's something nicer than passion?' She glanced at her doughnut. 'Apart from food, obviously.'

'Obviously,' I agreed. 'Food first. Passion second. Love third.'

'Hmm. I think love and passion should have equal positions. And speaking of positions, you still haven't told me what's happened to make you need my advice, other than you begged him to have sex with you.'

'Nearly begged him. I ran before I made an even bigger fool of myself.'

'Is that possible? Sorry. Continue.'

I regaled her with my latest run in with Aaron and when she eventually stopped laughing, she tapped the screen and peered at me.

'Earth to Katie. You might want to take notes. Right. It sounds as if he's one of the following. One – gay. Two – dating someone and he's the faithful type. Three – a player who's reeling you in. Or four – and this is the one I'm laying my money on – he's falling for you too but he doesn't want to admit it, either to you or to himself.'

'Yeah right. And I'm not falling for him. I just want to have sex with him. And that's

something I never thought I'd hear myself
say. Except I don't want to have sex with him
because I still love Cal. It's all so confusing.
I'll tell you something though. Aaron has a
secret. I'm sure of that. I don't know what it
is yet but I'm determined to find out.'

'I'm skipping over the part about Cal.
You don't love him. You just think you do.
But back to Aaron. Will you be running to, or
from him, while you're finding out this
secret?'

'That's why I need some advice. How do
I get close enough to ask about his private
life, and yet not seem interested in him?'

'You don't. Because you clearly are
interested in him. If you weren't you
wouldn't want to know what secret he's
hiding. And for once, I do have some advice.
Real advice. Forget about Cal. No.' She raised
her hand in a stop gesture. 'Don't argue with
me. Just listen. Forget about Cal for now, and
just go with the flow. Don't worry about
whether or not you're falling for Aaron. Let
your feelings guide you. Let your heart show
you the way.'

'Er. Have you been smoking something
you shouldn't?'

She rolled her eyes at me. 'Just try it.
Now I'm sorry to say this but I need to cut
you short. My boss is video calling me in five
minutes and I'd better tidy up his desk. I

don't know, it's like being in the salt mines, working here. I never have any time for myself or my friends. We'll catch up later. Love you.'

'Love you too.'

Twenty-six

I was confused about my feelings but I decided Tori's suggestion wasn't as mad as it sounded, although it wouldn't be as easy as she made it seem. If I'd gone with the flow just now, I probably would've thrown myself at Aaron. And that would've been even more embarrassing than running away.

But if I could stop worrying about whether I'd upset Aaron, or exactly what he was thinking, and I could stop wondering if Cal was missing me at all, then maybe I could sort out my emotions. It was certainly worth a try.

Nan still had her head in her magazine when I went back downstairs.

'Fancy a cup of coffee?' I asked, but I had to repeat myself when she didn't reply.

That's when I noticed she had nodded off. That was very unlike Nan. Then again, we hadn't got to bed until gone one-thirty and she was up long before me as per usual.

I decided to go for a walk and let her rest. I covered her with one of Emma's fleece, Christmassy throws that I'd found with all the decorations, and put another Christmas-themed cushion behind her head. I wrote her a note saying I was popping out and to call me when she woke up.

I know it sounds silly, especially as Aaron was probably in bed himself by now, but I looked through the window and opened the front door ajar before I left the house. The last thing I wanted was to bump into him again this morning.

I made my way to Conqueror's Court via Mulberry Park. I wanted to see if there had been much more damage to the building after the fire had taken hold again. I expected to see quite a lot of fire and water damage but I hadn't expected the place to look so bleak and desolate. It was hard to believe that only a couple of days ago I was inside that once grand building, helping to decorate a massive Christmas tree.

And now, instead of seeing a myriad of twinkling lights adorning the stone façade, all that stood before me was a blackened and broken shell. But that was thankfully only the central section. Both wings looked relatively unscathed.

I can't tell you how sad I was to see it. I could only imagine how all the residents would feel.

Last night, in Mary's car, Donald and Nan had both said they would be back inside before Christmas.

'We'll still have our Christmas Eve party,' Nan had said. 'Even if the walls aren't repainted in time, and the carpets aren't replaced. And I know I won't be allowed into my flat until all the mess is cleared away and the building is declared safe, but that won't take more than a week or so, I shouldn't think.'

I knew she was being optimistic, but I didn't want to upset her.

'I'm looking forward to it,' Donald said, beaming. 'I missed the Christmas tree lighting, but I won't miss Christmas Eve.'

'We all get together for that,' Nan told me. 'No one will want to miss Christmas Eve.'

'I think you might,' said Mary, clearly not one to worry about shattering people's dreams. Or maybe she was simply a realist. 'You'll be lucky if anyone gets back in that place before February next year. You definitely won't have Christmas Eve there. And besides, weren't all the presents kept under the tree? They'll all be gone. Either burned, or damaged by water. But don't worry, Dad. You can spend Christmas Eve with us.'

The expression on Donald's face suggested he'd rather spend Christmas Eve in Siberia or somewhere. Nan looked as if she'd like to join him. I'd never seen her so downhearted. At least, not since Mum had passed away.

'Never mind,' I'd said, attempting to cheer them both up. 'We'll find somewhere else to have your Christmas Eve party if you can't have it at Conqueror's Court. And we'll replace the presents.'

'Is it wise to give them false hope?' Mary asked me, as if Nan and Donald weren't there, and she gave me an icy glare via the rear-view mirror. 'You'll never find anywhere big enough for all those old people, especially so close to Christmas. And even if you did – which you won't – have you considered the cost? I hope you've bought a Lottery ticket because you'll need a lot of money to cover the expense of all those meals, a venue, the presents, the decorations, the Christmas tree, the band. Need I go on?'

I shook my head. 'No thank you. I think you've said enough.'

She gave me another frosty look via the rear-view mirror and I decided then and there that I didn't like Donald's daughter.

I hadn't thought any more of it, until now. Nan and I had gone to bed soon after Mary dropped us at Emma's, and this morning, to be honest, I had other things on my mind. Like whether Aaron was safe.

But standing behind the police and the fire and rescue cordon tapes, I made Nan a silent promise. I wouldn't be able to get her and her friends back into Conqueror's Court any time soon, but I would do everything in my power to save their Christmas. I had no idea how, but that Christmas Eve party would go ahead.

Twenty-seven

Mary was right about me needing to win the Lottery if I wanted the Christmas Eve party to go ahead.

After I left Conqueror's Court, I walked into town and had a browse around the shops, and let me tell you, I got quite a shock.

I knew how much I'd spent when I was Christmas shopping with Nan, and that was only on gifts for my family and friends. Buying gifts – even small ones – for all the residents and staff of Conqueror's Court would cost a tidy sum.

There were about sixty residents at the Christmas tree lighting and at least ten staff, so allowing for residents – like Donald – who were absent that day, plus all the staff who weren't on duty, I was probably looking at gifts for at least seventy-five people. Maybe more.

And gifts were just the tip of the iceberg. This party meant providing at least seventy-five Christmas lunches; seventy-five Christmas crackers; seventy-five Christmas cards; seventy-five serviettes; seventy-five plates, glasses, cups, saucers and cutlery for that many. Not forgetting the small matter of finding the seventy-five chairs those people would sit on, not to mention however many tables would be needed for those seventy-five people to sit around and eat those seventy-five Christmas lunches.

My head was already spinning and I hadn't even begun to address everything else the party would involve. As Mary had said, there was a band. How much did it cost to hire a band? And all those decorations; the fairy lights; the massive Christmas tree? More importantly, where were the seventy-five people, that band, the decorations and the Christmas tree going to be?

I had to agree with miserable Mary; finding a venue that was available on Christmas Eve would be like finding the lost city of Atlantis. Scientists and explorers had been searching for that for hundreds of years; I had exactly two weeks until Christmas Eve.

And even if I did, by some major miracle, find a suitable venue, that posed another logistical problem. How was I supposed to contact all these people?

Several of the residents were taken to the two hotels in town and the various guest houses that had vacancies. Others had gone to stay with family members, like Nan and Donald had, but what about everyone else? The staff probably all lived close by, but some of the residents might be miles away by now.

It simply couldn't be done. I had no choice but to admit that miserable Mary was right. It was a nice idea, but not even Father Christmas could make all this happen in just two weeks. Oh, and I'd forgotten about him. I would also need a Father Christmas to hand out all the presents.

Except I wouldn't. Because it definitely couldn't be done.

That was such a depressing thought. So depressing that I had to leave the town and go back to Emma's.

I avoided going via Conqueror's Court and Mulberry Park and instead I took the long route. It was bitterly cold but I had wrapped up warmly and the frosty air helped clear my muddled head.

So what if there wasn't a Christmas Eve party for all the residents, or I suppose I should say former residents, of Conqueror's Court. Nan and Donald could still enjoy a party on Christmas Eve. They could come to Alberto's restaurant.

Silvio had said the Christmas Eve party was going ahead, just as it had done every year, and I knew he wouldn't mind if Nan and Donald came. I might be working, of course, but I could still enjoy seeing them have fun. And it would be fun. Those parties at Alberto's always were.

That thought cheered me up and by the time I got to Conqueror's Convenience Store, I was smiling.

I spotted the local paper, *The Weekly Conqueror* in the newspaper stand near the entrance and as I expected, there was no mention of the fire at Conqueror's Court. An event like that would be front page news. It seemed sad that such news would be a week old by the time the local paper reported on it.

Nevertheless, I picked up a copy for Nan. She said she liked to read her news in paper form. Many people of Nan's era probably preferred that. I knew for a fact that Nan and others of her age regularly checked the obituaries. She'd also told me that there were always copies of the paper at Conqueror's Court, so lots of the residents no doubt read it.

'That's it!'

I hadn't meant to say the words aloud, let alone shriek them.

Several other customers gave me the strangest looks, but I didn't care. I'd thought of a way to get word out to all, or at least many, of the residents of Conqueror's Court.

Now all I had to do was have a word with Meg and see if she thought the owners of the paper might agree to run an article asking all those people to get in touch with Nan, via myself and the internet, or possibly via the offices of the local paper itself. Nan was on the Conqueror's Court Christmas Committee after all, and all the residents and staff knew that.

As if I'd had a revelation, which in a way I had, the ancient bells of Holy Trinity church rang out.

Someone must be getting married. Or maybe the bells were announcing morning service or something. I wasn't exactly a churchgoer. I think the last time I'd gone to church was for Mum's funeral. I definitely hadn't visited Holy Trinity since then.

Although I had gone to the Summer Fayre they'd held in the church hall a couple of years ago on a very wet, cold and windy Sunday in May, which had coincided with my visit for Nan's birthday.

The Summer Fayre was usually held outside in the field opposite which was common ground, but due to the inclement weather, the event had been moved into the church hall. It was just as well it had, because it poured with rain all afternoon.

Nan, Emma and I went to lunch at Alberto's and then popped into the church hall to shelter from a sudden downpour of biblical proportions. We ended up staying most of the afternoon and we spent a fortune on handmade items and home baked treats from the numerous stalls lining every wall of the hall.

There were even trestle tables running down the centre, I seem to recall. And dotted here, there and everywhere, were little groups of fold-up chairs, where people sat and drank tea, coffee and hot chocolate while waiting for the rain to stop.

Those chairs were normally used for lectures, pantomimes, meetings of the W.I. and such, organised by the church or local groups, but they certainly came in handy that day and the event made the most profit it had ever done, so Nan told me she had later read in the local paper.

'Oh. My. God!'

Honestly, I should learn to stop yelling my thoughts out loud.

But I'd had another brilliant idea. The church might be busy on Christmas Eve, but the church hall might well be available.

Seventy-five people, a band, a massive Christmas tree, trestle tables, fold-up chairs, and Father Christmas along with all his reindeer could easily fit inside that hall.

I expect there would be a cost to hire it but it would be cheaper than any other venue I might find. And, bearing in mind it was owned by the church, and this Christmas Eve party was for a good cause, I might even be able to get it at a discount. Or, if miracles really did happen, possibly even for free.

There was no time to waste. I must visit the church and find the vicar without delay.

But wait a minute. Hadn't I decided this party wasn't possible? Hadn't I realised it would cost a small fortune?

Oh! What the hell.

There was no harm in having a chat with the vicar, was there?

Twenty-eight

Mum used to say, 'from tiny acorns, mighty oaks grow' – and she was right.

Standing in front of the charred façade of Conqueror's Court that morning I'd made a silent promise to Nan, a tiny gesture in the hope that something good might come of it.

That night, on my way home from my shift at Alberto's, shortly after midnight, that promise stood a good chance of being fulfilled.

The first shoots had sprung to life when I'd spoken to The Reverend Charles Chesterfield of Holy Trinity Church. He wasn't the man in charge when Mum had passed away and he had only been the vicar since the beginning of this year.

I'd known the old vicar had retired, again because Nan had mentioned it, and I had doubts as to whether this new one would be as nice. Those doubts were completely unfounded. He was better than nice – he was fantastic!

He was also younger than I'd expected. Probably not that much older than me. And he was quite good looking too; almost angelic even, with wavy, golden blond hair and soft, baby blue eyes encased with golden lashes. The man even had dimples, cherubic lips and his teeth were definitely pearly white.

I wanted to take a photo of him to show to Tori; not as a prospective boyfriend for her, but simply because she wouldn't believe me when I told her how perfect he looked for his job.

He was also incredibly kind and generous. Not only did he tell me that the church hall was available on Christmas Eve, he had immediately insisted there would be no hire charge, once I'd explained the reason why I wanted it.

'There are enough trestle tables and fold-up chairs to seat at least seventy-five people,' he assured me, in an equally angelic voice. 'We also have a number of plates, glasses, cups and saucers, although possibly not enough for seventy-five. There's some cutlery too.'

'This is nothing short of a miracle,' I said.

When he smiled, I wouldn't have been surprised to hear a choir of angels.

'Well, it is the season for miracles,' he informed me, and confirmed that by adding: 'I'm certain I've seen a box or two of Christmas decorations and some fairy lights in the store room. If you give me your phone number, I'll call you later and let you know.'

'Thank you so, so much,' I said as we exchanged numbers. 'You're my saviour.'

'No, Katie. That would be our Lord and Saviour, Jesus Christ.'

'Oh right. Yes, of course. Well, say thanks to him for me, please.'

He raised one brow. 'I take it I won't be seeing you in church tomorrow then?'

'I'd be lying if I said yes. I'm really, truly grateful for everything you're doing, but religion isn't for me. I mean no disrespect.'

'None taken. You've got a good heart. I can see that. Would it help if I mentioned the fire and what you're doing during my sermon tomorrow? And perhaps we could put the details in our weekly Parish pamphlet. I'll see what can be done.'

I almost kissed him, but I didn't think he'd approve.

'That would be wonderful! Oh, but please don't say I'm the one doing this. It's going to take a lot of people to get this organised and to make it happen. Can we say it's the Conqueror's Court Christmas Committee that's heading the campaign and that we'll give credit to all the fundraisers, sponsors and those who donate? I'm not sure how we do that exactly, but I'm sure someone will know.'

'That sounds like a good idea. I'll be in touch about the decorations.'

'Thanks so much,' I said. 'Now all I've got to do is organise the food, the band, the presents, and a few other things and we'll have ourselves a Christmas Eve party. I didn't think this was possible, but thanks to you ... and Jesus Christ, we're halfway there already.'

After leaving the church, I'd called Meg and I'd run my plan by her. Not only was she happy to help by having a word with the owner of the local paper, she said she could do better than that.

'We'll be running a four-page spread, maybe more, on the fire and even if I say so myself, I've got some fantastic photos. Worthy of an award, in my humble opinion. I'll make some calls to local businesses and see if we can get them interested, both in buying advertising space in our 'special edition' and also donating to the event. The fire and the fallout from it, is big news in this town, Katie. I can't say too much, but criminal charges will be brought, there's not much doubt of that. As you witnessed yourself, the fire alarm didn't go off, neither did the sprinklers. The front doors were locked and no one seemed to know where the fire exits were. There're standard procedures and laws for care homes, and fire and safety inspections have to be carried out regularly. Something sinister was going on at Conqueror's Court and *The Weekly Conqueror* will get to the bottom of it.'

'Crikey! That sounds serious. I had no idea. But if that's the case, should we still be calling this the Conqueror's Court Christmas Eve party?'

'Hmmm. Possibly not. Let's give that some thought. But in the meantime, I'll get the ball rolling at my end. Or should that be snowball, bearing in mind the weather and the season?' Meg laughed, and so did I for a second.

'What about that?' I said.

'Sorry. What about what?'

'What about calling it the Snow Ball? Or the Snow Ball Party? Or the Conqueror's Snow Ball?'

'Or the Conqueror's Snowy Balls if we make it a regular event?' Meg roared with laughter. 'This could be the first of many.'

'I'm not sure the residents would approve of that, Meg. Most of them are over eighty and might not appreciate smut. Although Nan's the only one having a sex life in my family, so maybe they would.'

Meg smirked, and then her tone changed completely. 'Speaking of sex lives, what do you think of Aaron?'

I almost tripped on the pavement.

'Aaron? Your brother?'

'Y-e-s. Is there another Aaron? I realise there is, but what I mean is, another Aaron we both know.'

'Er. To be honest, I'm trying very hard not to think of him.'

'Oooh!' She sounded pleased. 'Does that mean you're trying to resist him? Or you've fallen for him and can't get him off your mind? Or – and I say this with love – does that mean he drives you mad with his moody and grumpy manner?'

'Possibly a mixture of all three. The thing is, I still love my ex. Whether I should or shouldn't is another matter. The fact is, I do. And part of me is hoping Cal will come to his senses and realise he still loves me. Aaron's ... gorgeous, I can't deny that, but he told me he doesn't date, and he's as good as told me he isn't interested in me, so I really don't see the point.'

'He told you he isn't interested in you? When?'

'This morning.'

'This morning?' She snorted with laughter. 'Well, well. I wonder what he's playing at? The not dating bit is true, but we're all working on that. There's something you need to know about him, Katie. But … damn it. I've got a call on the other line and I've got to take it. We'll continue this later. And I like Snow Ball, by the way.'

She rang off before I had a chance to say I didn't mind holding. What had she been about to tell me concerning Aaron? And why did she laugh when I told her he wasn't interested in me?

But more importantly, why was I thinking about Aaron Holt again when I had a Christmas Eve party to plan and only two weeks in which to do it?

I hurried back to Emma's. Nan was in the kitchen, stirring a pot on the hob.

'There you are, sweetheart,' she said. 'I was starting to wonder where you'd got to. I'm making sausage casserole for lunch. It'll be ready in half an hour.'

'I left you a note to call me.' I threw off my coat, scarf and gloves and went and gave her a kiss on the cheek. 'It's freezing out today. What would you like to do this afternoon? I got you the local paper.'

She glanced at it as I placed it on the kitchen table and I knew exactly what she was thinking.

'Anything about the fire?' she asked, turning her attention back to the pot.

'No. But I've just spoken to Meg and she says there's going to be a special edition with a four-page spread. She also said there's something dodgy going on at Conqueror's Court and the police will be bringing charges, no doubt against the owners, but possibly others too.'

'Really?' Nan looked me in the eye. 'Meg said that? Good gracious. That doesn't sound good, does it? Do you think they'll let us go back there?'

I shook my head. 'I honestly don't know. I went and had a look at it this morning and the central section's really little more than a shell. Both wings of the property look relatively unscathed but what they're like structurally, who knows? The insurers, the police and the fire service will be carrying out their investigations, and then I suppose decisions will be made.' I went to her and wrapped my arms around her shoulders. 'But if the owners are prosecuted, then I'm not sure who would run the place. I know this is dreadfully upsetting, Nan, but I think you may have to start facing the possibility that you'll need to find somewhere else to live.'

Her eyes filled with tears as she met mine.

'Somewhere else to live? You make it sound so simple. But it isn't, is it, sweetheart? Now you and I are in the same boat, but for different reasons. And neither of us is to blame. We think we know what life has in store for us, but we don't, do we? After we lost your mum, I thought life had dealt me its final blow. It seems I was wrong.' She took a deep breath and wiped a tear from her cheek. 'No point in crying over it though. All that'll do is give us blotchy faces.'

I hugged her tight and kissed her cheek again. 'I love you so much and it hurts to see you like this. Is there anything I can do to help? Or to cheer you up?'

'I love you too. More than you will ever know. But right now only a miracle could help. And I think everyone wants one of those, especially at this time of year.'

'It is the season for miracles,' I said, easing myself away. 'What about if I said there might be a chance – just a slight chance, that you could still have your Christmas Eve party? Would that cheer you up at all? Even a little?'

'If only we could, Katie love. But you and I both know that isn't possible. You just said so yourself. The building is a wreck. I suppose I ought to at least find out when I can go and get my belongings. All my clothes, and books, and treasured possessions are in that flat. I'm almost dreading going back, knowing I won't be going back to live there, just to pack my things and move to somewhere else. And I suppose I'd better start looking. Everyone from Conqueror's Court will be doing the same, I suppose.'

My heart was breaking but I didn't know what to do. I wanted to tell her about my plans for the party but if I did that and it all fell through, would that make things worse? In a couple of days I would know more. If Meg got interest from local businesses and if I could organise the food, or at least start to, then the party could happen and I could tell Nan all about it. Once we got the basics sorted, things should only improve from there.

As for Nan finding somewhere to live, well, that was another matter. And she wasn't the only one, of course. As she said, everyone from Conqueror's Court, or almost everyone, would be looking.

And let's not forget about me. Either I had to return to London after the New Year, which was now only three weeks away, or I had to move somewhere else. If I planned to stay in Norman Landing, I would now be one of many looking for a new home.

At least I had a job, albeit temporary, and I had five hours until my shift began. Plenty of time for Nan and me to cheer ourselves up, or so I thought, until I had a phone call from the police officer who had wanted to take my statement.

As the weather was too cold for Nan to spend long outside, we suggested he come and take both our statements that afternoon. We thought it might take a while but it was surprisingly quick. Even including the time it took for us to make him and his female colleague, plus Nan and me a pot of tea, and for us all to drink it, talk and sign our statements, it was all over and done within thirty minutes.

After that Nan and I watched two Christmas movies. They did a pretty good job of lifting our spirits, and, as the characters overcame almost impossible odds and still achieved their happy endings, Nan and I smiled at one another.

'There's always hope,' Nan said.

'Absolutely,' I agreed. 'And miracles do happen. Things will get better for both of us and for everyone else who's going through a bad time this year. You just wait and see.'

'And if they don't,' Nan added with a grin and a wink. 'We can always watch Christmas movies on TV.'

I knew she was putting on a brave face, but at least she seemed much happier. As I was myself.

And even more so as I walked home from my shift at the restaurant because Silvio and his dad, Alberto had heard about the fire and as soon as I told them of my plan, they immediately offered to help.

'We could supply some food,' Silvio said. 'Perhaps not your traditional Christmas meal, but maybe a buffet, like the one we have here, no? We will talk. Two weeks is plenty of time. No need for you to worry.'

In just one day, several elements of the party had come together. It was looking as if, with a lot of help from several wonderful people, I might be able to save Christmas, after all.

But when I turned into Emma's road and saw Aaron walking Ember, it wasn't thoughts of saving Christmas that made me smile.

Twenty-nine

I wasn't sure what to do at first. We hadn't exactly parted on normal terms that morning but the second he saw me, he did a double take, smiled, waved a hand in the air and leant against a snow-covered cherry tree waiting for me.

'Hello,' he said, that utterly gorgeous smile of his fixed firmly in place. 'Had a good day?'

I covered the couple of metres between us in a matter of seconds.

'Yes, thanks. Much better than I expected after the start I had this morning.'

He ran a hand through his hair and threw me a sheepish look.

'Yeah. About that. I'm sorry if I said the wrong thing. I was so tired I'm not sure what I did say. I hope I didn't … upset you.'

'Upset me? No. Why would you think that?'

There was a hint of devilment in his eyes.

263

'Because I seem to recall you shoving me and dashing out of my house as if the hounds of hell might be at your heels. Or maybe I dreamt that.'

'Yes. I think you might have.'

We both knew he hadn't and we grinned at one another.

'May I walk you home? Or would you find that as irritating as me saving you?'

'As we're both going in the same direction, I think that'll be okay. So how was your day?'

'I slept for most of it. Mum and Dad brought Ember round about five and Meg joined us for dinner. So basically, nowhere near as exciting or productive as yours.' He threw me a sideways glance and then reached out a hand and placed it gently on my arm, almost imperceptibly turning me to face him. 'Meg told us what you're trying to do, Katie, and we all think it's wonderful. I'd like to offer my assistance. Unless you don't want me involved? But I genuinely think I can help, if you'll let me.'

'Oh! Er. It's not that I don't want you involved. I would love your help. We need all the help we can get to pull this off. The thing is, we do seem to ... always end up disagreeing.'

His brows knit together. 'That's mostly my fault.'

'It's entirely your fault. You see! We can't even agree on that!' I burst out laughing as his expression changed from one of apology to shock and then amusement. 'Sorry. That wasn't fair.'

He shook his head. 'No. I expect I deserved that.'

'Not really,' I said. 'If anyone should apologise, it is probably me. You have saved my life three times, after all. The adventure in the snow. The fall down the stairs. And … what was the third time?' I joked. 'Oh yes. That fire. Sorry, Aaron.'

The laughter vanished from his eyes and mouth for a second and he looked away into the distance.

'You have no idea how worried I was when Meg told me you were in there.'

'Meg told you?'

'Yes. Thanks to several of the people you helped get out, I knew roughly where you were, but even so…' He shook his head.

'Well, thank you again. I'll admit I was terrified for a moment or two and so relieved when I knew I was safe. I honestly don't know how you do the job you do. You're not working tonight, I assume?'

'Nope. I've got the next two days off. I should've been off last night but I'm so glad I got called in. As I think I said this morning, we're so short-staffed at the moment, we're all working extra shifts. We're not really supposed to but someone has to be on duty.' He shrugged. 'They're recruiting all the time at the moment. Some of the guys are off sick, some are retiring. It's the same story everywhere. But what about you? Are you enjoying your new job?'

I laughed. 'It's actually an old job. I worked at Alberto's years ago. My best friend Tori and I were waitresses. That's where I met Cal and … um. Yes. I love it. It's good to be earning again too. I wasn't quite sure what I was going to do.'

I shouldn't have mentioned Cal and I saw something flash across Aaron's eyes as I did so, or perhaps I imagined it, but he quickly dropped his hand from my arm and resumed our walk towards home.

'It's just temporary though, isn't it? That's what Meg said anyway. Or is there any chance you might decide to stay?' His gaze was fixed on Ember.

'I honestly don't know. I haven't thought that far ahead even though I suppose I should have. And now, all I want to concentrate on is getting this party organised.'

'Saving Christmas, you mean? Meg says you've decided it's best not to call it anything to do with Conqueror's Court, in case of negative connotations.' He gave a quick burst of laughter. 'But I'm not sure The Conqueror's Snowballs is fitting.'

'No.' I sniggered. 'I'm not trying to insist we use any of my suggestions or anything but I've already vetoed that one. Maybe The Christmas Snow Ball or something. But that sort of suggests that other people can attend – and they can't.'

'Or you could simply call it Saving Christmas. That is, after all, what you'll be doing for all the former residents of Conqueror's Court.'

'That's true. And that's sort of how I've been thinking of it. But I've been calling it Saving Christmas Eve. Saving Christmas is much better. Concise and to the point. I like it. Thank you, Aaron. It seems you really are the one to call when anything or anyone needs saving.'

'I'm not,' he said, as we arrived at the bottom of Emma's drive. A cloud had crept over him once more. 'Good night, Katie.'

'Good night, Aaron. And Ember.'

Thirty

Meg, The Reverend Charles Chesterfield of Holy Trinity Church, Silvio and Alberto of Alberto's restaurant, Mr and Mrs Trewberry, the owners of *The Weekly Conqueror*, and several of the local businesses that Meg had spoken to, all liked, *Saving Christmas*.

'The Trewberrys told me we'd call it, The *Saving Christmas* Campaign, in the paper,' Meg said. 'That way even more people might feel inclined to donate either money, or gifts, or other things we need, like decorations et cetera.'

'I think that's a great idea. There's only one tiny thing that worries me. I haven't told Nan about this yet, and when she and the other residents hear about it, I don't want them to think it's charity. Even though it is, in a way. Nan's not rich, by any means, but she does have savings of her own and so do many of the others, I should think. It hadn't occurred to me until this morning but I don't want anyone to feel awkward about any of this. And if businesses are donating either money or items, will that be a problem?'

'Why should it? This isn't about whether those old people have money or not, is it? It's about the fact that they look forward to this big treat and get-together each year and now it's not happening. It's gone, along with the roof over their heads and the place they've called home, many for a number of years. It's not charity. It's community spirit. As for the businesses, it's great publicity, plus they can probably claim it against their taxes, either as charitable giving or something, or maybe even advertising and marketing. Who cares? As long as they donate, that's all that matters to us. And the more people who do that, the better.'

'That's a good point. About it being to do with community spirit. That's what I'll tell Nan.'

Meg laughed suddenly. 'When Aaron told me he and the rest of the guys at the fire station would love to help, I suggested they do one of those firefighter calendars. I even offered to take the photos, on condition they all get naked. For some reason, he didn't jump at the idea.'

'I'd buy one,' I said. 'And so would everyone I know. Can't you get him to change his mind?' The thought of seeing Aaron naked had a definite appeal. 'What about one of those things where dates with various men are offered in exchange for money?'

'Isn't that called prostitution? I'm joking. I know what you mean. It's called a bachelor auction, I believe. And that's not a bad idea.'

'Except Aaron doesn't date, does he?'

'I think he might for a good cause,' Meg said. 'Start saving your pennies, Katie. If I can persuade him to do this, you'd better bid for him – and win.'

'Me? Why me? I can't. He wouldn't want me to. I ... Do you think he'd actually agree to do it? The auction, I mean. Not go on a date with me.'

'I'm sure he would. And all the other firefighters, of course.'

'Of course. But maybe only the single ones. We don't want to cause any jealousy, do we? Christmas is stressful enough for relationships as it is.'

'I wouldn't know about that. I can't remember the last relationship I was in over the festive season. I might bid for someone myself. Right. I'll say goodbye for now. I'm going to call Aaron and get this ball rolling, so to speak. He may be a grumpy git at times, although not without good reason, but his heart is in the right place. I think we can safely add 'Flaming Hot Dates Auction' to the list of fundraising activities.'

Hmmm. I was going to have to call Tori or Emma and ask them for a loan. Possibly a large one. I was pretty sure I wouldn't be the only woman bidding for a date with Aaron Holt. And if he wondered why I was bidding, I had the perfect excuse. I could say I was only doing it because I wanted to help Save Christmas for Nan and the other former residents of Conqueror's Court. He couldn't say no to that.

Could he?

Thirty-one

'Flaming Hot Dates Auction!' Tori wolf whistled and fanned herself before leaning closer to the screen on our video call. 'If you think I'm going to lend you money to buy yourself a date,' she said, looking impressively reproachful before cracking into the largest smile imaginable. 'You're right. No. Scratch that. I won't. Consider it your Christmas present. I didn't know what to buy you this year so a hot date with a hot man is the perfect gift. And one that hopefully keeps on giving.'

'I'm joking,' I said. 'Well. Sort of. I do like the idea of bidding for a date with him. But on the other hand, it's pretty tacky, isn't it?'

'Absolutely not! What's more, I'm coming to this auction myself. When is it?'

'Oh. I don't know yet. Aaron hasn't actually agreed to it. But Meg's certain he will. And so will the others. I'll let you know. As it's a fundraiser, it should be before

Christmas Eve. But wouldn't it be great to hold the auction on Christmas Eve itself?'

'I could think of worse ways to spend my Christmas Eve. Except I'll be with my parents in Brighton. And aren't you working on Christmas Eve?'

'I should be. But Silvio and Alberto have been real superstars and have said I can have the night off to be at the *Saving Christmas* party. I told you they're also providing food for it, didn't I? Probably a buffet like they'll have at theirs. I feel guilty in a way. Their parties are so fantastic and I'm worried that this event is stealing some of the wind from their sails.'

'They wouldn't have offered to help if they were concerned about that. So what else has been happening down there? London seems so boring now compared to all the excitement you're having. I may have to call in sick and come down there and join you.'

'I wish you could,' I said. 'But you've got the whole week off between Christmas and New Year and you'll be just along the road in Brighton so we'll see one another then.'

'Assuming you can drag yourself away from the strong arms of your hot new man.'

'What hot new man? Oh. You mean Aaron.'

'Yes. The one I'm buying you for Christmas. And to think, all I got you last year was a sweater.'

'That was better than the present Cal got me.'

'Why did you mention him?' Tori glowered at me. 'Please don't tell me you think you're still in love with Callum bloody Blake?'

'Okay, I won't. But sadly, yes I am.'

'Katie!'

'I can't help it, Tori! I can't just fall out of love with him, you know.'

'Unlike Callum.' She grimaced. 'What's the point in loving someone who has said he no longer loves you?'

'Unfortunately, it's not a choice. But equally, what's the point of paying for a date with someone who has said they don't date and that they don't want to sleep with you? And by 'you', I mean me.'

'Obviously. Because everyone wants to sleep with me.' She stretched out her arms, leant back in her chair and glanced out of her window. 'There's even a queue forming as we speak. No. Wait. That's the queue for the number 21 bus.'

I laughed out loud. 'I miss you so much, Tori. I know we chat every day but it's not the same as being with you.'

'I know. I feel the same. I can't wait until Christmas week when I can see you in the flesh. Which is a phrase a certain firefighter will be saying to you before long. Oh hell. I've got to go. The old bag from HR is standing outside my closed glass door, tapping her watch. I've been telling her for the last week or so that my days are hectic at the moment, but does she care? She insisted on doing my annual report today at nine o'clock sharp.'

'Er. I hate to tell you this but it's nine-thirty.'

'God, Katie. You sound just like her! Let me know the date of this auction and I'll be there. Assuming I can escape from this prison.'

I laughed as she ended the call. How she still had a job was nothing short of a miracle.

'Was that Tori?' Nan asked, joining me in the kitchen.

'It was. And she's as crazy as ever. I love her so much, Nan and I really miss her. Oh, but I love you more. And Emma. I wish I could stay here in Norman Landing but I love my life in London. Sorry. I loved my life. Now I feel kind of lost. As if I'm in the middle of two worlds and I don't know which one is best for me.'

'I understand, sweetheart. All I can say to that is to follow your heart.'

I smiled. 'That's what Tori said the other day. But how do you know whether your heart is doing what's best for you? I followed my heart when I moved in with Cal and look how that turned out.'

'You have to trust it. And you have to listen to it. Really listen. I don't think you followed your heart when you moved in with Cal. I think you followed *his* heart. And that's an entirely different matter.'

'Then why didn't my own heart stop me? Why didn't it tell me not to do it?'

'It probably tried. But you'd turned the volume down so low you didn't hear it above the noise of his. Putting other people's hopes and dreams before your own might seem like a selfless act, but it's often the biggest mistake we'll ever make. You only have to look at the divorce rate to see that.'

That was a cheerful thought. But in a way Nan might be right. When I'd moved into the flat with Cal, I wanted Tori to come with us. He told me there wasn't room but I didn't feel happy about it. I know Tori bought her own place, but I also know that if I'd asked her to come with us, she would've done so without hesitation. Maybe that was my heart telling me that moving in with Cal wasn't the best choice for me. But I didn't listen.

And I still wasn't listening, was I? I still loved Cal and I couldn't seem to help myself.

'That's your phone, Katie love,' Nan said.

'It's Meg.' I jumped to my feet. 'Excuse me for a second. I was meant to check something for her and I forgot,' I lied, hurrying into the hall.

'He's in!' Meg yelled with unbridled excitement. 'He wasn't keen at first but when I told him you were going to bid for him, he didn't need any further persuading.'

'You told him what! Oh, Meg! How could you? I'll never be able to face him again.'

Meg laughed. 'That might make your date a little awkward.'

'What if I don't win? Have you thought of that?'

'Yep. Dad's going to be the auctioneer. That's what he did before he retired. So your bid will win, don't worry.'

'That's cheating, Meg. Your dad won't agree to that.'

'He will. Mum's already told him he's got to. And besides, it's not as if you're bidding for a Rembrandt or something. It's just a date with my brother.'

Personally, right now, I'd take a date with Aaron over a Rembrandt any day of the week. But then again, other than the fact a Rembrandt's worth a fortune, I don't know much about art. And money isn't everything. It can't buy you happiness, so I'm told.

But I'm not sure a date with Aaron will do that either.

Thirty-two

'You're wrong, Donald,' I said. 'And so are you, Nan.'

Nan, Donald and I were in the kitchen having a discussion about which fillings make the perfect Christmas sandwich and frankly, their suggestions left me cold.

Donald had called Nan while I was on the phone with Meg, and she had invited him to lunch. We were having hot sausage sandwiches, using up the rest of the large pack of sausages that Nan had opened to make the sausage casserole we'd had the day before, hence the debate.

'You've got to have pigs in blankets in it,' Donald argued, but good naturedly, 'along with stuffing. Sage and onion preferably.'

Nan had agreed with him.

'Stuffing in a sandwich? Are you both mad?' I had, not unreasonably, questioned.

The chime of the doorbell meant I was still explaining why stuffing should *not* be in a sandwich when I opened the door to Aaron.

'Who has stuffing in a sandwich?' he asked, confusion clearly etched on his face.

'My point precisely. Come in and help me fight my corner.'

I was so engrossed in the friendly argument that I momentarily forgot about my conversation with Meg just a couple of hours earlier.

Aaron glanced down. 'I've got Ember with me.'

'Oh. Er. That's all right. As long as he promises not to pee on any of the decorations. I haven't replaced the tree so he can't pee on that.'

Aaron smiled and they both came inside, Ember scampering into the kitchen the moment Aaron let go of his lead.

'Hello gorgeous,' Nan said. 'And hello Ember.'

She winked at Aaron and he blushed. Or maybe the warmth of the room sent a flush to his healthy-looking cheeks.

'Would you like a sandwich?' I asked.

'Stuffing?'

'No. Hot sausage. Or something else if you prefer.'

He grinned. 'Hot sausage sounds good. But I don't want to invite myself to lunch.'

I frowned at him. 'You didn't. I did. And what about you, Ember? Would you like a hot sausage? Or maybe a cool one?'

I swear to you that dog said, 'Sausages.' Just like that famous dog did on TV many years ago. I remember watching it with Mum and Nan. Or maybe it was with Tori, on You Tube. Anyway, everyone heard Ember say it because we all laughed.

'A cool one, please,' Aaron added.

I turned to the worktop and made Aaron his sandwich, taking another two sausages from the oven where they were being kept warm. I also took one out for Ember and left it on a plate to cool.

'What do you think makes a perfect, Christmas sandwich, Aaron?' Nan asked, while I was working.

'Not stuffing,' he replied.

'You see!' I said, glancing over my shoulder.

'I think it depends on my mood and what day it is. What I'd like on Christmas Eve, for example, might not be what I'd like on Boxing Day.'

The mention of Christmas Eve reminded me of the auction and my conversation with Meg and I dropped one of the sausages on the floor. It was immediately snuffled up by Ember, regardless of the fact it was still, perhaps, a little too warm. He didn't seem to mind. I'm not sure the sausage even touched his sides.

But I could feel myself blushing. Was Aaron's comment his way of telling me that even if he had to go on a date with me on Christmas Eve, it didn't mean we'd have another date after that? Or was his remark simply about sandwiches and nothing else? Was I becoming paranoid about Aaron Holt and what he thought of me?

I decided to put on a brave face.

'You know the saying, 'Your dinner's in the dog?'' I nodded towards Ember. 'Well, your sausage is in the dog.'

'He's a sausage dog,' Nan joked.

'I'll get you another one,' I told Aaron, who frowned at Ember and then laughed.

'Sorry,' Aaron said. 'My dog is even less well-mannered than me.'

'Really?' I grinned. 'I find that hard to believe.'

'So?' said Nan. 'What do you like on Christmas Eve and what do you like on Boxing Day? And we're still talking about sandwiches, here.'

Aaron grinned too, saying, 'Thank you,' as I handed him a plate with his sausage sandwich cut in two. 'On Christmas Eve I think it has to be freshly baked bread, thickly sliced, with ham from the bone, Dijon mustard, sliced tomatoes and melted cheddar cheese, washed down with a glass or two of good whisky. On Boxing Day, it's sliced turkey, sliced ham, sliced leftover sausage meat, streaky bacon, cranberry sauce, sliced brussels sprouts and pickled onions on wholemeal bread with lashings of butter. And a good red wine to wash that down.'

'Not bad,' I said. 'Apart from the sprouts. Oh, and the whisky.'

'For a moment there I thought we might've actually agreed on something.' His eyes danced with merriment as he bit into his sandwich.

'Close, but no.' I smiled. 'We don't have whisky, as far as I know, or even red wine, sadly. But I can offer you tea. Or coffee.'

'Tea would be great. So what's yours?'

I switched the kettle on and put a tea bag in a Christmassy mug.

'Mine also depends on the day and my mood, so we do agree on that. My favourites are – and please take notes in case I come round for a sandwich over Christmas – freshly baked white bread, butter, pickled onions and lashings of pickled onion vinegar.'

'What?' He stared at me in disbelief. 'A pickled onion sandwich is your favourite?'

'One of my favourites. I'm a woman of simple pleasures.'

'I'll remember that when we...' He coughed and studied his sandwich. 'If we should ever go on a date.'

'If you take my granddaughter out on a date and buy her a pickled onion sandwich,' Nan said. 'I'll box your ears. My Katie deserves the best.' But she was laughing as she said it. 'Is that a possibility? Going on a date?'

'Nan! I haven't finished. My other favourite sandwich is ciabatta still warm from the oven, butter, ham off the bone and stilton.'

'That does sound nice,' said Donald. 'But all of those would be so much better with stuffing.'

'I agree,' said Nan, tapping Aaron on the arm. 'So this date? Where would you–'

'Nan!' I stopped her mid-flow and glowered at her. 'Ignore her,' I said to Aaron as I made his tea and handed it to him. 'Oh. I've just realised I haven't asked you why you came round. Did you want something?'

'Thanks.' He took the mug from me and smiled. 'Er. No. Not really. I was taking Ember for a walk and ... um ... I just thought I'd ask if you needed anything while I'm out. Or ... or if you wanted to come with me.'

'On a date?' Nan asked, excitement written all over her face.

'Nan! Will you please stop going on about dates! Would you like more tea?'

'No thank you, sweetheart.'

I picked up my own mug of tea, threw her a warning look and took a couple of sips.

'We went for a walk on our first date,' Donald said, giving Nan a look so full of warmth and love that it almost took my breath away.

How did I not know about this relationship before now? They must've been dating for ages for Donald to look at Nan like that.

'We did,' Nan confirmed, mirroring that look. 'Three weeks ago today, if memory serves me.'

I spat out the mouthful of tea I had been about to swallow and when I'd stopped choking, I stammered, 'Th-three weeks? You-you've only been dating for three weeks!'

Nan stared at me. 'Yes. Is that a problem, Katie love?'

I shot a look at Aaron before shaking my head.

'No,' I mumbled. 'I just … I just assumed you'd been together longer. But I suppose you've known one another for years.'

'We met when Donald moved in to Conqueror's Court.' They reached out to one another and held hands. 'Three weeks ago today.'

Even Aaron seemed surprised by that.

'You asked her out the day you met?'

Nan and Donald laughed.

'Not exactly,' Nan said, as Donald lifted her fingers to his lips and kissed them. 'I told him that I was in my eighties and I wasn't getting any younger. I said, "If you don't ask me out today, you might miss your chance." He said, "What makes you think I want to ask you out?" I replied, "I've seen the way you've been looking at me for the last ten minutes. You want to ask me out. You're just not sure you should."'

'Nan was right,' Donald said, beaming at her. 'So I asked her out and we went for a walk.'

'And we had our first kiss that afternoon,' Nan added. She looked at me and then at Aaron. 'Life is short. We never know how long we've got. I lost both my husband and my daughter, far too young. Donald lost his wife several years ago. Don't waste time wondering and wishing. If you want something, or someone but you're not sure how they feel, just ask. What's the worst that can happen? They can say no but they might say yes. And that can lead to something wonderful.'

Aaron shifted uncomfortably on his chair and coughed before forcing a smile.

'I'm pleased for you both,' he said, 'but sometimes "wonderful" doesn't last.'

He got up so fast that the chair almost tipped over but he grabbed it and steadied it as Ember dashed towards him.

'I didn't mean your relationship wouldn't last,' he added, a look of dismay etched on his face. 'I was ... It doesn't matter. I think Ember's getting restless. I'd better take him for his walk. Thanks for the sandwich and the tea.'

'Er. You're welcome,' I said, as he hurried to the door. I jumped up and followed him. 'Aaron? Is everything all right?'

He threw on his coat, took hold of Ember's lead and opened the front door.

'Yes. Of course. Why wouldn't it be?'

And with that he was gone, leaving me standing on the doorstep.

I had no idea what on earth had just happened.

Thirty-three

'I agree that holding the Flaming Hot Dates Auction on Christmas Eve is a great idea,' Meg said, when we met for coffee the following morning, 'And instead of the proceeds going towards the *Saving Christmas* campaign, the funds could be given to another deserving cause or charity. That way the former residents of Conqueror's Court will, effectively, be giving something back.'

'Ooh!,' I said. 'I like the sound of that. And I think it'll make the residents feel better about it too.

'Excellent. That's another thing ticked off the list.'

'Ah. There is one tiny problem. Tori, my best friend, won't be able to come on Christmas Eve and she wants to be at the auction.' I blushed a little. 'She's buying me a date as my Christmas present. I thought it was just a little joke between us but this morning she sent me a 'voucher' she's made, with a photo of a very sexy firefighter and the words, 'one flaming hot date' and several pound signs. Look.' I scrolled through the emails on my phone and showed Meg the one from Tori.

Meg laughed. 'I wish I had a friend like Tori. Er. Has she set a price limit?'

'No. Actually she hasn't. I suppose I ought to ask.'

'Aaron could sell for a tidy sum. Maybe fifty pounds or more.'

'Fifty pounds would be an absolute bargain! But I suppose this is Norman Landing, not London. Whatever it costs, she's determined, and I can pay her back any difference, by instalments. It's for a good cause, after all.'

'Yes. We'll make sure the money goes to something worthy. We can discuss it with the Trewberrys and the vicar.'

I grinned at her. 'No. I meant the good cause is my sex life. Oh! Not that I'm suggesting for one minute that Aaron has to have sex with me on the date, obviously. Or ever. It was a joke!'

Meg roared with laughter. 'Don't look so worried, Katie. I know it was. Although my brother needs to have sex with someone soon before he forgets how to. It's been over five years now since he had a relationship, and that's a long time for any fit and healthy young man to shut love out of their lives. Although, having said that, it's been years since I had a relationship, and it hasn't done me any harm.'

I was just going to ask Meg about Aaron's last relationship but at that precise moment, he walked past the window of the café we were in and Meg spotted him.

'Aaron!' She called out, waved and tapped on the glass and he turned to see who was hailing him.

He smiled at Meg and then he saw me and the smile formed a sort of happy frown. It was as if he was both pleased and irritated to see me and his brain couldn't decide which emotion to express on his face.

He finally went with a happy expression and pointed at himself and then the vacant chair at our table, silently asking if he could join us. Meg nodded and beckoned him in and I couldn't stop the sigh from escaping. I had half hoped he would walk on, so that I could interrogate Meg about his love life, but I was also pleased he joined us after he'd left Emma's house so abruptly yesterday. Luckily, the café welcomed dogs and Ember, to my surprise, curled up quietly under the table.

'Shouldn't you be at work?' Aaron asked Meg as soon as he sat down.

'This is work,' she replied. 'We're discussing the *Saving Christmas* campaign. Oh. We've decided the Flaming Hot Dates Auction should be on Christmas Eve, and we'll give the proceeds to some other worthy cause.'

'Any good cause would be grateful for the fifty pence it's likely to get from the bids for me,' he said, grinning. 'But are you sure about Christmas Eve? It's a nice idea but won't most people want to be with their families? And I thought only the former residents and staff of Conqueror's Court are going to be at the Christmas Eve party. Don't you want the auction to be open to as many people as possible?'

'That's a good point,' I said. 'I hadn't considered that even though I just said my best friend Tori can't come because of that! I don't know where my mind is at the moment.'

'I do,' said Meg, grinning at me and winking. 'I suppose that's true. But we're running out of time. The paper's coming out on Saturday and the following Saturday is the big day itself.'

'Christmas Day is Sunday this year,' I said.

Meg tutted. 'I meant this big day. The *Saving Christmas*, Christmas Eve party.'

'This is all such a rush,' I said, suddenly feeling the weight of everything we still had to do. 'We don't have a tree, the church hall only has a few decorations and lights. We've got lots of gifts, thanks to your efforts, Meg, but we need wrapping paper and someone to wrap them! There's so much to do. And now we've got to organise this auction before Christmas Eve.'

'Leave the auction with me,' Meg said. 'I'll get Dad on to it. Mum and her ladies from the W.I. can donate the wrapping paper and they can wrap the presents.'

'The guys from the fire station will help with the decorating,' Aaron said. 'And we'll get some more decorations and lights donated from shops and businesses in town. Don't worry about that. The guys can be very persuasive. In a good way. Not in a heavy handed, thuggish manner.' He grinned.

'Why don't you take Katie to Barnard's Christmas tree farm today?' Meg suggested. 'You can get the tree for the church hall, and get one for me while you're there. I haven't put any decorations up yet at my place. And maybe you could get yourself a tree this year?' She gave Aaron a hopeful look but his eyes had glazed over as if he'd gone off into the distance again.

'I need a tree for Emma's,' I said. 'I've got a car so I can go myself. If you tell me where to find Barnard's Christmas tree farm. I don't remember that from when I lived here.'

'I'll take you,' Aaron said, coming back from wherever his mind had led him. 'We'll need a truck if we're going to get three trees, plus the big one for the church hall. Although they'd probably deliver that one if we ask.'

'They will,' said Meg. 'Okay. I think we're nearly there. You can go as soon as we've all had our coffees. So, what are you getting me for Christmas, brother dear?' She gave him a playful nudge.

'How about a Christmas tree?' he joked.

We spent ten minutes or so exchanging ideas on what presents Aaron and Meg could buy one another and then we went our separate ways; Meg to call her dad and sort out the Flaming Hot Dates Auction, and me, Aaron and Ember to go and get the Christmas trees.

'My sister can be so bossy,' Aaron said when Meg was out of earshot. But he was smiling affectionately.

'I couldn't have done any of this without her. And you, of course.'

'I haven't done much. And you need to take more credit. None of this would be happening if it hadn't been for your idea. And you got the church hall, the food, and so much more sorted without anyone's help. Plus, you got Meg on board in the first place.'

He gave me an odd smile. 'And wasn't the Flaming Hot Dates Auction your idea?'

I blushed suddenly. 'Yes, And one I'm beginning to regret.'

I knew I shouldn't have said it the moment the words left my mouth. Aaron tensed and even moved a little distance away.

'Why? Because Meg's forcing you to bid for a date with me? You know you don't have to do that. Hopefully, someone else will outbid you. I know a date with me isn't exactly a thrilling prospect, but it is for a good cause.'

'That's not what I meant at all!' I was cross that he'd think Meg had forced me, but even angrier that he clearly hoped I would be outbid. 'But don't worry. I'll keep my bid low if that'll make you happy. After all, neither of us wants to go out on a date together, do we?'

He glared at me. 'No. Obviously we don't. It wouldn't work if we did. You're still in love with your ex.'

I couldn't argue with that, even if I wanted to.

Thirty-four

Barnard's Christmas tree farm was massive and sat on the opposite side of town from Emma's, and also from the road via which I always arrived during any of my visits – which explained why I hadn't seen it.

When I'd lived in Norman Landing this farm was a sheep farm owned by an elderly couple whose names, I'm ashamed to say, I can't remember. We visited several times in my childhood, when Dad was still with us, during lambing season. The owners were friends of his and that was why we never went there after Dad left.

The place was almost unrecognisable now, although the farmhouse itself looked unchanged. There was a long lane leading to the farmhouse with fields either side, once full of sheep and now full of Christmas trees of various shapes and sizes.

A large rickety barn had stood to the right of the farmhouse but now a posh, newly-built two-storey affair that looked more like someone's home than a barn, stood proudly in its place.

It was covered in fairy lights from its roof to its floor, even at this time in the morning, and as the sky was a forbidding shade of gunmetal grey, the brightness added much needed cheer.

Especially as Aaron and I had hardly spoken on the way here.

Snow still lay thick on the ground, thanks in part to the freezing temperatures of the last few days, but more snow was forecast and those clouds looked perfectly capable of bringing it.

'Wow! I can't believe how much this place has changed,' I said, turning on the spot to get a three hundred and sixty degree view once I got out of Aaron's car.

We hadn't gone to get a truck after our heated exchange and neither of us had discussed how we were now going to transport the trees.

Aaron didn't reply so I continued. 'We used to come here when Emma and I were kids, although Emma was very young and might not remember. It was a sheep farm in those days and Dad brought us to see the lambs. I can still remember how warm their little bodies were when we were allowed to cuddle them.'

'We came here too,' Aaron said, a slight smile forming on his mouth. 'Mum and Dad brought me and Meg when we were kids, like you, during lambing season. I can remember we fed some lambs and how hard they tugged on the bottles. Meg cried when she discovered those lambs had been abandoned by their mothers.'

'I know how that feels.'

Aaron shot a look at me and was still looking as he opened the rear passenger door to let Ember out of the car. I felt I had to explain.

'When I was ten and Emma was only five, Dad decided one day that he didn't want to pay the mortgage anymore, or the outstanding bills, or anything else and he packed his suitcase and left. Just like that. No explanation. No apologies. Nothing. He didn't even say goodbye to me and Emma. He didn't call. He didn't send us cards or presents, either for Christmas or our birthdays. It was as if he simply disappeared. Then one day, completely out of the blue, he got in touch with us. But I couldn't forgive him at the time. It took me years to do so, and by the time I finally did, he was ill. Shortly after, he died.'

'Oh Katie, I'm so sorry. That must've been awful.'

'Awful isn't the word I'd use.' I walked at a snail's pace towards the rows of Christmas trees and Aaron and Ember walked beside me. 'It really screwed me up. For years I thought Dad left because of something I did or said. The day before he left, he'd spent with me. The entire day. So it must've been my fault. Of course Mum and Nan assured me it wasn't. It was his fault and no one was to blame but him. But when you're ten nothing much makes sense about the way grown-ups behave. To be honest, I'm still not sure I understand other adults' behaviour. And then I heard Mum crying and telling Nan that she still loved Dad and she wanted him to come back. Nan had moved in with us to help out both financially and with all the day to day stuff. It was hard, and I believe sorrow and regret and that burden of unrequited love contributed to Mum's death five years ago. Sudden Adult Death Syndrome they called it. It's rare, but it happens more often than you might expect. Sorry.' I shook myself both mentally and physically. 'I don't know why that all came pouring out.'

'Maybe because this place stirred up memories of happier times,' Aaron said, his tone of voice almost a hug, and when I looked into his eyes, I saw real empathy.

He had known sorrow. Deep, heart wrenching sorrow and he knew exactly how I felt.

'Maybe,' I said. 'I vowed no man would ever do that to me. No man would break my heart the way Dad had broken Mum's and mine and Emma's. I never wanted to go through that again. And that's why I didn't date anyone until I was twenty-four. Don't laugh.'

His eyes had opened wide as had his mouth but he'd quickly regained his equilibrium.

'I wasn't going to,' he said.

'Thanks. I thought I'd got over it, although I still had insecurities. But we all have those, don't we? And then, out of the blue, my boyfriend of almost six years does virtually the same. I couldn't believe it and I still can't. I couldn't deal with it. All my insecurities and doubts flooded back. This was my fault. He no longer loved me. Just like Dad. And there was nothing I could do about it. And the worst part is, just as Mum still loved Dad, I still love Cal. How bloody stupid am I?'

Aaron's eyes narrowed with a mixture of what looked like sadness and anger and then, to my surprise, he took me by the arms and held me a few paces from him.

'You're not stupid. You're not. I know how it feels to love someone who's no longer there for you. This is not your fault. Your ex is an idiot if he can't see what he had. It's hard to get over someone, I know. But what did Nan say yesterday about life being short? You might not believe this now, but one day you'll meet someone and you'll begin to realise that maybe – just maybe – you could love again. Love someone else as deeply and as passionately as you loved her. I mean, him. You'll fall in love again, Katie. I'm sure of it.'

We looked into each other's eyes, and for a moment, one brief and almost blissful moment, I thought he was going to kiss me.

'Is this your dog?' a female voice called out, breaking whatever strange magic was happening between us.

'Ember?' Aaron looked at the dog in the woman's arms and then, almost comically to me, scanned the ground around us before rushing to the woman. 'I'm so sorry. Yes. Thank you. I thought he was by my side. Where was he?'

The woman gave him an amused but vaguely reproachful look. 'I'm not sure you want to know. He's a bit of a terror, isn't he?'

Aaron half laughed, half sighed. 'I'll pay for any damage he's caused.'

'No need. I've been trying to make my hubby cut down on bacon sandwiches, so in a way, this little chap did me a favour.'

'Ah,' Aaron said. 'Please say sorry to your husband for me. I hope he's not too upset.'

'Oh get away with you. He almost died laughing.' She chuckled. 'Do you two lovebirds need any help?'

'Lovebirds?'

Aaron's eyes darted in my direction and this time I was the one who had to quickly regain my equilibrium.

'We need some Christmas trees,' I said. 'Four to be precise. One very large one if you have it and three smaller ones, please. Do you deliver?'

'You've come to the right place.' The woman smiled. 'Let's have a look and see what we've got, shall we?'

Thirty-five

Having ordered the perfect trees, not just for the church hall but also for Meg and Aaron and me, we needed even more decorations for when they were scheduled to be delivered the following day.

Thankfully, Emma had several beautiful baubles, all carefully packed and labelled, so my decorating needs were covered. Meg had plenty too. Aaron's mum, Daphne had lots to spare so Aaron's tree requirements were also sorted. It was only the tree for the church hall that would be looking a little bare.

But not for long.

With Nan and Donald conveniently out of the house, Aaron, Meg and I were sitting at Emma's kitchen table, drinking coffee and eating mince pies, discussing the decorations, when my phone rang and a delighted, Reverend Charles Chesterfield of Holy Trinity Church almost sang out over my speakerphone.

'We have more decorations! Far more than I know what to do with! Boxes and boxes of them, of all shapes and sizes, all colours and varieties. When will the tree be delivered?'

'Tomorrow!' I said, unable to contain my excitement. 'Who gave the decorations? We'll need to add them to the thank you list.'

'It'll be a long list,' he said. 'I think the entire town is chipping in. And it's not just decorations that have been arriving. As we speak, there are cars and vans queuing – yes queuing, to drop off donations of all manner of things.'

Clearly the vicar had his phone on speaker too because a woman said, 'At this rate there'll be enough to hold parties on every one of the twelve days of Christmas.'

'Mum?' Aaron and Meg said in unison, exchanging glances.

'Yes darlings. I'm here. And so is your father. Plus most of the W.I. We've come to wrap the presents as we promised we would.' She laughed suddenly. 'One of the women said that the last time the town had come together like this was in the second World War!'

'Crikey,' I said.

'With bells on,' said Meg.

None of us could quite believe it and we sat in silence for a moment or two after the call ended.

'You know what this means, don't you?' Meg looked serious.

'That people obviously feel strongly about this?' Aaron said.

Meg shook her head and then turned it into a nod.

'Well yes, but mainly it means that this could be about saving Christmas for others, too. Not just the former residents of Conqueror's Court. We'd need to get agreement from our main sponsors, of course, and from anyone else who has donated, but imagine what a difference this could make to so many lives.'

'Er. I don't know about you,' I said, 'but I wouldn't know where to start. I'm not sure I'd be able to do what was necessary to pull something like that off. All I wanted to do was save Christmas for Nan and her friends. I wasn't planning on feeding the five thousand. I agree it's wonderful. It really is. All I'm saying is, are we the best people to handle that? Oh God! But you know what else it means.' I cast a horrified look at them. 'That word of this has got out! It was supposed to be under wraps until the paper announced it on Saturday. It isn't in the

Parish magazine until then either, so how do all these people know about it?'

'Oh don't worry about that,' Meg said, waving a hand dismissively in the air. 'The Trewberrys won't mind. And it'll help to sell more papers. Everyone will want to read about it and see if they can help. I think it's fabulous. But I agree it's taken on a life of its own and we may not be equipped to cope.'

'I don't think the paper is what Katie is concerned about,' Aaron said. 'I think it's Nan. Katie hasn't told her yet. Have you?'

That last part was directed at me and I shook my head. 'No. I need to do that now because if ... Oh, Nan! You're back.'

We all looked at Nan as the front door opened. She had a peculiar sort of smile on her face and she took off her coat in silence, as did Donald.

'Yes, sweetheart. We're back. Donald and I would love a cup of tea if there's one going. And also,' – the smile grew tighter as she came towards the table – 'an explanation as to why there are queues of people waiting to drop things off at the church hall, apparently in aid of the Conqueror's Court Christmas Eve party. Or *Saving Christmas* to give it its rather engagingly catchy new name. I'm told you are the person to ask.'

Thirty-six

Nan was brilliant, as I should've known she would be. I told her what I had hoped to do and how it was now taking on a life of its own. I wish I'd spoken to her about it from the word go.

Within minutes of Meg, Aaron and me bringing her up to speed she had come up with both suggestions and solutions as to how to manage the entire thing. I should've remembered she had been head honcho of the Conqueror's Court Christmas Committee and had spent the last few years organising events like the one we were arranging.

And when we discovered that Donald had worked for a large and prestigious charity throughout his career, Meg and I, and possibly even Aaron, wanted to kiss him.

'Does that mean you and Nan might be prepared to step in and take over?' I asked, hope springing to life within me. 'To work with the local paper and all the businesses and the church and...' I picked up a bundle of papers, '...all the others on these lists?'

It wasn't that I hadn't enjoyed what we'd achieved so far, it was simply that I knew we couldn't take it any further. As Meg had said, we were now in a position to do so much more than we'd ever imagined.

Nan and Donald exchanged thoughtful looks and then both smiled.

'We would relish the opportunity to get involved,' Nan said. 'We may be elderly but we're not dead yet. A project like this would not just make it even more worthwhile getting up every morning, I think it would put an even bigger spring in our steps. Falling in love with Donald has made me feel young again. What better way to spend my regained youth than to help as many people as we can have a wonderful, or at least a special, Christmas.'

That was music to my ears. 'I'm still more than happy to do anything you need me to,' I said.

'As we all are,' added Meg.

'Absolutely,' agreed Aaron.

'But the thought of all the red tape is daunting now that its growing?' Donald queried.

'Yes!' I said. 'The Trewberrys have helped keep us on track with all the necessary paperwork so far, but they've got a newspaper to run, so even they may want to take a bit of a back seat now that it's heading into the stratosphere. Although they'll still want to be involved, won't they, Meg?'

'Yes. But you're right. They will need to step back a little. As will I if I want to do my day job. Which I do.'

'Are we agreed then?' I looked around the table and everyone nodded. 'Okay. Nan and Donald, we're handing over the reins of *Saving Christmas* to you.'

'You'll want to come and meet the Trewberrys,' Meg said. 'I'll call them now.'

'We'll need to get in touch with everyone from Conqueror's Court,' Nan said, while Meg made her call. 'Not the owners, of course, but all the former residents and staff. I know you said the announcement will be in the paper and the Parish magazine on Saturday, but there are some people I can think of who could help us.'

I leant back in my chair, thrilled by the look on Nan and Donald's animated faces.

'I think they're happy,' Aaron said, leaning close.

So close that I could smell his aftershave and that sent another but completely different thrill through me.

'If I'd known they would react like this, I definitely would've told them the second I had the idea. I thought I had to save

Christmas for them and their friends, but I realise now that it's often better to give people access to the tools they need to help themselves.'

Thirty-seven

Meg, Aaron and I were all relieved that Nan and Donald were now at the helm of the *Saving Christmas* campaign. The moment *The Weekly Conqueror* appeared on the counters and in the newsstands of all the shops, stores, cafés, hair salons, florists and other local businesses, things went crazy.

National newspapers called, radio stations near and far, Breakfast TV shows, and so many other businesses, celebrities and such, all wanting to be a part of *Saving Christmas*.

Nan and Donald, and the other former residents of Conqueror's Court they'd brought on board, were loving every minute of the attention. But when Nan mentioned me as the person who had started it, and I got requests for interviews, I politely declined them all. Nan and Donald were naturals at self-promotion. I came out in hives just thinking about being on the radio, let alone

TV. The last thing I had ever wanted was to be famous.

Unlike my former boyfriend, Callum.

The next few days flew by in a whirl of fun and laughter, with Aaron, Meg, their parents, the Trewberrys, Nan, Donald and I, together with, it seemed, the entire town of Norman Landing, making preparations for Christmas Eve.

We'd contacted all the former residents and the staff of Conqueror's Court and, I think without exception, every one of them able to do so, came to lend a hand.

And a decision had been made. This was no longer just a party for the former staff and residents; now anyone in Norman Landing, who was elderly and alone, was welcome to attend.

But that wasn't all. Now two well-respected charities were involved, and this wasn't the only party being held, and not just on Christmas Eve, and it wasn't only the elderly who were being invited to those.

I must admit though, the only one that was special to me was the one being held on Christmas Eve in the hall of the Holy Trinity Church.

The church hall had been transformed into a winter wonderland. A local artist named Luke had painted murals of snow-covered fields and mountains, a starry night sky, and Father Christmas and his reindeers flying through the air, his sleigh piled high with brightly-wrapped presents.

Obviously, as this was a building owned by the church, the murals had been painted on a number of specially prepared MDF panels that were temporarily fixed to the walls but could be easily removed. After Christmas, those panels would be going to the Norman Landing Amateur Dramatics Society, thanks to the generosity of the artist.

Decorations and fairy lights glistened and glowed all around those murals and the floor had been covered with a wonderfully realistic-looking, type of artificial grass that came in snowy-white.

Health and Safety officers along with Fire and Rescue had carried out inspections, and changes were made where necessary to ensure no lives were at risk and all standards and procedures were in place and were stringently adhered to. Unlike they had been at Conqueror's Court, I might add.

Tables were positioned; folding chairs unfolded; tablecloths were ironed and smoothed into place. Napkin rings and serviettes, cutlery, crockery, glasses and cups were washed and dried and laid on the tables, which all had festive runners down the centre strewn with sprinkles of Christmas-themed confetti.

'Look at this place,' I said to Tori, holding my phone so that she could get a good look at the hall as I walked around it. 'Doesn't it look magical? Replace Santa, his reindeer and his sleigh with a Cinderella-type carriage and white horses, but keep everything else exactly as it is, and this place could be the wedding reception venue of my dreams. I've always wanted a winter wedding. And one around Christmas would be even more romantic.'

'Wait! What?' she said. 'Turn your phone round right now, Missy. I need to get a look at you. Is there something going on that your best friend should know about?'

I laughed at the expression on her face.

'Sadly, no. But one can live in hope.'

'You're living in Norman Landing, with a certain hot firefighter as a neighbour. Are you saying things have progressed? Do I need to buy you something else for Christmas instead of a date?'

I'd already told her about the row I'd had with Aaron when we'd both said that neither of us wanted that date. Tori had, of course, dismissed that as nonsense.

'That just tells me how much you two *do* want it and just how badly you both need it.'

Aaron and I hadn't mentioned it since that day at the café and Barnard's Christmas tree farm but when the trees were delivered to the church hall and to each of our homes, there was definitely a lot of sexual tension in the air. Or maybe that was just me imagining there was.

But when Nan told us that they had agreed, together with Meg and Aaron's dad, Roger, that the Flaming Hot Dates Auction would definitely be held on Christmas Eve, I did see Aaron dart an odd sort of look at me; one that was a mixture of excitement and dread.

I wasn't quite sure what to make of it and my face was so hot and flushed that I had to go outside briefly to get some fresh air.

I will admit a tiny part of me – okay, a huge part of me ... all of me – hoped he would follow me outside. And he did.

But sadly, only to take Ember for a pee. At least that was what he told Donald who had been right behind him and had come to call me back inside so that I could hear all the details for the auction and why the decision had been made to hold it on Christmas Eve.

'Then you had better go back and get Ember, hadn't you?' Donald had said, roaring with laughter as he linked his arm through mine and led me back into the kitchen.

Apparently, quite a lot of adults like to go out on Christmas Eve. Especially, single adults.

314

Who knew?

'So you can see why Christmas Eve is perfect for the Flaming Hot Dates Auction,' Nan said. 'We believe it will be a fun way to bring the night to a close. And we also feel we need to open the night up for other adults to attend. Not just those connected to Conqueror's Court. The daytime will be for the former residents and staff, but the evening will be open to anyone who is prepared to buy a ticket to attend.'

'Wait,' I said. 'You're saying that people have to buy a ticket to be able to buy a date?'

'Exactly,' said Donald, beaming.

'So … they're paying twice, effectively. Once to get in, and then whatever it costs them to get their date in the auction?'

'Yes,' Nan said, looking even more thrilled than Donald. 'That's what they do at lots of things like these. And in Hollywood and such places, the entrance tickets cost a fortune!'

'We're not in Hollywood, Nan. We're in Norman Landing.'

'Which is why the tickets to our event will be a snip.'

'And by snip, you mean how much, exactly?'

'Oh, there's no need for you to worry about that, sweetheart. You don't have to buy a ticket. You'll get in for free, as will Meg, of

315

course. This was your idea, after all. If Tori wants to attend, however, I'm afraid she'll have to pay. And tickets will be like gold dust, so she'll have to get in quick. We announced the Flaming Hot Dates Auction in the newspaper but we didn't give the date, and we've been inundated with calls, texts, emails. The place should be packed.'

'I've created a monster,' I said, laughing.

But I was beginning to understand how Dr Frankenstein might have felt.

I was almost glad I had to go to work that evening, but before then, Meg, Aaron and I went over to Aaron's for half an hour or so to start decorating his Christmas tree.

We'd decorated our tree – the tree that I'd put in Emma's living room, earlier that day, while listening to more updates from Nan and Donald. Meg had decorated hers the moment it arrived, with help from her parents, apparently. Aaron said that he would decorate his 'at some stage'.

'We'll decorate it today,' Meg had insisted. 'But I can't stay long because I've got to meet some friends. I wish you didn't have to work, Katie. You could've come with us. But there's always another time. Anyway. Let's get to Aaron's now. I can spare half an hour.'

'That's all I've got too,' I said, wishing I could spend all evening with Aaron, decorating the tree, listening to Christmas music, drinking Baileys in front of a roaring log fire, looking into each other's eyes, and maybe–'

'Come on then, daydreamer,' Meg said. 'I've got my car, so I can give you a lift into town in half an hour.'

The restaurant had been packed, so all the staff at Alberto's were rushed off our feet and then, when I got home just after midnight, I spotted Lou, the stunning paramedic, at Aaron's house.

She was standing in the front window beside the Christmas tree that he, Meg and I had been decorating before I left for my shift that evening. Aaron had said he'd wait to finish decorating it until I was free on Tuesday. Clearly, he had called Lou instead and asked her to step in after Meg and I had departed.

I was tempted to go and ring the doorbell and make a sarcastic comment, but instead I went indoors and opened the bottle of wine that Silvio had given me that evening.

I switched on all the Christmas lights, including a beautiful battery-powered candle that I'd won in a raffle at the restaurant, also that evening, and I listened to a variety of Christmas music via earbuds so as not to wake Nan, and possibly Donald, who had stayed one or two nights recently.

I thought it was thunder at first and then I realised my phone was also ringing and so was the doorbell. Whoever was thumping on the door really wanted to get my attention.

I rushed to open it and nearly died when I saw Aaron, wearing an expression of anger and terror in equal measure.

'Shush! You'll wake Nan!'

He pushed past me and raced into the living room, and although I was astonished by his actions, I noticed he had what looked like a thick piece of material in his hands as I followed him.

'I hope I have,' he growled. 'You never, ever leave candles burning. Especially when you're falling asleep. And you've been drinking too.'

He glared at the bottle of wine and my half full glass on the table as he ran to the window and then he stopped, as if he'd hit a brick wall, when he reached out for the candle.

Realisation dawned on me. Aaron had thought it was a real candle with a flame, and for some reason he'd panicked. He must've come over, seen me through the window, lounging on the armchair with my eyes closed, and overreacted. He'd thought he was saving me again, when all he was doing was making enough noise to wake everyone in the house. But I suppose that was his intention.

'How foolish do you feel right now?' I was still annoyed about Lou. 'It's a battery-powered candle. Not that it should make a difference. One candle can't do much damage, can it? Has anyone ever died from leaving a candle burning?'

I knew that was a stupid remark even as I said it. Candles could cause fires, so I'd heard. But even so.

'Yes, they can. And yes. People have died after leaving a candle burning.' The anger in his voice and eyes was so intense I actually took one step back. 'All it takes is one little breeze to send the curtain into the flickering flame and before you know it...' His voice trailed off and he shook his head.

'The windows are all closed, because it's freezing out there, so there was no breeze. And there's no flickering flame. At least not a real one. So no need to panic.'

He looked as though I'd punched him, really, really hard. But I hadn't touched him.

'I'm surprised you even saw it. I would've thought all your attention would've been focussed on the lovely, Lou.'

'I saw it after Lou and her boyfriend left. All your lights were on and I came to see if ... if you were in the mood for a chat. I looked through the window when you didn't answer the bell. I thought you'd fallen asleep. I saw the candle and I ... panicked.'

He frowned at me but he still looked crestfallen.

And then I knew why. Just like that. I knew why he got so moody. Why he sometimes seemed a million miles away. Why a certain word or phrase in a conversation could suddenly change his demeanour.

'Oh God! Is that what happened? Did someone leave a candle burning and they died before you could save them?'

'Yes,' he said, after a second or two. I could hardly hear him now.

'That must've been horrendous. But you can't blame yourself. I don't mean to sound cold hearted but surely you accept that death can be one of the worst aspects of your job?'

The anger flared again. 'You have no idea what you're talking about.'

'Excuse me. But people die every day. In fires. In car accidents. From illness and disease. During surgery. You can't save everyone, Aaron.'

'Stop.'

'Of course it must affect you. I realise that. But you can't let bad things rule your life. I know that from experience. You have to let it go. Don't you have counselling after traumatic events?'

'Stop now!'

'Okay. I'm sorry. I just don't understand.'

'No, you don't. Of course I accept people will die. That doesn't make it any easier. But this – tonight – this isn't about my job. This is personal.'

'Personal? Oh no! Was it … was it someone you knew? That must've made it so much worse. I'm so, so sorry. But you need to come to terms with it. You need to try to move on. Was it a friend? A close friend? How long ago did it happen? Do you want to talk about it?'

'It was five years ago and no I don't. I do my very best never to talk about it. It was far worse than you can possibly imagine.'

'I'm sorry, Aaron. Truly I am. I know how terrible I would feel if anything happened to my best friend, Tori. But isn't it better that you had that friendship? Would they want to know that their death is still affecting you? Still making you so unhappy.'

I really shouldn't drink. I say and do the stupidest things after just a couple of glasses of wine. And I simply couldn't seem to stop.

'Do you want to put your life on hold forever? No true friend would want you to do that.'

'Please stop.' He moved as if to leave.

'I'm trying to help you, Aaron. Talk to me. Tell me what happened. It might make you feel better to share your pain.'

A snort of bitter laughter escaped him and he stared at me for a second.

'Help me? Is that what you're trying to do? One minute you behave as if you care. Really care. The next, you're telling me how much you still love your former boyfriend.'

'What's Cal do to do with this?'

'Nothing. And everything.'

'Now you're making even less sense. I do care, Aaron. Tell me about the friend you lost.'

He met my eyes and held my gaze and I wasn't sure if he wanted to kiss me or kill me.

'It wasn't a friend.' Again his voice was little more than a whisper. 'It was my fiancée.'

I didn't mean to gasp. Or to shout, 'Your fiancée!'

Before his words had sunk in, he marched out and closed the front door.

I wasn't sure what shocked me more. That Aaron blamed himself for his fiancée's death five years ago. Or the fact that Aaron had had a fiancée.

Thirty-eight

Thinking about the stupid things I said. The hurtful comments. The way I'd pushed Aaron to tell me about it, kept me awake for most of the night.

The worst part of it, for me, was that I was jealous. Jealous of his fiancée. A dead fiancée. How insane and uncaring was that?

My dreams throughout the night – when I did manage to get some sleep – were all about me wanting him, and in some of them, almost getting him, only to have him taken from me by a stunningly beautiful woman who, every time she appeared, he went to instead of me.

Don't ask me how I knew she was stunningly beautiful. I just did. I didn't see her face in any of the dreams, and I had no idea what Aaron's fiancée looked like, having only just discovered he had a fiancée. But I knew she would've been beautiful.

One of the main thoughts troubling me was – how do you compete with a ghost?

That, along with my guilt and my genuine contrition, meant I didn't get much sleep.

So you can probably understand why I thought I must be dreaming when, at eight a.m. on Tuesday morning, which, let's not forget, was the Tuesday before Christmas, I received a phone call from none other than my own former boyfriend, Callum Blake.

'I've missed you, Katie,' he said. 'But I expect you've been too busy to give me a moment's thought. And don't think I'm calling because I've heard you're involved in this *Saving Christmas* campaign. I'm not. I'm calling you because … well, because I've realised I've made the biggest mistake of my life. When I knew I was going to lose the restaurant, I span out of control. I wasn't thinking straight. I wanted to shield you from further debts, additional worries, all the problems closing down the restaurant entailed. I knew how hurt you were and I was trying to protect you from further pain. I see now that I went about it all the wrong way. I thought you'd be better off without me. And clearly you are. The problem is, Katie, I'm worse off without you. I can't stop thinking about you, no matter how hard I try. I dream about you. I even stop women in the street who *look* like you in the hope it *is* you. How crazy is that? I know I've got no right to ask, and I understand if you want to tell me to get lost. But I'm hoping you still love me, Katie. Just a little bit. And that, perhaps, you'd be willing to see me if I came down and paid you a visit. Would you, Katie? Could you find it in your heart to hear me out? I love you, Katie. And if it takes me the rest of my life to prove that to you, I'm happy to do it. As long as I can be with you, nothing else matters.'

I didn't say a word. I couldn't.

'Katie? Are you there?'

'Callum? Is that really you?'

His laughter rang into my ears – and all around the bedroom, because I'd pressed the button for the speaker, still being half asleep.

'Yes, my darling. It's me. Are you pleased to hear from me? It's so great to hear your voice.'

'Er. I'm surprised to hear from you.'

I pulled myself up and flopped back against the pillows as I scanned the room, still not completely certain this wasn't just a dream.

Nope. This was Emma's guest bedroom. Those birds I could hear, no doubt squabbling over bird food Nan had put out for them, were real.

Two of the first things Nan had brought with her from her flat at Conqueror's Court when we had gone to collect her belongings, were the bird feeder and bird bath.

'Priorities,' Nan had said.

'Clothes might be a more important priority,' I had replied.

'Katie?' Callum's voice held a hint of doubt. 'Are you really surprised to hear from me? Surely you knew, deep down, that it wouldn't be long before I realised what an idiot I'd been? Surely you knew I loved you really?'

'I ... I didn't know for sure,' I said. 'But I did hope you would.'

I heard his sigh of relief.

'How could I not? I may be an idiot, Katie, but I'm not so stupid as to let the best thing that's ever happened to me, get away. I can't wait to see you, darling. To hold you in my arms again. To kiss you. To make love to you. Are you still in bed?'

I nodded even though he couldn't see me. This wasn't a video call – thank God. I must've looked a wreck after no sleep, and with no make-up. Not that I ever wore much make-up.

'Katie?'

'Sorry, Cal. Yes. I'm still in bed.'

'Oh God, Katie. I wish I was there right now. What would you say if I jumped on a train this minute and came to see you?'

'I'd ask why you were so close to a train. Are you at a station?'

He laughed. 'No. But I can be. Just say the word, my darling. I'll be on the very next train. No. Don't. Don't say a thing. I love you. You love me. We don't need words, we need action. I'll see you very soon, my darling.'

Thirty-nine

'Please don't tell me you agreed to see him,' Tori said, when I phoned her right after Cal's call.

The odd thing is, Callum phoning me wasn't the first thing I spoke to her about. The first thing I told her about was what had happened last night with Aaron.

She had been as amazed as I was about Aaron having a fiancée, and as uncertain as to what I should do next.

Should I go and apologise? Should I tell him I was too drunk to remember last night at all? Should I wait and see if he came to me?

As for his remark about Cal having nothing and everything to do with whether or not I cared about Aaron – well, neither of us could work that one out. We spent at least twenty minutes or so trying. She even cut off three other phone calls so that we could discuss it.

But when I eventually went on to tell her that Cal had called, I thought she would explode before my eyes. I mean literally explode. Her face turned red, her eyes bulged and she screamed and tossed her head from side to side. One of her colleagues shoved open the closed glass door of her office and rushed in to check if she was all right.

'Get out!' she yelled. 'Can't you see I'm having a major meltdown here?'

'Are you okay?' I meekly asked.

'No, I'm not okay! How can I be okay when you are obviously considering seeing Callum bloody Blake?'

'I haven't actually said yes. I told him I needed to think about it. He's going to call me again later today. I know you think I'm mad, but I can't help it, Tori. I do still love him, you know that.'

'You've said it often enough. But just because you say something several times it doesn't make it true. Just like Cal calling you to tell you he's made a mistake and he loves you – again – doesn't make it true.'

'You think he's lying? Why?'

'Why do I think it? Or why would he lie?'

'Er. Both.'

'I think it, because it's all a bit too sudden and it happens to coincide with your star now being on the rise. If you want it to be, that is. You could get a lot of good publicity out of this *Saving Christmas* stuff, for, oh I don't know, let's say a certain chef and a certain restaurant.'

'You think he's using me? But the restaurant is closed. He's forfeited the lease and the tenancy.'

'Doesn't mean he can't start up a new one.'

'But how would I be of any help to Cal? Nan and Donald and the Trewberrys, along with a couple of charities, are running it all now. Nan simply mentioned it was my idea.'

'Yes. But you could make more of that if you wanted. Get more publicity for yourself.'

'I don't want publicity. I never have. I don't want to be famous. All I've ever really wanted was to have a little shop – a bakery or something – where I could bake cakes and sell enough to cover all my overheads and have some cash for a few luxuries. I've always been a woman of simple pleasures.'

'Do you know that's the first time I've heard you mention your bakery in years? We used to play shops when we were kids, remember? Your shop was called Katie's Kakes. With a K.'

Tori and I both went a little dewy-eyed at the memory.

'I was never very good at spelling,' I joked. 'What happened to our dreams, Tori?'

'Life. And Callum Blake. Look. You know I love you. And I mean it, unlike some. So I will support you whatever you do. Even if it's something as mind-numbingly stupid as seeing a guy who dumped you without a single thought for you and how you felt. But I honestly don't think you should see Cal.'

'So what are you saying? Exactly?' I didn't hide my sarcasm, either on my face nor in my voice. 'That I should tell him not to come and see me? But shouldn't I give him a chance to explain?'

'You should tell him not to come and see you, or call you, or get in touch with you ever again. You should tell him that you don't love him. You should say you've met someone else. You should make it clear that you don't want him in your life and that you wish him well but you never want to have anything to do with him ever again.'

'So ... that's a 'no', then?'

She let out the loudest sigh imaginable.

'You're going to say you'll see him, aren't you?'

'I'm not sure. I would like an explanation. And I'd like to know where Felicia features in all this. I was so surprised that he'd call and then by the things he said, that I completely forgot to ask about her.'

'Are you expecting him to tell you the truth? Or will you be happy as long as he says what you want to hear?'

'I know you don't like Cal that much, but I don't think he ever lied to me before. Well, maybe small lies. But not big ones. He hid how serious our finances were, but he said he did that for me. I don't know, Tori. I think I just need to see him and see how I feel. Surely you understand that? After all, wasn't it you who said that I should go with the flow? That I should follow my heart?'

'Bugger!' she said. 'I knew all that psycho-babble stuff would come back and bite me on the bum.'

Forty

Making a decision that could affect the rest of your life, is something that should not be done lightly or when your mind is on other things. That was what both Mum and Nan had often told me.

Taking that on board, and having wrestled with my thoughts and feelings for most of the day, when Cal called back, I told him that I did still have feelings for him, but I had too much on my plate at the moment and couldn't give our relationship, or whatever it was now, the time and serious consideration it required.

'What is there to think about?' he asked, and he didn't sound happy. 'You either love me or you don't. If you love me, we should be together. Especially as it's almost Christmas. I want to spend Christmas with you, Katie. I want to be with you on Christmas Eve. And every other day.'

'What about Felicia?'

'Felicia!'

'Yes. I know you've been seeing her, Cal. Tori saw you together in The Fulcrum.'

'What? When?'

'Have you been there with her more than once?'

'No. Maybe. The thing is, Felicia and I are friends. And now that she's famous, she says she'll put in a good word for me with everyone she knows. We've had a few drinks together, but we haven't had sex, so you needn't worry about that. She's great, but she's far too young for me. I could never have a serious relationship with Felicia, Katie. You know that.'

'I've got to ask this, Cal. Is your deciding you still love me, anything to do with the fact that I could get you and any restaurant you might be connected with, some publicity?'

'Katie! How could you think that? I love you. Not because of this *Saving Christmas* stuff, but because you're you.'

'You didn't love me three weeks ago. You told me you'd fallen out of love with me.'

'I explained that. I was worried. I was an idiot. I was wrong. I do love you. You have to believe me, Katie. Don't throw away almost six years just because I made one silly mistake. We're good together, darling. We could be great. You and I could have a wonderful future. All you have to do is give me a second chance. You won't regret it. I promise. We met on Christmas Eve. Do you remember?'

'Of course I remember.'

'Then let's spend this Christmas Eve together, darling. And every coming Christmas Eve after that.'

'I don't know,' I said. 'I'd decided to tell you we should wait until after Christmas. And I do think that would be wise. I'll be so busy on Christmas Eve, and between today and then, it'll be manic here. Let's meet on Boxing Day and see how things go from there. If things go well, we can spend New Year's Eve together instead.'

'I could come and help. And you won't be busy all Christmas Eve. You've got to go to bed at some stage. Look. I know this has been a bit of a shock. Everything. You and me. This *Saving Christmas* stuff. It's no wonder you feel so confused. So mixed up. I'll go now and give you a bit of time to think. Just remember I love you. And I'm going to make sure you know just how much. Good bye for now, my darling.'

That seemed weird, but I didn't have time to think about it because Nan called out that she needed my help and, after going to see what she wanted, I definitely didn't have time to think about Cal.

'Alberto's are now providing all the food for the buffet in the evening,' Nan said. 'Silvio and his dad are perfectly happy with that. And we've got two other local restaurants who are combining their supplies to provide traditional Christmas lunches for the daytime. I just need you to check with the local vineyard and make sure we'll have enough wine. I can't remember the woman's name, sweetheart, and you were the one who dealt with her.'

'It's Juniper, I seem to recall. But don't worry. I'll check and get that sorted.'

'Now that we've got so many cash donations coming in we can pay for anything the businesses can't afford to supply for free, so perhaps who could mention that.'

'I'm on it,' I said.

'And the cakes are being delivered today. I don't suppose you could be at the church hall to check there's enough, could you?'

'Of course. Just tell me when and I'll be there.'

The original plan was for me to bake cakes for the event, but now I didn't need to. In a way I was a little sad about that, but I had been baking almost every day, just for Nan and Donald, and for Meg, Aaron and me. And for anyone else who wanted them.

Everything was coming together now and the time just flew by. I saw Aaron quite a bit, but oddly we didn't seem to talk much. We were both dashing about doing things for the event, plus I worked every night in Alberto's and Aaron was on duty. We were like ships passing in the night.

I suppose this seems appalling, but I was tempted to pretend there was a fire in the kitchen at Emma's, just so that he could come and save me again. I would never have done anything so dreadful, of course, but as crazy as it sounds, I missed him. I even wondered if I could start a row, just so that we could talk.

I couldn't wait for the Flaming Hot Dates Auction on Christmas Eve. I had to get a date with Aaron, no matter how much it cost.

And Tori told me that this year she would miss out on spending the evening with her parents and would come to the auction instead. I'm not sure if that was because she had decided to bid for a date herself, assuming there was anyone she fancied, or because she wanted to make sure I got my date with Aaron, but whatever the reason, I was so delighted she would be there.

And her parents didn't mind. They phoned on the Thursday beforehand and offered to help if they could. I think they might have regretted that though. With Christmas Eve only two days away, Nan soon found plenty of things for them to do.

Daphne and Roger were still being brilliant, as were the W.I. Some of them got together and made Ember a lovely little, embroidered coat with *Ember's Saving Christmas* emblazoned on either side. He was declared an official, Therapy Dog, and Daphne and Roger, or Meg, or Aaron, depending who was free, took Ember to visit some of the former residents of Conqueror's Court – the ones who had been in the care home section, who were now having to spend time in hospital or at other care homes nearby, where there had been vacancies.

Ember was so popular that he soon found himself visiting the children's wards at the hospital too.

Everyone was so pleased to see Ember. And he did look exceptionally cute in his coat. His white fur was groomed to perfection and he even had a sparkling red and green bow tie that lit up with twinkling lights.

There were only a couple of tiny incidents. One when he peed on the Christmas tree in the reception area of a rather posh care home and one when he nipped into someone's office and pinched their turkey sandwich.

Everyone forgave him though. No one could stay cross with Ember. Although I must say, he did push the boundaries sometimes.

I was pleased to see him on Christmas Eve morning, although sadly with Meg, not with Aaron.

'All ready for the big day?' Meg waved and hurried towards me.

I'd opened the front door because I'd seen her arrive and I wanted to check that Aaron would still be at the Flaming Hot Dates Auction. I hadn't seen him at all the day before and as foolish as I knew I was being, I was worried that something had happened.

'As ready as I'll ever be,' I said. 'You?'

'More than ready. I know who I'm going to bid on tonight – and no, it is *not* my brother!' She laughed.

'Will Aaron definitely be there?' I tried to sound curious, not desperate. I think I failed.

'Don't worry. He'll be there. And Dad has promised he'll do his bit. You'll get your date with Aaron. But you know that he wants to ask you out, anyway, don't you?'

'Does he? No. I didn't know that.'

Meg pulled a face. 'Oh come on! You'd have to be blind and stupid not to see how much he likes you.'

'Then I must be both. We never seem to agree on anything. And not once has he said anything about asking me out. In fact, he's always said the opposite. The day we went to get the Christmas trees he said neither of us wanted to go out with one another and he hoped someone would outbid me.'

She frowned. 'He said that? Really? How weird. But then he can be weird sometimes. He still hasn't got over losing his fiancée. Not completely.

'I was so surprised when he told me about that.'

'He told you? Wow. He never tells anyone.'

'He didn't tell me much. Just that she had died in a fire caused by a candle. I hadn't known he was engaged until he said that.'

'He still blames himself. Not that there was anything he could have done. He was miles away at the time. He and his mates had gone up to London for a former colleague's bachelor party. And I think that's the real problem. Aaron blames himself for not being here when it happened. He knows the other guys did everything they could and he also knows if he had been here he couldn't have saved her. The place went up in minutes and was completely gutted. But it was the smoke that killed her, thank God, so she didn't know anything about it.'

'One candle did that?'

'Yep. Aaron goes crazy if anyone leaves a candle burning. Bat-shit crazy.'

'I know. That's why he told me. He thought I had a candle in the window but it was a battery-powered one.'

She smirked. 'Sorry. That's not funny. Poor Aaron. He would've flipped out.'

'He did. And I made things worse because I had no idea why he had. So that's why he told me. But he said he didn't want to talk about it and he left.'

'Yeah. He still finds it tough. But since you arrived, he's a changed man. That's why I don't know what he's playing at. Why he said he doesn't want to date you. Because believe me, Katie, there is nothing my brother wants to do more than that right now.' She grinned. 'Well perhaps there is one other thing he wants to do, but hopefully that'll happen too. He should be home any minute so we can ask him. He was working last night which is why I've got Ember.'

'Then I ... Oh. My. God!'

'What?'

Meg spun round, but she wouldn't have known why I was so astonished.

She had never seen Callum Blake before today.

'What the hell are you doing here!' I couldn't believe my eyes.

'It's our anniversary,' Callum said, holding out the biggest bouquet of flowers I had ever seen and beaming at me. 'You didn't really think I'd miss our anniversary, did you?'

'I told you not to come. I told you I was busy.'

'And that's fine. I'm here to help. I won't get in the way.'

'I think maybe I am,' Meg said, looking utterly bewildered.

'No,' I said. 'You're not. This is Cal, my former boyfriend. Cal, this is Meg.'

'Hi, Cal.' Meg still looked bemused.

'Hello, Meg. I'm pleased to meet you. Any friend of Katie's is a friend of mine. But as for former boyfriend, well, I hope we can do something about that. In fact, I'm pretty sure we can.'

He reached into his pocket, got down on one knee and with the bouquet secured under his arm, he opened a blue velvet box and a huge diamond ring sparkled in the pale lemon sunshine.

I don't believe Meg moved but although I heard her gasp, she sort of faded into the distance as I stared at the gorgeous ring. I also heard tyres as a car close by skidded to an abrupt halt and I think I heard a car door open but I was in a daze as I listened to what Cal was saying.

'I adore you, Katie Barr. Will you make me the happiest man this Christmas Eve, on our six-year anniversary? Will you be my wife?'

And then, out of the corner of my eye, I spotted Aaron. And the expression on his face was one of abject horror.

Forty-one

I don't know exactly what happened after that.

I do remember looking at Aaron and bizarrely wondering how he had proposed to his fiancée.

I remember Nan and Donald coming out of Emma's front door.

I remember Ember barking and growling, I believe at Callum.

And I definitely remember hearing the words, 'Katie? I said I love you. I adore you. I want to spend the rest of my life with you. Will you please say yes, you'll be my wife?'

And I did.

'Yes. I'll marry you. Yes. I'll be your wife.'

The only problem is, I don't remember saying those words to Cal.

Everything went a little crazy after that.

Actually, everything went *a lot* crazy.

Cal jumped up, tossed the bouquet to one side and pulled me into his arms.

I think he kissed me but I don't remember kissing him back.

I do remember Meg shouting something, but I'm not sure what.

I also remember seeing Aaron walk away from me and I definitely called out his name but he ignored me.

I distinctly recall the sound his front door made when it slammed shut.

Nan and Donald came and stood beside me.

'Are you sure about this, Katie love?' Nan said.

'Does this call for a celebration?' Donald asked, looking slightly unsure.

And that's about it.

I don't remember much more.

I think I turned and somehow walked back into the house. And then – don't ask me why – I opened a bottle of champagne; one that we were going to have later, and I took a massive gulp. And several more. And more after that.

But thankfully, despite my very best efforts, I couldn't seem to get drunk.

At least, I hadn't thought I had.

Forty-two

The room was spinning when I woke up in my bed in Emma's guest room. The curtains were drawn but there was a chink wide enough for me to see that it was dark out.

Tori was sitting on the edge of the bed and she was looking annoyed and yet amused.

'What day is it?' I asked.

'Christmas Eve,' she said.

'Still?'

'Still.'

'What time?'

'Time you were up and in the shower. Don't worry. You haven't missed the ball. You've missed the entire day. Or most of it. But not the ball.'

I groaned. 'It's not a ball. It's a party. And an auction. Is Nan very cross?'

'Surprisingly, no. She was rather pleased when I last saw her. But you do know that you've made a complete mess of things, don't you?'

'Yes.'

'And that this will take a major miracle to put right?'

'Uh-huh.'

'And that you need to make a big gesture now to prove how you really feel?'

'Believe me, I know that. I just don't know how. Or what.'

'Well for a start, we need to make sure you look the best you've ever looked. And looking at you now, that may take some time. Get up.'

She virtually dragged me to the shower and threw me in.

'Meg's angry with you.'

'I can imagine.'

'And obviously, Aaron's not too happy.'

'What if he hates me? What if he won't forgive me?'

'There's only one way to find out.'

I don't think I've ever been so nervous in my life. But I only had myself to blame.

Why hadn't I just said no?

How we made it to the auction I'm still not sure.

But I am sure that Aaron was astonished to see me there.

The place was packed and everyone was having so much fun. I was angry at myself for having missed it. Especially after all the hard work everyone had put in to make it happen.

But the truth is, it didn't really matter to anyone other than me, that I hadn't been there. It didn't matter to them that I hadn't seen Father Christmas arrive and hand out all the presents. No one was bothered that I hadn't eaten one of the scrumptious Christmas lunches, or drunk a glass of the delicious sparkling wine.

And let's face it, I'd already had quite enough champagne for one day.

No one even noticed that I wasn't there. No one asked, 'Where's Katie?'

Or maybe they did. I've no idea.

But my absence hadn't spoiled anyone's day today. Everyone had, and still was having, a truly wonderful time.

And that's exactly how it should be. I was very glad of that.

Aaron was the last 'date' to be auctioned and he looked truly miserable.

'Give us all a twirl, Aaron,' Roger said, as Aaron stepped into position.

How Aaron didn't storm off is beyond me. He glowered at his dad. But then he did try to force a smile. It just didn't seem to want to come.

'How much am I bid for a date with this handsome young man,' Roger said.

As Roger finished his sentence, Tori helped me get up onto a chair and, before anyone had a chance to bid, I waved a wad of twenty pounds notes in the air, and I yelled at the top of my voice.

'I don't care how much it costs, or how much anyone else bids, I'll outbid them. No matter what happens tonight, I'm the one who is going on a date with this extremely handsome, incredibly kind, unbelievably brave and wonderful man. Because although I did something exceedingly stupid today, I love him. And I need him to know that. Even if he doesn't love me. And I'm going on a date with him whether he likes it or not. Not just so that I can say I dated Aaron Holt, but hopefully also because I can make him see how good we could be together. Because I think we can be. I know we can. And I'll pay whatever I have to pay to make sure that happens.'

Aaron's eyes opened wide, as did his mouth. Everyone in the church hall turned and stared at me but I didn't care.

'Well,' said Roger, grinning from ear to ear, 'I'm not quite sure I've ever had a bid like that before. I think we should let this determined young lady have her date, don't you? And we'll say if she agrees to match the highest bid for a date so far tonight, that it's fair.'

He banged his gavel on the make podium and a huge cheer went up around the room. Everyone clapped. Many wolf-whistled. Several laughed.

'Sold,' Roger said. 'Would you like to come up here and claim your purchase?'

Tori helped me down and the crowd parted as I hurried towards Aaron who stood on the little stage at the end of the church hall. He was like a statue, possibly in shock but I didn't care. I was going on a date with Aaron Holt and I couldn't be happier.

I walked up to him and he just stared at me. A slight furrow between his brows as if he wasn't quite sure what was happening.

I knew how that felt.

I think people were still cheering but all I could hear was him.

'You love me?' Aaron queried, as if he might have misheard.

I nodded. 'Yes. I do. And I know it isn't the first time I've said those two words today, or similar at least. But I told Cal it was a mistake. That I hadn't meant to say yes to him. I had been looking at you at the time and as crazy as it sounds, in my head I thought it was you proposing to me, not Cal. That's the only reason I said yes. And then, I'm not really sure what happened. It was as if I was dreaming or something. I know it's weird but then I went inside and got drunk.'

'But you love me? *Me*?' He sounded genuinely surprised.

'Yes. I know we haven't known one another long but I've fallen in love with you, Aaron. And I know you still love your fiancée. But I think you might be falling for me too, if you just give yourself a chance. If you give us a chance.'

Suddenly he smiled. A huge gorgeous, sexy smile.

'I think I fell for you the very first day we met. I've been trying to fight it ever since because I'm scared of losing someone I love, again. But I think I'm ready to take that risk. In fact I know I am. I love you too, Katie.'

He pulled me into his arms and kissed me and all I can say is, 'WOW! The second our lips met I knew that Aaron Holt was The One. Without a shadow of doubt.

An ear-splitting cheer went up as everyone clapped even louder than before, and when Aaron and I finally eased apart, he swept me up into his arms.

'Thank you for saving me, Katie,' he said, and his eyes were filled with love and passion.

'You're most welcome, Aaron,' I replied. 'And thank you for saving me. Again.'

Coming soon

A not so secret Winter Wedding

Meg's at this wedding to get an inside scoop – not to fall for the best man's charms.

Meg Holt loves being a photo-journalist for her local newspaper and writing her quirky, Bridal advice column, Aisle, Altar, Hymn. But Meg has bigger dreams; she's just not sure how to achieve them. Until one particular bride-to-be, Pop icon, Lucinda Revere announces she is marrying ski-racer, Cody Clayton.

There's only one problem. Meg's not on the guest list for the wedding of the year in an exclusive, winter wonderland resort. But she's determined to get the inside scoop, and not even world-famous photographer, Rick Price will be able to stop her.

Rick doesn't 'do' weddings. He's here as a favour to his best friend, Cody, but when he discovers what Meg is up to, he resolves she won't succeed. And if being direct and downright rude won't work, a charm offensive might. Even if that means he'll have to keep Meg close, both day and night.

But Meg's got more important things to do than be swept off her feet by Rick's sexy smile, dreamy eyes, seductive voice and super-fit body. When this wedding looks like it might be cancelled, Meg discovers she's the only one who can get it back on track. Now nothing can stop her from getting what she came for.

And what she came for was to get the scoop of the year. Not to fall in love with Rick Price.

Pre-order this new book to ensure you get it on release day.

A Note from Emily

A little piece of my heart goes into every one of my books. I can't wait to bring you more stories that I hope will capture your heart, mind and imagination, allowing you to escape into a world of romance in some enticingly beautiful settings.

I really hope this book brought a smile to your face. If so, I'd love you to tell your friends. And if you have a minute or two to post a review (just a few words will do) or even a rating, that would be lovely too.

A writer's life can be lonely at times. Sharing a virtual cup of coffee or a glass of wine, or exchanging a few friendly words brightens every writer's day. Pop over to Facebook or Instagram, or better yet, there's my lovely Facebook group for book news, chats and general book-related fun.

You can sign up for my newsletter. It's absolutely free, your email address is safe and won't be shared and I won't bombard you, I promise. You can enter competitions and enjoy some giveaways. You can unsubscribe at any time.

You'll find all my contact links on my website and in the Contact section in this book. Hope to chat with you soon.

To see all my books, please go to the books page on my website.

Also by Emily Harvale

The Golf Widows' Club
Sailing Solo
Carole Singer's Christmas
Christmas Wishes
A Slippery Slope
The Perfect Christmas Plan
Be Mine
It Takes Two
Bells and Bows on Mistletoe Row

Lizzie Marshall series:
Highland Fling – book 1
Lizzie Marshall's Wedding – book 2

Goldebury Bay series:
Ninety Days of Summer – book 1
Ninety Steps to Summerhill – book 2
Ninety Days to Christmas – book 3

Hideaway Down series:
A Christmas Hideaway – book 1
Catch A Falling Star – book 2
Walking on Sunshine – book 3
Dancing in the Rain – book 4

Hall's Cross series
Deck the Halls – book 1
The Starlight Ball – book 2

Michaelmas Bay series
Christmas Secrets in Snowflake Cove – book 1
Blame it on the Moonlight – book 2

Lily Pond Lane series

The Cottage on Lily Pond Lane – four-part serial
Part One – New beginnings
Part Two – Summer secrets
Part Three – Autumn leaves
Part Four – Trick or treat
Christmas on Lily Pond Lane
Return to Lily Pond Lane
A Wedding on Lily Pond Lane
Secret Wishes and Summer Kisses on Lily Pond Lane

Wyntersleap series

Christmas at Wynter House – Book 1
New Beginnings at Wynter House – Book 2
A Wedding at Wynter House – Book 3
Love is in the Air – spin off

Merriment Bay series

Coming Home to Merriment Bay – Book 1
(four-part serial)
Part One – A Reunion
Part Two – Sparks Fly
Part Three – Christmas
Part Four – Starry Skies
Chasing Moonbeams in Merriment Bay – Book 2
Wedding Bells in Merriment Bay – Book 3

Seahorse Harbour series

Summer at my Sister's – book 1
Christmas at Aunt Elsie's – book 2
Just for Christmas – book 3
Tasty Treats at Seahorse Bites Café – book 4
Dreams and Schemes at The Seahorse Inn – book 5
Weddings and Reunions in Seahorse Harbour – book 6

Clementine Cove series

To see my books, or to sign up for my
newsletter, go to

www.emilyharvale.com/books

Or join my Facebook group for exclusive
news and giveaways.

www.emilyharvale.com/FacebookGroup

Scan the QR code below to see all my books
on Amazon.

Stay in touch with

Emily Harvale

If you want to be the first to hear Emily's news, find out about book releases, see covers and maybe chat with other fans, there are a few options for you:

Visit: www.emilyharvale.com

and subscribe to Emily's newsletter via the 'sign me up' box. Or, if you really love Emily's books, apply to join Emily's Open House here:

www.emilyharvale.com/MembersClub

Or ask to join Emily's exclusive Facebook Group here:

www.emilyharvale.com/FacebookGroup

Alternatively, just come and say 'Hello' on social media:

 @EmilyHarvaleWriter

 @EmilyHarvale

 @EmilyHarvale

Printed in Great Britain
by Amazon

10331328R00212